#5

Good Reading
DR

FIND HER BEFORE DARK

A GRIPPING SERIAL KILLER THRILLER

DAN PADAVONA

GET A FREE BOOK!

I'm a pretty nice guy once you look past the grisly images in my head. Most of all, I love connecting with awesome readers like you.

Join my VIP Reader Group and get a FREE serial killer thriller for your Kindle.

Get My Free Book

www.danpadavona.com/thriller-readers-vip-group/

TUESDAY, JULY 1ST 5:30 P.M.

"Relax."

Darcy sets her feet shoulder-width apart and exhales, waiting until the tension leaves her shoulders. She raises the Glock-22, the same model she carried for the FBI, and aims. The blast is like thunder, even with the earmuffs for protection. The earmuffs are cumbersome, a distraction. But not protecting her ears invites permanent hearing loss.

Standing beside her with his arms crossed, Detective Julian Haines, Darcy's husband, raises his hand toward the target.

"You're still pulling with your right shoulder," he says. The bullet hole punctured the paper two inches away from the target's head. "Again. This time, concentrate on keeping your upper body steady."

Darcy waits until she's clear to shoot. Pulls the trigger. The bullet tears through the paper along the target's ear.

"I'm still pulling my shoulder," she says.

"Not as much as before. You're making progress."

"I'm stuck at this level, and I don't get it. I was a better shot with the FBI."

"Coming to the shooting range a few times per month isn't a replacement for consistent instruction. You're out of practice."

Darcy removes the magazine, racks the slide, then locks it. She sets the gun down and removes her safety goggles. Darcy shakes her head as Julian brings the target forward and rips the paper free. No direct hits. She's regressing, allowing frustration to throw her concentration off. Mick, the range instructor, is a heavyset man with a red mustache and beard. He nods at Julian. The men have an easy rapport. Men like Mick welcome women to the range, yet watch them from the corners of their eyes. The old boys' club will never accept her, though she carried a weapon for the FBI's Behavior Analysis Unit and hunted Michael Rivers, the nation's most-infamous serial killer. Nicknamed the Full Moon Killer by the national media, Rivers murdered teenage girls and young women in the days surrounding the full moon.

"Try again tomorrow?" Julian asks, patting Darcy's arm. She shrugs. "Don't get down on yourself. You have the ability inside you. It's just a matter of cleaning up your technique and pulling the trigger without thinking about your form. Just let it happen."

Darcy nods and holsters her weapon. Her history with the Glock remains a troubled one. Though she shot and disabled Michael Rivers, she missed the mark and didn't kill the murderer. As a private investigator, she hasn't fired her weapon on the job. Most cases deal with infidelity, corporate fraud, and tracking down missing people. Last September, Julian's sister hired Darcy to track down her daughter after the girl went missing from college. The serial murderer responsible for kidnapping Julian's niece captured Darcy during the investigation and locked the women inside an unlit root cellar. Without a weapon, Darcy survived by defending herself with her hands. Julian saved her, firing the two shots that felled Dustin Gendron, a graduate student at New Sherill College.

"I'll meet you back at the house after I swing by the grocery store," she says, throwing the bag strap over her shoulder.

"Sounds good. Want me to fire up the grill?"

"Wait until five. Rush hour is tough with all the tourists in town."

Opening the door to her Prius, Darcy lowers the windows before she slides into the seat. Summer heat rolls out of the vehicle as she reaches inside to set the climate controls. Julian beeps his horn and pulls out of the parking lot ahead of her. Traversing the North Carolina coastal village of Genoa Cove shouldn't take so long. With the calendar flipping to July, vehicles with out-of-state plates clog the roads. Honks call out when traffic comes to a standstill. It sounds like an army of ducks overran the village.

Adjusting the mirror, Darcy spies a black SUV forcing its way into traffic from a side street. The aggressive maneuver draws more horns and a derogatory shout through an open window. Damn, she can't wait until summer ends and Genoa Cove returns to normal. Traffic flows after she hits the coastal highway. She bypasses village congestion until the exit dumps her off near the sprawling supermarket on the east end of Genoa Cove.

Darcy is forever attuned to people following her. Some would call it paranoia, but it's survival instinct. Ever since she left the shooting range, the same black SUV has stayed in her mirror, always a few vehicles behind. Shooting glances at the mirror, she searches for a plate number but can't find one. A pickup truck rumbles between the Prius and the SUV. Darcy swerves out of the left lane and turns right, cutting down a residential street. If she circles the block, she'll come back to the supermarket parking lot. No vehicles trail her while she passes through an upscale neighborhood with gated driveways and manicured lawns.

But as she turns into the supermarket parking lot, she isn't surprised when the black SUV pops into her mirror again. She finds a parking spot near the entrance and throws a glance over her shoulder. No sign of the vehicle now. A gust of chilled air greets her and blows her brunette hair back when the automatic doors slide open. Grabbing a shopping cart, she passes the Independence Day display and snatches a box of sparklers off the shelf. While she collects groceries, Darcy stays attuned to her surroundings, cognizant of anyone paying her too much attention. No suspicious shoppers. No shadow following her from one aisle to the next.

On her way out of the store, she spies a man in a black suit and sunglasses leaning against her bumper. A fed. She considers turning around, but he already spotted her. Darcy groans and shoves the cart toward the Prius. The last time she spoke with the FBI, the Genoa Cove Police Department had wrapped up the Michael Rivers case. Her old FBI partner, Eric Hensel, died on the night Julian shot the Full Moon Killer in a forest outside Genoa Cove. That was two years ago. No reason the FBI would contact her today.

"Darcy Gellar?" the man asks, flipping his sunglasses over his head as he moves off the car.

"It's Darcy Haines now," she says, opening the trunk. "And I'd appreciate it if you didn't sit on my hood."

The agent stands a hair taller than Darcy. His lined forehead and rutty face mark him as a senior agent. He rounds the vehicle and grabs a bag from the cart, placing it in the trunk.

"I've got it, Agent..."

"Ketchum," he says, hauling a second bag into his arms. "Agent Adan Ketchum, Federal Bureau of Investigation."

"I don't know why you're here, Agent Ketchum. Michael Rivers died two years ago. It's quiet in Genoa Cove these days."

Ketchum reaches up and closes the trunk. He positions

himself between the Prius and a neighboring Honda, a subtle move to block Darcy's path to the driver's side door.

"Perhaps we can find a quiet place to talk," Ketchum says, making it clear he's not moving until Darcy agrees.

If he means to intimidate her, he fails. She quit the FBI after Michael Rivers stabbed her, opting for an early retirement so she could raise her children. As a private investigator, Darcy only answers to her clients. She isn't beholden to the FBI.

"I need to get these groceries home. Milk and eggs spoil in the heat."

She tries to slip by, but he won't give her room.

"Please, Mrs. Haines. It's important."

The corner of his eye twitches. She knows why he called on her.

"This is about the Doll Face Killer."

She follows the Michigan killings on the Internet and evening news. Grisly murders in a lake community. The media named the murderer the Doll Face Killer after the police discovered multiple victims, their bodies positioned on the shore or before windows facing the water, porcelain masks covering their faces and making the victims appear doll-like.

Ketchum waits until a woman pushes a cart past the Prius.

"Yes." Ketchum pauses. "If we could discuss this somewhere more private. Inside your car, perhaps."

"You can't convince me to help you with this case. After I walked away from the BAU, it took me several years to reclaim my life. This is the first year I've slept without constant nightmares. I won't open myself up to another killer."

"The Doll Face Killer exhibits many traits similar to Michael Rivers."

"That's not true. The Full Moon Killer murdered young women around the lunar calendar. Doll Face kills all age groups and genders."

"So you have followed the case."

Darcy chews the inside of her cheek. She admitted too much. It's impossible to ignore the grisly news stories coming out of Veil Lake every week, though she's compartmentalized the murders as best as she can. This isn't her responsibility. The FBI has to catch Doll Face.

"Mrs. Haines, I'm aware Eric Hensel discussed your return to the BAU."

"Please don't speak of my dead friend. There's a difference between Hensel and you, Agent Ketchum. Hensel asked me as a friend, and he didn't push me after I declined." Darcy clicks the key fob and unlocks the doors. "And he didn't track me through Genoa Cove."

"Please hear me out."

"Stop following me, Agent Ketchum. I don't answer to the FBI."

Darcy pulls out of her parking space and swerves around a stalled pickup. Ketchum hasn't moved. She can see him in the mirror, his eyes following her behind the sunglasses.

2

Her body tremors as she pulls to the stoplight and turns out of the lot. Darcy can't stop searching for his SUV until she crosses the village to her neighborhood. Pulling into her driveway is like crossing a moat that shields her from a dangerous world.

"Hey, Mom."

Hunter's voice pulls Darcy away from memories of Agent Ketchum. Back from college for summer vacation, her son brushes dark, spiky hair off his brow and jogs out of the open garage. He wears a half-shirt with the sleeves cut off, showing off the muscles he built at the Coastal Carolina student gym.

"Let me grab those," he says when Darcy pops the trunk.

Hunter hoists a bag under each arm and carries two more by the handles. Her son is strong enough to haul four bags into the house, but he's likely to drop a bag if he rushes.

"Thanks, Hunter. Watch the stoop."

"I can see it."

He stands in the entryway to hold the door open. Darcy slips past with two bags in her arms. Unloaded in one trip. Having her son home comes with advantages.

"Did you get oat milk?" her teenage daughter asks, peeking her head out of her bedroom.

"I didn't forget," says Darcy, grunting as she lifts the bags onto the kitchen counter.

Jennifer claps her hands. Her hair a shade lighter than midnight, Jennifer wears it in a ponytail like Darcy. While Darcy unpacks the groceries, Jennifer fishes through the bags until she locates the oat milk.

"Save your appetite. Julian is grilling steaks."

"Mom," Jennifer says, placing her hands on her hips. "I'm a vegan."

"This again? I thought you went Paleo last week."

"Ugh. I can't look at another piece of meat. Do you know what they do to cows when they kill them?"

"Not now, Jennifer. It's been a long afternoon."

Jennifer huffs and rummages through the cupboards for the blender. Two scoops of frozen berries, a cup of oat milk, a banana, and a handful of greens. Darcy has to admit the smoothie looks delicious. Burning coal scents waft from the deck into the house when Julian opens the sliding glass door. Her mouth waters, thinking about the filet mignon. Julian kisses her cheek and opens the refrigerator. He retrieves the steak from the meat drawer and winks.

"I craved steak all day," he says.

"Hey, can I talk to you?"

"Sure. What's up?"

"Not here," she says under her breath.

"Meet you on the deck."

After Darcy unpacks the last of the groceries, she finds Julian hunched over the grill. Muscles ripple beneath his t-shirt. The cuffs of his shorts touch his knee caps, and he wears sandals and a baseball cap. Julian proposed last September after the Dustin Gendron investigation. Until that moment, their relationship had hit the rocks, and Darcy felt sure he wanted to leave her. Then he dropped to one knee with Jennifer in the kitchen and Hunter watching from college through the wonders of modern technology. Her kids had known for twenty-four hours. Julian, old-fashioned and romantic, asked her children for permission to marry Darcy. She'd wondered how her kids would take to a man in the house. She lost her husband, Tyler, to an aneurysm when Hunter was a child and Jennifer too young to remember her father. Julian is great with the kids. He helps Jennifer with school and drives her to parties and sleepovers. A good way to be a step dad while sending a message he's keeping an eye on her. This past spring, he made the four-hour drive to Coastal Carolina to hang out with Hunter for the day. Darcy's throat tightens. How did she wind up with a guy this perfect?

"Smells incredible," Darcy says, drinking in the smoky scent when Julian flips the steak.

"You wanted to talk?"

Darcy glances over her shoulder. Inside the kitchen, Jennifer giggles and shoves Hunter. He's razzing her again. It's good to have her kids together, even if it's only for three months.

"I ran into an FBI agent at the grocery store. To be more specific, he followed me from the shooting range."

Julian drops the tongs, his expression blank until understanding spreads across his face.

"The Michigan murders."

Darcy slumps into an Adirondack chair overlooking the yard. The wind ushers the salty tang of the Atlantic across the deck.

"They want me to construct a profile of the killer."

Julian pulls his chair across from Darcy's and faces her.

"What did you tell him?"

Darcy recounts the conversation, not concealing her anger that Agent Ketchum followed her.

"He could have called first," she says. "It would have been the professional thing to do."

"Would it have changed your mind if he had?"

Darcy ponders the question.

"No." Chewing a nail, she fixes her eyes on a painted-over patch of siding on the back of the house. Three years ago, a kidnapper and murderer painted the Full Moon Killer's symbol, a leering smiley face, on the siding. It was the same symbol Michael Rivers branded his victims with. "I can't go back to those days, Julian. Stepping inside a killer's head space, looking at crime scene photos."

"You're doing so much better," he says, touching her arm.

Darcy hasn't needed anti-anxiety medication in four months. After years of therapy, she conquered her debilitating fear of the dark. At the peak of her addiction, she abused the medication, sometimes consuming three to four times the recommended dosage. When a serial murderer abducted Jennifer in Georgia, Darcy overdosed and passed out in her cousin's living room. Alone in the house, Darcy could have died.

She pushes herself out of the chair and grabs the tongs, giving the steak a flip. It soothes her to stay busy, to concentrate on matters unrelated to kidnapped teenagers and murdered families.

"I just don't know what profiling Doll Face would do to me. But I feel obligated to help. Nobody wants to see another family murdered."

"It's not up to you. The FBI has profilers. Let them do their jobs. Why is Agent Ketchum determined to pull you into the investigation?"

"You know the way it's been since the Rivers case. They've done a lousy job hiring new recruits, and their best profiler left for a teaching position."

"*You* were their best profiler, Darcy. The FBI needs to get its business in order and do a better job at hiring. And they can't keep calling you when they're in a bind."

"It would just be a consulting position. I can't imagine they want to hire me back."

The steak hisses, drawing orange flames around the fatty sides. A chunk drips down and perishes on the coals. Julian takes the tongs back and eyes her. He slides the steak to the side, removing it from the fire.

"I wonder what they're posting on the website today," Julian says, eyeing the steak.

She'd wondered as well. Since she began hunting the Full Moon Killer for the FBI, Darcy has monitored a website devoted to serial killers. The forum activity perks up when a new killer becomes active. Doll Face must have the board in an uproar. Goosebumps crawl down Darcy's arms when she remembers posts tracking her activity. One forum member, who hid behind the name *FM-Kill-Her*, penned fan fiction, which depicted the bloody murders of Darcy and her family. The moderators took the post down and suspended the author's account. But not before Darcy saw.

"I'll check the site after dinner."

"Don't."

"It's amazing the information they dig up. Like they're on the front lines, watching the murders."

Plating the steak, Julian shoots Darcy a warning glance.

"Watch yourself. Remember your theory about Michael Rivers and his henchmen using the forum under assumed names? You never know who's tracking you online."

Darcy removes a glass bowl of pasta salad from the refrigerator and sets it on the table. Time never stops ticking. By the middle of next month, Hunter will be off to college again, and she won't see him until Thanksgiving.

Trepidation crawls from the hidden corners of Darcy's mind. What if the FBI can't catch the Doll Face Killer?

After dinner, Julian cleans the grill while Jennifer and Hunter double-team the dishes. Darcy opens her laptop and clicks the link to the serial killer forum. Every thread on the first page follows Doll Face's activity. She follows the rabbit holes, opening threads and scanning the comments. Theories about why he kills, who Doll Face is, and where they expect he'll strike next. None of it represents an informed opinion. Just sickos rubbernecking. Then there are the fans, the sociopaths Darcy worries about. They worship this new killer, cheering him on as they would their favorite football team. She's ready to give up when a new thread opens to photographs of Veil Lake. The sun reflecting bloody tones against the tranquil water. A worried woman hustling out of a hardware store at dusk, her haunted eyes fixed on the photographer. Someone on the forum is in Veil Lake, Michigan, documenting the horror.

Or is he causing the horror? The possibility the photographer could be the Doll Face Killer sends a tingle down Darcy's spine. She clicks on a picture of the lake, offering a larger view of the image. It also reveals the person responsible for uploading the photograph. *FM-Kill-Her*.

3

Seconds become minutes. When Darcy checks the time, she realizes she wasted two hours paging through the serial killer website forum. With an apology waiting behind her lips, she pads to the living room, passing the closed doors to her kids' bedrooms. Laughter and yelling emanate from behind Hunter's door. He's playing on the Xbox with his friends.

One table lamp shines in the corner as dusk fills the living room window. Julian sits on the couch, his back to her, eyes glued to the television. He's watching a cable news channel, one of those networks where shills scream at each other over politics. From the scene playing out on the television, something more ominous than political strife played out moments ago. The floor squeals under Darcy's foot. Julian spins around and finds her behind the couch.

"Are you watching this?" His gaze swings back to the television as Darcy slides beside him. "He got another family."

The Doll Face Killer murdered again. From the swirling lights of the emergency vehicles and the police officer holding the looky-loos at bay, Darcy can tell it's a fresh scene. In a village walking on pins-and-needles, any rumor of another murder will throw the populace into a panic. A female newscaster with perfect teeth and auburn hair holds a microphone in front of a two-story residence on Veil Lake. Except for the row of bushes along the house, Darcy can't discern much about the residence, the darkening sky casting gloom over the house. At the bottom of the television screen, the news announces the residence belongs to Jim and Carol Lieberman.

"Turn up the sound," Darcy says, pointing at the remote on Julian's lap.

So far, it's all conjecture. The police aren't prepared to give a statement. Just then, a grizzled officer with gray hair curling up beneath his cap crosses the yard. The camera jostles as the operator rushes toward the officer. The breathless reporter shouts questions, demanding to know if the killer struck again. A second officer rushes in front of the reporter and cuts them off, the camera angling toward the sky as he forces them behind the barricades. As the cameraman rights his camera, Darcy spies two men on the porch stoop wearing baggies over their shoes.

"The CSI team arrived," Darcy says, leaning forward.

The reporter retrieves her fallen microphone and fixes her hair as the camera zooms in.

"Jim and Carol Lieberman, both fifty-nine-years-old, are lifelong residents of Veil Lake. Police aren't saying if the married couple is inside the house, but we just learned an anonymous caller phoned 9-1-1 about a disturbance inside the Lieberman household. As you can see over my shoulder..." The reporter shifts her body, and the camera focuses on the two-story house. "The lights are off inside the Lieberman house, and a neighbor tells us the lights have been off for the past three days. We don't want to speculate. But the Doll Face Killer, the murderer terrorizing the tiny village of Veil Lake, keeps his victims for three days before killing them."

Her voice trails off when Julian lowers the sound.

"Why did you turn it down? I wanted to listen."

Julian waves his hand at the television.

"They don't know what they're talking about. If they had anything to say, they would have told us already."

"Then why were you watching?"

He clears his throat and flips the channel, settling on a baseball game.

"I came across the news while channel surfing." Darcy swivels and hurries toward the bedroom. Julian rises from the couch and follows. "Slow down. Don't pull the story up on the Internet. Darcy, neither of us can stop what's happening in Michigan."

She clicks off the forum and scans the websites for the major news networks. All of them display headlines from Veil Lake, speculating on rumors. Two more people died at the hands of a psychopath. Julian stands beside the chair, staring down at her.

"What?"

"You're considering Agent Ketchum's offer."

Darcy folds her arms and shakes her head. Standing up from the desk, she paces the bedroom, searching for words which match her feelings.

"It's not my responsibility. But there must be something I can do to help, even if I work from here."

"Darcy, don't go down that hole. You know where it leads."

"Yes, I'm aware of the risks." Her eyes stop on the nightstand. She expects to find a bottle of anti-anxiety pills beside the bed. The space now holds only a lamp and the new Dean Koontz novel. Her fingers curl and uncurl. "Julian, I can't decide."

He holds her arms and kisses her forehead. Resignation softens his face. He's afraid she'll run off to Michigan, and he's willing to negotiate.

"That's not a bad idea. Aiding the FBI from home. You can run searches for Ketchum, send him profiles based on the information the FBI feeds you. That keeps you here with your family and out of the field."

And out of harm's way. That's what he really means. She slumps into the chair and buries her face in her hands.

"What's the murder count now? It's growing by the week."

"Take it from a cop. The only people responsible for solving these murders are the Veil Lake PD and the FBI." He kneels beside Darcy and rests his hand on her shoulder. "If you can't stop yourself from getting involved, consult with the FBI from home. That way you'll keep up with your P.I. caseload."

When she doesn't reply, Julian gives her time to think through the situation. The door closes, and she's alone with her guilt. She should have listened to Ketchum.

Darcy understands the worst thing she can do is open the laptop again and read the updates. She can't help herself. The headline stares back at her as though mirroring her desperation.

The Doll Face Killer Murders Two More.

4

The clamor inside the Veil Grill gives the teenager a headache.

Dishes clink together, the cook calls out orders, and patrons at the bar and tables shout as if they aren't sitting three feet apart. But it's good to see this many people inside the restaurant. Faith appreciates Rosanna for giving her a chance to prove herself a worthy employee, and business has been good. Even with the police searching for a criminal inside their tranquil village. Mom and Dad won't tell her more. A criminal is loose in Veil Lake, and she needs to be careful. Be careful of what? Criminals steal things, and Faith has nothing worth stealing. She doesn't even own a car. Faith used an app on her phone to order rides home after work until last month. And that stunk, because she lost a third of her wages to Uber and Lyft. Now she's not even allowed to use a ride sharing service. Dad drives her because of the stupid criminal running loose. Wouldn't it be easier if Mom and Dad bought her a cheap car? Something small and used with rust around the edges.

What's the use in pretending? They'll never trust her to drive. No one will. It's not as if she can't learn. She watches Mom and Dad drive. All you need to do is press your foot on the left pedal when you want to stop and stomp the pedal on the right when you want to go. The harder you stomp, the faster you drive. There's other stuff, of course. She'd need to memorize which direction to push the blinker lever and figure out how to turn the lights on and off.

"Faith, you daydreaming again?"

Faith pauses mid-wipe and lifts the cleaning cloth off the polished bar. Her reflection merges with the long row of patrons, turning everyone blurry. She lifts her head and grins at her boss. Rosanna wears a handkerchief over blonde curls. She has a button nose and high cheekbones that flare in pink tones as though someone told her an embarrassing joke.

"Sorry, Ms. Noble. I was just thinking about driving a car someday."

Clutching a handful of receipts, Rosanna pulls Faith into a hug and kisses the top of her head. Just like Mom did when Faith was younger.

"You can accomplish anything you set your mind to," Rosanna says, whispering in her ear.

The woman's breath tickles, but Faith doesn't break into a fit of giggles. Rosanna's words warm her. Lots of people tell Faith she can do anything, even Mom and Dad, but sometimes she catches them glance away when they say it, concealing their beliefs. When Rosanna encourages Faith, the teenager believes. Faith hopes she grows up to be kind and helpful like Rosanna.

"Now, can you help me with the phones? Jill called in sick, and my hands are tied running orders and payments."

"Yes, Ms. Noble."

Rosanna hesitates. She places the receipts beside the register and draws Faith into another hug. This one lasts longer.

"I'm really gonna miss you this fall," Rosanna says with a

tear behind her words. "You don't know how proud I am of you. College. Do you realize how special you are, Faith?"

"Lots of kids go to college."

"But they didn't work as hard as you did to get to this point. Remember your promise."

"Yes, I'll email you every week to let you know how I'm doing."

"And if you ever need someone to talk to..."

"I'll call you on my cell phone."

Rosanna touches Faith on the cheek and presses her lips to the teenager's forehead. Faith closes her eyes. She'll miss Rosanna, maybe even more than she'll miss Mom and Dad. Oh, that was a mean thought. She's glad she didn't say it out loud. Family comes first, and she loves her parents more than anything in the world. But the possibilities seem endless when she's with Rosanna. What if she didn't go to school and stayed in Veil Lake? She could work right here at the restaurant. In time, she could save enough money for driving lessons. If she worked hard, Rosanna would give her a raise so Faith could buy her own car. Her parents couldn't say no if she paid for everything herself. She's eighteen, a legal adult. But that's her fear talking. The scared side of her that feels intimidated. Though North Chadwick University isn't as big as Michigan State, eight thousand students attend the school. That's two hundred times larger than her high school's senior class.

Taking a composing breath, Faith moves down the bar and cleans a spill. The messy person left five dollars. Maybe because he felt bad. Keith is the server, but he's busy taking an order from a loud couple at the end of the bar. Faith sets the tip aside and affixes a sticky note with Keith's name written on it.

"Hey, hey!"

Faith smiles at the drunk guy in the flannel shirt struggling to stay upright. He wears his sleeves rolled up. There's an anchor tattoo on his forearm that reminds her of the Popeye cartoon. The man's eyes droop, his smile more of a sneer. An equally drunk woman props him up, snickering every time he almost topples off the stool.

"Hey, I'm talking to you. You understand words, right?"

The woman spits her beer and doubles over, an overreaction to the man's joke.

"May I help you, sir?"

"May I help you?" He mocks in falsetto. The drunk man waves a dollar bill in her face, supporting himself against the bar. "How about you pour me a refill?"

Faith glances over her shoulder. Rosanna is busy talking to the cook. Something about a problem with an order. Faith remembers Rosanna telling Keith not to serve this man more alcohol tonight.

"Beer costs more than a dollar, you idiot," the woman laughs.

He leans into her ear and proclaims, "Yeah, but she doesn't know that," as if Faith can't hear.

This inspires both to clutch their sides in laughter. The woman hacks, a smoker's cough.

Faith tells the man she's cleaning tonight and Keith will help him. Now the laughter and good times flee the man's eyes. He slams the mug on the bar, sloshing foam over the rim.

"Listen here. It's a free country, and I'm allowed to have a freaking beer when I want one. If I give you money, you have to serve me. Capeesh?"

"I'm sorry, mister. I'm not allowed to take orders, but if you wait for Keith—"

"Then what the hell good are you? Can't believe they let dummies work in a restaurant. Soon we'll have blind taxi drivers and deaf music critics. Entire world is going to shit, if you ask me."

"Knock it off."

The man who slides onto the neighboring stool looks familiar. He's younger than the drunk. Kind hazel eyes. Sandy hair parted on the side. Where does Faith know him from?

"I wasn't talking to you, jerk off," the drunk man slurs.

The woman narrows her eyes on the new man.

"I know you weren't, but you are now," says the familiar man. "Leave the girl alone."

"She wouldn't take my order."

"Come on now, friend." The man with the kind eyes drops his hand on the drunk's shoulder. "How about we call it a night? Save your cash for next time. Hell, it's a weeknight."

"Take your fucking hand off me."

The drunk throws the kind man's hand off his shoulder and takes an aggressive step off the stool. He stands chest to chest with his smaller foe. A mass of patrons step between the men to diffuse the fight before it can begin.

"You're dead," the drunk says, pointing at his new enemy as three men prod him toward the exit.

The woman's eyes shoot bullets back at Faith.

"It's her fault. The freak started it."

Faith flinches. The door closes, drowning out the angry shouts from the parking lot.

"Are you okay?" Rosanna asks, touching Faith's arm.

"Yes. You don't have to worry about me."

Keith is on the phone with the police. He's arguing because they can't send a cruiser to the restaurant for another fifteen minutes. Faith wonders if the criminal Mom and Dad mentioned struck Veil Lake tonight.

Rosanna gives Faith a concerned stare before she returns to her backlog of receipts. Faith wishes everyone would stop yelling and not treat her like a child. She grabs a dry rag and cleans the spilled beer. Her cheeks burn. Everyone is staring at her. Ignoring them, Faith scrubs the bar clean until she can see her reflection.

"That was brave of you, standing up to that man."

Faith raises her eyes. It's the familiar man with the kind eyes speaking to her.

"You were the brave one," Faith says, trying hard to remember where she's seen his face before.

"Brave? It scared me. He was about to punch my lights out before Tom and the others stepped in."

The kind man raises his soda and tips it toward three men at the end of the bar. Tom nods back at him.

"I was afraid they'd start a fight and break something in the restaurant. That would make Mrs. Noble sad."

"Yeah, it sure would," the man says, playing with his napkin. He sips his soda. "You're a hard worker, Faith. You don't take any breaks, and you're the first person to show up on the job. I wish we had someone with your work ethic at the post office."

She remembers him now. Mr. Funes. He delivers mail around Veil Lake, though another postman took over in her neighborhood the last two years. Faith's Dad said their routes change all the time. That must be tough, memorizing all those streets and names.

"Keith works the hardest," Faith says, tilting her head toward the young man carrying a cardboard box toward the office.

Funes takes another sip and skims his eyes over the restaurant as if worried the drunk man and the woman will come back. Business is booming, almost every table filled. Impressive for a Tuesday evening.

"So the Fighting Red Hens," Funes says, stopping Faith when she moves toward another spill further down the bar.

She cocks her head at him.

"Come on, Faith. You have to learn your school's mascot if

you want to be a fan. Their basketball team will be good this year. I bet you'll have good seats, being a student and all."

"I didn't know that was their name."

"Heck, yes. The North Chadwick Fighting Red Hens. That's an elite school too. With a degree from North Chadwick, you might be famous someday."

Faith blushes. Mr. Funes is a nice man, but she's falling behind. How do her workmates balance talking with people and keeping up with their jobs?

"Bet you're psyched about going to college," he says. "Excited, I mean."

Faith knows what psyched means. Mr. Funes looks embarrassed. He tears the corners off his napkin and fidgets.

"Yeah, I can't wait to meet my roommates. They'll know all the fun things to do at college, and I'll be able to call Mom and Dad when I miss home."

Funes nods and points at Faith.

"You're gonna be an enormous success at college, Faith. When you come home, you need to tell me all about school and the neat things you learned."

Faith gives Mr. Funes a nervous laugh. She hardly knows the man. Why is he so interested? Funes lowers his eyes when he catches Keith glaring at him. The postman clears his throat and sets a five-dollar bill on the bar.

"I need to use the little boy's room. Can you watch my drink?"

"Sure," Faith says.

It doesn't seem fair to accept five dollars. He's only going to the bathroom, and it's silly to watch over his soda when there are so many other jobs she should be doing. Besides, her shift ends in fifteen minutes. What if Funes takes longer than fifteen minutes? She slides down the bar, unable to see Funes anymore amid the throng of patrons. Then the phone rings. Shoot. Faith

promised Rosanna she'd answer phone calls, but she's behind
on her tasks. The garbage behind the bar smells and needs to go
in the dumpster. People are scattering peanuts and pretzels
everywhere. A man in a tight gray t-shirt knocks his knuckles on
the bar, holding a wad of dollar bills in his hand. Nobody is
available to take his order. And the phone keeps ringing.

Faith blows out a flustered breath and picks up the phone.

"Veil Lake Grill," she says. "This is Faith."

"Faith Fielder?"

She doesn't recognize the man's voice, but he has a sing-song
voice that reminds her of Mr. Funes.

"Yes."

"This is Glen Filmore at North Chadwick University."

Faith's heart pounds. Who is Glen Filmore, and why would
anyone from the university call her at work? She hopes they
aren't rescinding her acceptance. With everyone shouting inside
the restaurant, Faith needs to plug her other ear to hear Mr.
Filmore.

"Do you remember me, Faith? We met at the Learning
Disabilities Center. Or as we like to call it, the Learning Abilities
Center."

Faith squints her eyes and tries to recall. She met so many
people at North Chadwick during the tour.

"Hello, Mr. Filmore," Faith says with a pang of guilt. She
doesn't remember Mr. Filmore, though she's sure they met. "I
still get to go to North Chadwick in August, right?"

Mr. Filmore's chuckle sets Faith at ease.

"Of course, of course. We're all very excited you're coming to
our school."

"I wish it was already August."

"I'm sure you do, Faith. The first week at college is memora-
ble for all students. So many new friends."

"I want to make new friends."

"Well, you'll make more friends than you ever dreamed of. North Chadwick has over eight thousand students."

"So many people." A motor rumbles in the background. "Are you outside somewhere, like on a street, Mr. Filmore?"

"Why, yes. That's very perceptive. You're an incredible talent, Faith."

A glass shatters. Keith rushes to clean the mess, glancing at Faith as he sweeps the shards into a dust pan. Faith doesn't want Keith and Rosanna to be angry. She's answering phone calls as she was told. But this call is taking a long time.

"I should get back to work, Mr. Filmore. It's busy tonight, and someone broke a glass."

"I won't keep you, Faith. Listen, the reason I called is I'm in town."

Faith touches her forehead.

"Why are you in Veil Lake?"

"Because you're an extra special student, and we need to start working immediately. We're not hiding you in remedial classes. You're getting a real college degree, just like everyone else. But it won't be easy. College is much harder than high school."

Faith bites her lip. The high school sheltered her to a degree, kept her out of the grueling classes until she proved herself capable.

"I'll do whatever it takes to graduate college."

"That's the spirit. How would you like to complete three course credits this summer and get a head start on the other students?"

"Is that why you came here? To get me started?"

"Not only that. I'll be your first professor."

She grins and bounces on her toes.

"When does my first class start?"

"Tomorrow. But I'd like to show you the coursework tonight.

I'm downtown now. I can swing by the restaurant when you finish work and drive you to the place I'm renting."

A voice whispers danger in the back of her head. She's not to accept rides from strangers. Mr. Filmore isn't a stranger, is he? They met during orientation. But she met a hundred or more people. The faces are a blur. If only she could remember.

"May I ask my parents first?"

Mr. Filmore chuckles.

"I got off the phone with your mother five minutes ago. She's excited for you to work with me. And no surprise—she'd prefer I drive you home and save Dad the trip."

"I don't know."

"You don't have to take my word for it. Your mother left you a message. I have it on my recorder. Would you like me to play it for you?"

"Mom said I can go with you?"

There's a pause as Mr. Filmore plays the recording. Her mother's voice sounds tinny and distant coming through the speaker. Yet it's her.

"She really said it was okay," Faith says, breathing a sigh of relief.

"Faith, the parking lot at the restaurant is probably overflowing at this time of night. Could you do me a favor and meet me at the corner of Spruce and Church? It's only half a block from the restaurant."

"Sure, Mr. Filmore. And thank you for teaching me. I can't wait to see you."

"I'll be there in ten minutes, Faith Fielder, future North Chadwick graduate."

The call ends. Faith tingles with energy. A smile etched to her face, she finishes her tasks, keeping one eye on the clock. She enjoys her work, but the ten minutes feel like an hour.

When it's time to leave, she waves to Keith and Rosanna and promises to work harder next time. Rosanna cocks an eyebrow.

Starlight bathes the sidewalk, turns the lakeside village silvery and magical. With the restaurant commotion behind her, cricket songs swell, and her footsteps become loud. Every house on Spruce appears asleep. Shades drawn, lights doused. Somewhere a car door closes.

She stands alone at the corner. Where is Mr. Filmore? Sometimes kids play jokes on her. Many did during her school days. Is this an elaborate prank to play Faith for a fool? She scrolls through the contacts on her phone and pauses over her mother's number. At that moment, a pair of headlights slice through the night. A vehicle crawls down Church. Please, let this be Mr. Filmore. A friendly toot of the horn announces his presence. He pulls to the curb in a minivan and rolls down the window.

"Hop in, Faith. The night isn't getting younger."

A moment of indecision freezes her on the sidewalk. She can't see his face. Too many shadows inside the car, the lights blinding.

"Everything all right? Perhaps we should call Mom again."

"No," Faith says.

Her mother already gave permission, and Faith doesn't wish to make a fool of herself.

She grasps the door handle and slips inside.

WEDNESDAY, JULY 2ND 10:15 A.M.

D amn these weeds.

Darcy grabs a clump and pulls them from the garden, roots and all. The app on her phone identifies the offending weed as mugwort, a plant with medicinal benefits. It spreads faster than she can remove it from the garden, choking off her lettuce, tomatoes, and pepper plants. Wiping the sweat off her brow, she squints at the North Carolina sun. It hasn't been this hot in two years. Not since the summer Michael Rivers came to Darkwater Cove.

The memory pulls her gaze to the neighboring house. A young couple owns the house now. Janelle ringed the home with rose bushes and blooming perennials, and Derek installed a concrete deck off the back door and a fire pit on the lawn. They've brought Darcy, Julian, and Jennifer over for cookouts. Two years ago, the house stood vacant. The black-eyed windows watched her at all hours of the night. Grass and weeds grew knee high. And the Full Moon Killer hid inside the master bedroom and stalked Darcy for days without her knowing.

The deck door slides open. A toolbox in hand, Julian waves to Darcy and sits down to replace a warped board. Darcy fans her face. Damn this heat. Not even eleven o'clock, and it's too hot to work in the garden. As she hauls a bucket of weeds to the compost bin, a black SUV pulls to the curb. Agent Ketchum. Darcy glances toward Julian, but he hasn't noticed the vehicle. The FBI SUV idles curbside until the engine shuts off.

Ketchum wears black slacks and sunglasses. Even with his suit jacket thrown over one shoulder, he must feel uncomfortable in a long sleeve button down. Not noticing Darcy in the backyard, Ketchum angles toward the driveway and heads for the front door. If Julian sees the FBI agent, the argument will turn ugly. Dropping the bucket, Darcy rushes around the corner. Ketchum notices her before he presses the doorbell.

"You shouldn't be here," Darcy says, looking over her shoulder for Julian as she marches across the lawn.

"Please, Mrs. Haines."

"I gave you my answer yesterday evening."

Julian shouts behind her. Too late. Removing his baseball cap, Julian approaches the federal agent. Though Julian would never start a fight, his muscular physique outweighs Ketchum's by twenty pounds, and the bull rush is meant to intimidate the intruder.

"It's all right, Julian," Darcy says, placing a hand on her husband's chest. "Agent Ketchum and I are just talking."

"Do you realize how long it took before the nightmares stopped?" Julian yells over Darcy's shoulder. "And you want to toss her into the fire again. She sacrificed enough."

Ketchum slides his sunglasses off. He barely glances at Julian, his eyes fixed on Darcy.

"If there's somewhere quiet we can speak," Ketchum says. "I'll only take five minutes of your time."

"She gave five years—"

"I can handle it," Darcy tells Julian.

His lips stretch tight.

"I'll be on the deck if you need me."

Julian kisses her forehead and shoots a glance of admonition at Ketchum. After he rounds the house, Darcy opens the door and motions Ketchum inside. She offers Ketchum a chair, but the agent prefers to stand. His hands slide into his pocket as he leans against the counter. Darcy stands opposite Ketchum, arms folded.

"I considered your offer," Darcy says.

It's quiet inside the kitchen. A clock ticks in the living room. Jennifer and Hunter are still asleep. For once, she's grateful her kids stayed up past two o'clock and slept in late.

"What did you decide?"

"I'm willing to work from home and give you a profile. But I can't enter the field again. I won't do that to my family."

"You mean you won't do that to Julian."

"He supports me. This is my decision, not Julian's."

"Mrs. Haines...may I call you Darcy?" She nods. "When I joined the FBI, Agent Hensel fought hard for you to rejoin the Behavior Analysis Unit."

"I told you not to bring up my friend's name again. Eric was the best agent I worked with. He gave his life to save my family, and I won't allow you to use his name for your own benefit."

"It's not for my benefit, Darcy. It's for Veil Lake, the victims. And for you."

"For me?"

"Let's be honest, Darcy," he says. "Private investigative work? That's beneath someone of your considerable talents. You spend your days tracking fraud and catching spouses in moments of infidelity. How will you feel the next time Doll Face butchers another family? Or a child? The FBI trained you to find kidnappers and serial killers. Nobody in the BAU has your gift, Darcy. We need you. *I* need you."

Darcy sits in a chair and scrubs her hands across her face.

"Agent Ketchum, I have two children."

"And you're a newlywed. Congratulations."

She narrows her eyes. Though his eyes display kindness, she takes the compliment backhanded.

"It's ridiculous you haven't filled your profiler positions. What's happening at the upper reaches of the FBI? Someone slashing budgets again?"

Ketchum pauses. He slides a chair out from the table and sits across from Darcy, his eyes locked on hers.

"Darcy, he took a girl with Down syndrome this time."

Darcy catches the next argument in her chest.

"Down syndrome?" She blinks. "When did this happen?"

"I take it you saw the report on the Lieberman couple? It was all over the national news."

"We did."

"The bastard has balls. Two hours after he murdered the Lieberman family and phoned the police, he abducted Faith Fielder."

"How old?"

"Eighteen. The girl was on her way to college this fall."

Drumming her fingers on the table, Darcy slows her mind before it spins out of control.

"What do we know about Doll Face?"

"We identified several similarities to Michael Rivers. But this guy doesn't wait on lunar cycles. Doll Face keeps his victims seventy-two hours before he murders them and phones the police. The son-of-a-bitch wants us to view his work. He faces the victims toward the lake. We don't understand the significance."

"It doesn't sound like you know much about this guy."

Ketchum's gaze moves to the sliding glass door, then falls to the table.

"We don't. That's why I'm here."

Over Ketchum's shoulder, Julian pounds a deck board into place. Julian keeps looking into the kitchen. He won't be pleased with Darcy for agreeing to Ketchum's request. Doll Face kidnapping any teenager would tug Darcy's heartstrings. But a girl with Down syndrome...

"I'll help you. But this is a onetime deal. I have no intentions of returning to the FBI."

Ketchum nods.

"You'll receive your full prorated salary, plus a consulting bonus."

Darcy and Julian could use the money. Though the GCPD pays its detectives well, and Darcy's investigative business thrived the last year, Hunter's college payments took a bite out of their savings. Jennifer's college days are closer than Darcy wants to believe.

The FBI agent crosses one leg over the other.

"And except for visiting crime scenes, you won't be in the field. We'll take Doll Face down. Your sole job is to find him."

"I can't promise my husband will take this well."

"If it smooths things over, he can accompany you. But the contract is for you alone."

"I'll speak with Julian."

When she looks through the deck door, Julian is gone.

6

Julian isn't difficult to track. He walks the cove when he's under pressure.

Darcy follows his footprints down the beach until she spots seagulls swirling over a figure at the far end of the cove. His back turned to her, Julian doesn't see Darcy approach. A smile curls her lips as she watches him leap and toss pieces of bread into the air. He's kind and childlike, and the last thing she wants to do is spend the next two weeks away from him.

"You're going with Ketchum to Michigan."

It isn't a question.

Darcy halts, wondering how Julian knew she was behind him. He brushes the crumbs from his hands and spins back to her. Disappointed, the gulls screech and swoop toward the public beach for their next free meal.

"I'm sorry."

He touches her cheek. The pained look in his eye forms a lump in Darcy's throat.

"Are you sure about this?"

She half-nods, half-shakes her head. Wandering along the shore with her hands buried inside the pockets of her shorts, Darcy steps through the breakers. The Atlantic feels bathwater-warm, the waves sparkling with a million reflections of the sun.

"The only thing I'm sure of is the FBI won't catch him on their own."

"What did Ketchum tell you about the killer?"

"Nothing we didn't already know. The killer's a psychopath, another Michael Rivers."

"Leave him to the feds. This is how they earn their paychecks."

"This isn't an ordinary killer, Julian. Guys like this come around once every twenty or thirty years. It's extraordinary this decade produced two mass murderers the public will remember forever."

"You act like you can't wait to go. Something changed your mind."

She stops and cups her elbows with her hands, tracing a line in the sand with her toe. The tide washes the drawing away.

"He took a girl with Down syndrome this time."

"Jesus."

Darcy's eyes glaze. She swipes a tear away with her thumb.

"Ketchum says Doll Face holds his captives for seventy-two hours before he kills them."

"Why three days?"

"Why did Michael Rivers murder under a full moon? There's always more mystery than fact with serial killers."

"Then I'm coming with you."

Darcy stops and places her hands on Julian's shoulders. If Julian had heard Ketchum's invitation, Darcy couldn't have stopped him from coming. Julian won the bid for the detective position after his predecessor, Detective Ames, retired. The mayor likes Julian, and whispers around Julian becoming a future police chief candidate have already started. Now isn't the time for Julian to ruffle feathers.

"You can't. As much as I want you with me, I'd feel more comfortable with you watching Jennifer than Hunter. Besides, you saved your annual leave for the Outer Banks in August."

He paces like a rat in a cage.

"If I talk to the chief, he'll get me a few days off. I can borrow leave from next year."

"Stop," Darcy says, shifting in front of him. "All I have to do is find the guy. It's up to the FBI to capture Doll Face."

Unconvinced, Julian scrunches his brow.

"And if Agent Ketchum isn't around when this psycho shows his face?"

"The Doll Face Killer won't know I'm in Veil Lake."

"Until your fan club reports your position on the serial killer website."

"I'll speak with Ketchum," Darcy says, caressing his cheek. His skin holds the sun's warmth. "I'll make him promise to keep my name out of the press."

"They'll find out. And when they do, there'll be a firestorm. The agent who caught the Full Moon Killer tracks a new psychopath in Michigan." He laughs without mirth. "You'll dominate every headline for the next week."

"I'll have Ketchum and the entire Veil Lake PD surrounding me. There's no danger."

"Please, there's always danger," he scoffs. "You'll miss everything while you're gone. The Genoa Cove fireworks celebration, the Independence Day parade. You're supposed to help the Women's Auxiliary plan the festivities."

"The Women's Auxiliary survived for over a century without Darcy Gellar Haines. They won't miss me."

"Maybe not. But we will."

She lowers her head. It's only a week or two. Why does it seem like she's never coming back? Ketchum wants her on the plane in two hours, and she hasn't packed.

The wind blows her hair back. His eyes fix on the lightning bolt scar running across her scalp, a permanent memory of the tornado striking the forest on the night they killed Michael Rivers.

He drapes his arm around her shoulder, and she leans into his body as they follow their footprints across the cove. Her stomach flutters. Michigan seems a world away. When the sun sets tonight, she'll be alone in a crowd and missing her family as she tracks the most vicious killer to strike the U.S. since Michael Rivers. Lest she forget, Rivers plunged a knife into her belly. She shouldn't be alive. Luck, not FBI training, saved her the first time she encountered the Full Moon Killer.

Back at the house, Julian helps Darcy gather her belongings. She takes enough clothes for five nights. If the case lasts longer, she'll do laundry. Her kids stumble bleary-eyed to the kitchen to scrounge for breakfast, Hunter's uncombed hair a rat's nest of spikes.

Jennifer pours oat milk into a bowl of cereal and catches Darcy watching in the entryway.

"What?"

"I'm leaving for a few days," Darcy says, letting out a breath. She sits across the table from Jennifer and Hunter, occupying the chair Agent Ketchum used when he convinced her to accept the FBI's offer. "It will just be the three of you. Promise me you'll behave for Julian."

Jennifer sets her spoon down and glares at Hunter. Her kids are perceptive. They've followed the Michigan murders.

"This is about that Doll Face maniac, isn't it?"

"The FBI wants me as a consultant, someone to help figure out who this guy is."

"And that's all you'll do, right?" Hunter asks. "Just consult."

"You can do that from here," Jennifer argues. "Why do you have to go to Michigan?"

"Because it isn't easy to track someone like Doll Face by reading articles. I need to see the crime scenes, interview the victims' families. Figure out how this guy ticks."

"Get inside his head. That's what you mean." Darcy braces herself for one of Jennifer's eruptions. To Darcy's surprise, her daughter composes herself. "Mom, what if the nightmares start again?"

"I don't think they will, honey," Darcy says, reaching across the table. She grasps her children's hands as Julian leans in the doorway. "But if they do, I swear I won't hide it. I won't go into a shell like last time."

Jennifer worries Darcy will fall off the wagon and overdose on anti-anxiety medication. Hunter holds a blank expression on his face. Blocking out problems is her son's coping tool.

Through translucent drapes dangling over the living room window, Darcy spots the black FBI SUV at the curb. Ketchum sits inside. She checks the time and jolts. They'll be late for the flight if she doesn't hurry.

"Don't do this," Hunter says, rising when Darcy stands.

"I'll call you as soon as I get there, and I'll talk with you every day I'm gone." She pulls her children into a hug. "I won't be gone long. A week or less. And I promise I'm coming back."

Julian grabs Darcy two protein bars for the trip. Though he's disappointed with her decision, Julian supports her. She loves that he believes in her.

"I'll text you when we reach the airport."

He presses his lips against hers. His kiss is warm. It draws the nervous energy out of her shoulders. Closing her eyes, she wraps her arms around Julian and wishes she could fast-forward through the next week. Being away from Julian and the kids slams against her chest and tightens her throat.

"Catch the bastard, Darcy."

She opens her eyes. In that moment, he's more than her partner and lover. Detective Haines understands the stakes.

"I'll find him."

7

WEDNESDAY, JULY 2ND 11:30 A.M.

Mr. Filmore allowed Faith to sleep late. She didn't awake until ten, and he had a plateful of strawberry-topped waffles waiting for her in the kitchen. After he watched her eat, his eyes happy and full of wonder as he washed dishes, she studied the downstairs. Faith saw little of the cabin last night. The long evening at the restaurant left her exhausted, and she retired to her bed after he showed her to her room. Her bedroom is tiny but clean, with a bed and a child-size desk.

"Like a dorm room," he'd remarked when she first entered the bedroom. "No better time than the present to live like a college student."

The living room isn't much larger than her bedroom. There's an ancient couch with a blanket covering the rips. A small television faces the couch, and a bookcase holds a small library of gardening manuals. He keeps his bedroom door locked. She knows this because the lock pops when he exits the room. A locked door also bars access to the room across the hall.

The tidy bathroom appears half the size of her family's bathroom. Hair dots the sink. The medicine cabinet holds a myriad of pill bottles with names she doesn't recognize. She felt embarrassed opening the cabinet, but she needed toothpaste for the brush he gave her.

Now the hour approaches noon, and the open windows welcome in a soothing breeze that carries the clean scent of Veil Lake. Birds chirp and caw beyond the window, and butterflies perch on the screen, unfurling multicolored wings. She hasn't seen his garden yet. Already, it fascinates her.

"You'll pay your tuition with your work in the garden," he says, covering his balding head with a bucket hat. Mr. Filmore removes his glasses and cleans the lenses on his shirt. He squints. "Ah, much better. Come, Faith. Let me show you the wonders of nature."

He's taller than she thought, even bigger than Dad. Though Mr. Filmore isn't muscular, he moves with a limber, athletic grace that reminds Faith of classical music. He keeps itching his hands. Red splotches like insect bites rise off the skin.

Mr. Filmore leads her out the door. When she arrived last night, it had been pitch black. Walking through the gated fence to the front door seemed like traversing a jungle, and she'd shivered at the possibility of wild beasts with wicked fangs crouching in the darkness. For the first time, she sees the garden in all its glory. This is not a jungle to fear. It's a kaleidoscope of colors. More butterflies wing over the plants, some of which grow past Faith's knees.

"Oh," she says. "It's so beautiful."

He places a hand on her shoulder.

"Calluna vulgaris. Heather plants."

The colors sweep her in—crimsons, sunrise oranges, and a rich man's gold. Dirt paths worm between the plants. His hands clasped behind his back, he strolls between the rows with Faith trailing him. Her gaze whirls from one color to the next. It's as if the garden is liquid, and she can dive in.

"How did you plant so many?"

"The heather plant represents change, becoming," he says as though he didn't hear her question. "Do you wish to be an exceptional student, Faith?"

"Yes, I do."

"Then there is much you can learn from heather. From humble beginnings come grand resolutions. You will care for my heathers, Faith, and they will care for you."

His words make little sense to Faith, but she nods along, intent on pleasing this man. She never met anyone like Mr. Filmore.

Above the rows, a wooden fence circles the yard. It's too tall to climb, and the horizontal slats lie across the other side of the fence. Not that she would climb the fence, but she wonders why he needs a barricade. As Mr. Filmore leads her through the rows, her gaze keeps moving to the fence. It circles the property. No way in or out.

"What's the fence for, Mr. Filmore?"

"Elementary." He removes the hat and wipes sweat on his shirtsleeve. "The garden attracts wildlife, dear Faith. Without the fence, deer, woodchucks, rabbits, and even the black bear would sneak out of the woods and take my garden."

My garden. Faith scratches her head.

"I thought you worked at North Chadwick, Mr. Filmore? Didn't you tell me you came to Veil Lake to teach me?"

"Did I say that?"

"On the phone, yes."

"Well, the truth is I live in Veil Lake."

Her eyebrows shoot up.

"I've never seen you in town before."

"I keep to myself. The college is only an hour up the road, so it's an easy commute."

"I'm lucky one of my teachers lives in town."

"Very lucky, yes."

Inside the house, it didn't appear anyone lived with Mr. Filmore. No perfumes belonging to a wife. Yet he keeps the extra bedroom locked.

"Is it just you living here, Mr. Filmore?"

"Just me, Faith. And you for as long as you wish to stay."

Mr. Filmore's face twitches with a nervous tic that reminds Faith of her Uncle Sal. Aunt Donna left Uncle Sal, and Mom said the divorce and living alone changed Uncle Sal. Perhaps that's Mr. Filmore's problem. He doesn't enjoy living alone.

"Come into the kitchen," he says, leading her inside.

It takes a long time for Faith's eyes to adjust from the bright sunshine to the dreary home. She bumps into the wall and hopes he doesn't notice.

"How about an ice cold lemonade?" he asks, pulling a pitcher from the refrigerator. "You have much work to do, and it's important to stay hydrated."

"Okay."

The ice cubes clink against the glass as she raises the drink to her lips. Faith hides her puckered lips, not wanting to offend him. Lemonade always tastes sour to her, even with extra sugar. Mr. Filmore pulls out a chair for Faith.

"You don't talk much."

"Sorry."

He tilts his head. An apology softens his eyes.

"No need to be sorry, Faith. You hardly know me. It's normal to be shy around new people. But you must trust me for our arrangement to work."

"I don't understand," she says, sipping the lemonade. "Is the class about plants?"

He studies the ceiling in thought.

"In a way. The class is about change. Heather represents the wonders nature can achieve when man gets out of her way. But you will study change in humans. Though I must warn you. To understand humans, you must enter darkness."

Faith sets the glass down and wiggles her legs beneath the table.

"Maybe I should start with the plants."

"Indeed. Come. You may bring your drink with you."

The summer heat slams her in the garden. She shields her eyes, thankful for the sour lemonade as Mr. Filmore instructs her. The soil he scoops with his hand is black and rich like chocolate cake or coffee grounds. Earthworms squirm under the dirt and escape the sun. She nods while he speaks, but her eyes wander back to the fence. There's a gate at the end of the row. That must be where they entered the garden last night. Two sturdy locks bar entry.

Faith raises her hand like she did in high school. When he stops, irritation flashes in his eyes. Then his smile returns, though it looks painted on. Like a clown's grin.

"Yes, Faith?"

"What's on the other side of the door?"

"Just the forest outside Veil Lake. Why do you ask?"

"Am I allowed to walk in the forest?"

"I'm afraid the doors must remain locked. These are your mother's orders, you understand. She wouldn't forgive me if you wandered into the woods and became lost, or a wolf came down from the hills and hurt you."

"Wolves?"

Faith shivers. She never knew wolves lived in the hills above Veil Lake.

"And bears. Even the occasional bobcat. The fence protects you. Never open the door and let the forest inside."

He swivels and marches down a row of golden heather. Two chairs and a table provide a relaxation area amid the beauty. Setting her lemonade on the table, Faith follows, holding her hands behind her back as Mr. Filmore does. So much to learn. He tells her about soil acidity and nutrients. Beside the house, he dips both hands into a compost bin and feeds the soil to the plants. Faith doesn't mind getting her hands dirty.

As he discusses soil enrichment, her gaze travels to the corners of the house. A camera points down from each corner. Another camera perches above the gate.

"What are the cameras for?"

He stops what he's doing. The corner of his mouth tics.

"Are you paying attention, Faith? The cameras aren't important."

"But you have so many of them."

He releases a loud exhale and drops the compost. Faith steps back. He seems different. Angry.

"Like the fence and locked door, the cameras protect you. Should the unthinkable happen, and some wild beast sneaks into my garden, I need to know your whereabouts and ensure your safety. Now if you'll let me continue the lesson..."

She bites off her next question. Sometimes Dad becomes irritated when Faith peppers him with questions. She doesn't wish to anger her teacher. Besides, she's a college student now, and she needs to figure things out for herself.

After a long afternoon digging through soil and spreading nutrients around the heather, Mr. Filmore allows her to come inside. Her neck prickles, sunburned and parched. He serves a grilled chicken salad with fresh strawberries and a vinaigrette. Sitting across from her at the kitchen table, Mr. Filmore chews faster than anyone she's met. A rotating fan blows the air around in the kitchen, ruffling Faith's hair with each sweep. He finishes his meal when Faith is only half-done. From a black leather bag at his feet, he pulls a notebook and a folder overflowing with pictures and newspaper articles.

"What's that for?" she asks, pointing with her fork.

"This is your next lesson. Starting now, you will study the human condition in its most evil form."

She coughs into her napkin.

"I don't want to do anything scary."

"Life is scary. Face your fears."

"What are the pictures of?"

"Patience, my dear girl. Finish your food, and we'll start on your assignment."

An old-fashioned telephone hangs on the wall. The phone has a rotary dial like her late-grandmother's.

"I want to talk to my parents."

"And you will." Her heart leaps. "But not until you complete your assignment. When I spoke with your mother, she insisted you immerse yourself in your work and not call home until you finished. She expressed full confidence in your ability."

"But I miss my family."

"Chin up. That's what college is all about. It's uncomfortable moving from home, sleeping in a new bed, meeting people from strange and faraway places. What will you do during fall semester? Call home every five minutes to tell your parents you miss them?"

"No," she says, lowering her eyes to her lap. "Is that why you won't let me keep my phone?"

"Dear Faith, phones are distractions. Besides, your parents know you're with me and studying hard. You'll get your phone back after you complete your coursework."

"How long will that be?"

"Your work will only take three days, if you're thorough. An entire semester crammed into seventy-two hours. Won't your friends be impressed?"

Faith chews a fatty piece of chicken. He's right. Three days will pass in the blink of an eye. No longer hungry, Faith leaves a quarter of her meal untouched. Mr. Filmore scrapes the remains into the garbage disposal. Despite Faith's offer to help with the chores, he washes the dishes. Afterward, he pours Faith a tall glass of water. He cracks the ice cube tray until three cubes plop into the glass and settle on top. Sliding the glass over to Faith, he holds her eyes as he opens the folder.

"Are you ready for this, my dear?"

Her heart drums. Faith doesn't watch frightening movies, and she worries what lies inside that folder is worse than any monster Hollywood can dream up. Beneath the table, she wipes sweaty palms on her shorts.

"I am."

"Good, because it's time to begin."

It takes all of Faith's will not to scream when he opens the folder.

8

Rustic cottages whip past the window as Agent Ketchum drives a black FBI SUV around Veil Lake. A law enforcement contingent met them at the airport and handed him the keys, and he didn't lower the speed below seventy-five until they reached the outskirts of the village. Partially hidden behind dense trees, piers and boats break up the monotony of the lake, the placid waters stained red by the setting sun.

"No prints found at any of the scenes," Ketchum says as he concentrates on the narrow road. A pickup truck driving in the opposite direction forces him to creep toward the ditch. The road doesn't have a shoulder. "His victims seem scatter shot. It's as if he doesn't have a preferred type."

"He might not," says Darcy, cracking the window open to let in the fresh air. "Michael Rivers targeted young women. Doll Face focuses on the placement of the bodies. Figuring out why will be our key to catching him. Tell me more about the murders."

Ketchum glances down when his radio squawks.

"The first victims were Paul Forsythe and Tracey Vassallo,

both twenty-one, murdered on the northwest shore of the lake. Lifelong Veil Lake residents, neither attended college. Friends say they drove to the lake at sunset to party. Police discovered beer cans and cigarette butts at the scene, and DNA tests confirmed they belonged to Forsythe and Vassallo. There didn't seem to be a motive. A random killing."

"Wrong place, wrong time."

"A contusion to the back of Forsythe's skull suggests their attacker struck from behind, disabling the male before he went after the woman. The killer slit their throats and positioned the bodies against a tree, sitting up and facing the water with porcelain masks covering their faces."

Darcy stares out at the water when the trees open. The north-south lake stretches as far as she can see. Shadows crawl down the ridges and obscure the shoreline.

"Who came next?"

"Cassy Regan, sixteen days ago. Regan was a sixty-eight-year-old widow. She owned a cottage on a steep grade overlooking the shore. According to the locals, the tax bill increases by one-hundred-seventy-five percent along the lake, but Regan had a partial view of the water from her backyard."

"Let me guess. The police discovered her at the back window, wearing a doll mask."

Ketchum slides a folder from the center console and hands it to Darcy. She opens the folder in her lap and scans the photographs.

"Tied to a chair with her throat slit end to end. No DNA evidence at the scene that didn't belong to Regan, but CSI discovered cornstarch powder in the kitchen. Could be from cooking, but cornstarch powder is used in latex gloves. Our killer is careful."

"What about the Lieberman family? I saw the network news coverage last night."

He hands her a second folder. This one is thinner and contains prints of downloaded crime scene photographs.

"Both in their late-fifties. Two daughters, one living in Wisconsin, the other in Texas. The Liebermans were supposed to be on vacation in Florida. Since they didn't cancel their reservations, the resort hit their credit card Monday night around the time they died. The killer bound the couple to chairs and positioned them in front of a floor-to-ceiling window in the master bedroom. Throats slit. Porcelain masks. The medical examiner found bruising on their arms, legs, and faces, suggesting Doll Face smacked them around."

Darcy scratches her cheek.

"How do we know the killer keeps his victims for seventy-two hours?"

"It's a working theory. With the two twenty-one-year-olds drinking at the lake, it's likely our unsub came across them by chance. The Regan and Lieberman cases suggest he targeted his victims ahead of time. The medical examiner concluded the bruising occurred well before their deaths. Also, interviews with neighbors and family suggest the Liebermans and Regan lost contact with their acquaintances three days before the murders."

"A young couple partying beside the lake, a single woman in her sixties, a middle age couple, and now a teenage girl with Down syndrome. You're right. It's scatter shot. This unsub isn't targeting types. Something else is driving him, and it's tied to the lake. What's the story with Faith Fielder?"

"The girl left the Veil Lake Grill at nine o'clock. The father drove to pick her up, but he was running a few minutes late. When he arrived at the restaurant, Faith wasn't there. Nobody saw her get into a strange vehicle. We checked her cell phone records. No calls or texts in the twenty-four hours preceding her disappearance, and now the signal is dead."

Poor girl. Name one teenager without a slew of texts and calls every night. Does Faith have any friends?

The sun dips behind the trees when Ketchum turns up a dirt and stone driveway. The climb concludes at a quaint cottage adorned with brown shingles. A rose bush with wicked thorns climbs along the iron rail leading up the steps. Black mulch circles a flowering cherry tree in the yard.

Wes Fielder opens the door as Agent Ketchum leads Darcy up the steps. Worry creases the rotund man's forehead. Circles around his eyes point to a sleepless night. The few strands of hair remaining drape across the top of his head. His jeans hang off his hips as though he dropped ten pounds recently. Ketchum flashes his badge.

"Mr. Fielder? I'm Agent Ketchum with the FBI, and this is Darcy Gellar...excuse me, Darcy Haines. She's helping us locate your daughter."

"Please, come in," Wes says, stepping aside and motioning them into a gloomy living room with two recliners and a couch. "There's no television. Faith's education has always been our priority, and television is nothing but a mindless waste of time."

The woman waiting in the room wears blue jeans and a green flannel shirt. She wrings her hands as she glances between Darcy and Ketchum.

"Zoe, these are the FBI agents looking for Faith."

Zoe sniffles and chokes on tears.

"Find her," Zoe says, her gaze settling on Darcy. "Faith is special, and she's all we have left in the world."

"It would be best if we all sit," Darcy says. Zoe appears wound tight, an emotional bundle of frayed nerves. "Tell us what happened last night."

Zoe and Wes fill in details for each other as they recount Tuesday evening. Zoe dropped Faith off at the restaurant at 4:45 p.m. Due to finish work at nine, Faith should have waited outside the restaurant for Wes to pick her up. He arrived at 9:05. No Faith.

"Does your daughter ever use Uber to get to and from the restaurant?" Ketchum asks, glancing at his notepad.

"I drove her until October," Wes says, picking at an invisible piece of lint on his pants. "Then I switched to second shift at the hospital. I'm on the maintenance staff. Zoe doesn't have a license, though I keep telling her she should take the test, so Faith needed to call a Taxi or one of those ride sharing options. I went back on day shifts last month, but we allowed her to use a ride sharing service. It made her feel independent. At least until the murders started. I put my foot down and demanded she let me drive her home at night."

"Given your daughter has Down syndrome, weren't you concerned about strangers driving her?"

Darcy cringes at Ketchum's comment, but neither Wes nor Zoe bat an eyelash.

"Our daughter graduated high school with honors, Agent Ketchum," Wes says, provoking Zoe to nod as she wipes a tissue across her nose. "She's a smart girl, and she has a level head. Whether or not it scares us, my wife and I must allow Faith to find her place in the world. We can't look over her shoulder the rest of her life."

Ketchum gives Darcy a confused glance before speaking.

"Did Faith have any enemies?"

Wes and Zoe share a baffled look.

"Why would Faith have enemies?" Zoe asks, wiping her eyes on the back of her sleeve. "She's a good girl. Never starts trouble."

"No bullying in high school."

"Never."

Darcy crosses one leg over the other.

"Did anyone pay too much attention to Faith?" Darcy asks.

"Someone who started a conversation with Faith and showed unusual interest. Maybe a neighbor or someone in town followed Faith."

Zoe glances at Wes, who shrugs his shoulders.

"Faith never mentioned anyone following or harassing her," Zoe says, pocketing her tissue and ripping a fresh one from the box. "But Faith might not have understood. It's true she's intelligent, but her interpersonal skills lag behind her classmates."

Darcy shifts to face Zoe.

"Has anyone called the house lately looking for Faith?"

Zoe scrunches her brow.

"Faith rarely receives phone calls. It saddens me that the other students don't involve her." The mother touches her chest. "Wait. A man from the North Chadwick Learning Disabilities Center called last week. Glen Filmore. That was the man's name."

Darcy glances at Ketchum, who jots the information down.

"He wanted to speak with Faith?" Darcy asks.

"No, only me." Zoe pauses, recalling the conversation. "He asked me to record messages for Faith. I found the request odd, but he explained students with Down syndrome require positive feedback during their first semester in college."

"What sort of messages did he request?"

"Positive reinforcement. I recorded pep talks. Something she could listen to if school became too difficult. Oh, and I told Faith to always listen to Mr. Filmore and follow his advice. We met him at orientation. The staff at the Learning Disabilities Center impressed us. They're so supportive. That means a lot to us, knowing Faith will be in good hands."

The hairs rise on the back of Darcy's neck. Something about this Mr. Filmore troubles her. Though the pep talks seem like a great idea, why did Glen Filmore ask Zoe to ensure Faith followed his advice?

"Is that the only time you heard from Glen Filmore?"

"Yes."

"And no one else at the center contacted you?"

"Just Mr. Filmore."

"All right, let's discuss last night. Are you certain Faith left work at her usual time?"

"The police checked with Rosanna—that's Faith's boss—and she said Faith left at nine o'clock. There was an incident at the restaurant. Something about a drunk couple starting trouble at the bar."

"Was Faith involved?"

"The man made a derogatory comment because Faith wouldn't serve him beer. She's not even supposed to take orders from the customers. Faith cleans tables and answers phone calls. Sometimes she helps in the kitchen when the restaurant is short staffed. So there's no reason the man should have harassed Faith."

"Do you know the man's name?" Ketchum asks, looking up from his notepad.

"No."

Did the drunk couple wait outside for Faith and cause trouble? Darcy wants to believe there's an alternative explanation for Faith's disappearance. A serial killer abducting a teenage girl with Down syndrome is the worst-case scenario.

Ketchum concludes the interview ten minutes later when it's obvious Faith's parents can't provide more clues which will lead the police to the lost girl. Inside the SUV, Ketchum checks his notes and glances at Darcy while he turns the key in the ignition.

"Let's swing by the restaurant. We need the names of the two creeps who started trouble last night."

Darcy nods. It's full dark now, the starlight mottled by patchy clouds and a thick tree canopy. He backs out with care. One wrong move on the narrow road, and the SUV will drop over the ditch and careen down the hillside.

As they follow the lake road into the village, Darcy catches Ketchum glaring at her.

"Something wrong?"

"You gave me a funny look back there when I asked the parents why they let a girl with Down syndrome use a ride sharing app."

Darcy adjusts the passenger seat forward.

"It came off as insensitive. I didn't want you to offend her parents."

"Does it make sense to you, allowing Faith to ride around in taxis and Ubers with complete strangers?"

"Down syndrome varies from person to person. Faith is high functioning. She must be, considering her grades and confidence."

Ketchum brushes the hair off his forehead.

"Sending my girl to college was scary enough. Can't imagine how I'd feel if she had Down syndrome."

"We've learned a lot about Down syndrome over the last four decades. Their life spans have tripled since I was a kid, many graduate high school and attend college, and a growing number attain graduate degrees. So I'm not surprised Faith is self-sufficient. Would I worry if I was Zoe? Sure. But she's right. Faith's parents can't protect her forever."

The village center rests on the southern shore of Veil Lake. A community pier arrows a hundred yards over the water, and upscale stores dominate the shopping district. Veil Lake brims with tourist money. The three-story bed-and-breakfast on the corner shines light upon the sidewalk. Vehicles with license plates from California, Florida, and New Jersey fill the parking lot. Could the Doll Face Killer be an out-of-towner?

"What did you think of the phone call?" Ketchum asks, knocking Darcy out of her thoughts.

"Glen Filmore?"

"Right."

"Something feels off about that situation."

"Why would this guy ask Faith's mother to leave messages, inspiring Faith to do whatever he asks?"

"Yeah, I wasn't buying that part, either. It doesn't strike me as protocol. I wonder if the man who called is really Glen Filmore."

"I'll phone the university first thing in the morning."

North Chadwick University is forty-five minutes from Veil Lake. Close enough for Filmore to kidnap Faith.

9

Laughter and raised voices boom from the open windows of the Veil Lake Grill when Ketchum pulls into an open parking space. Judging by the number of vehicles choking the parking lot on a weeknight, business couldn't be better.

The restaurant appears cobbled together. Wooden steps lead to the blue-shuttered building, but a glass sunroom that can't be over five years old offers additional seating, and an outdoor deck overlooks the lake. A full moon reflects off the water.

As Darcy climbs the steps, she swallows the lump in her throat. The Veil Lake Grill reminds her of Harpy's, her favorite restaurant in Genoa Cove. Missing her family, she checks her phone for messages from Julian, Hunter, and Jennifer. Nothing.

The clamor inside the restaurant rises to a fevered pitch when Ketchum pulls the door open. A teenage girl with auburn hair offers to show them to a table before her eyes fall to Ketchum's FBI badge. The girl points to Rosanna Noble behind the bar.

Noble's hair spills out from the band. The woman is torn in

multiple directions as she hustles between the kitchen window and the bar, a stack of menus beneath her arm. Darcy pegs the woman's age around forty, the stress lines on her forehead making her older than her years.

"Rosanna Noble?" Ketchum asks, displaying his badge.

Noble jumps and almost fumbles the menus. Placing a hand to her head, she says, "Sorry, I didn't see you come in."

"Is there somewhere quiet we can talk?" Ketchum needs to yell over the commotion.

"Sure, in my office." Noble waves to a tall, college-age male with blue eyes and ruffled brown hair. "Keith, I need you to take over for fifteen minutes."

Keith gives Noble a thumbs-up. Darcy and Ketchum follow Noble down a wood-paneled hallway. Darcy turns sideways when a harried waitress rushes past. Noble's office isn't large enough to accommodate the three of them. Offering the chair opposite Noble's desk, Ketchum stands in the corner beside a garbage can. A mess of receipts and bills cover Noble's workspace. A computer monitor wobbles on the corner of the desk, the cords running down to a PC at the woman's feet. The door closes and stifles the noise.

"Is it always this busy on a Wednesday night?" Darcy asks.

Noble blows a strand of hair out of her eyes.

"During the summer, it is. Tourism won't die down until after Labor Day, and then this place will look abandoned." The woman bit her thumbnail to the quick. A smudge of ketchup stains her black chamois shirt, her ponytail refuses to stay in place, and black circles around her eyes stand out against a pallid, sleep-deprived face. "Please tell me you know where Faith is. I'm worried sick and didn't sleep a wink last night."

"We're hoping you can help us find her," Ketchum says from the corner. "What time did Faith work last evening?"

"Until nine o'clock," Noble replies, confirming the Fielders' time line.

"We understand an altercation occurred last night, involving Faith and an inebriated couple."

Noble fixes the rubber band around her ponytail.

"I wouldn't call it an altercation. It never turned physical."

"But you witnessed the event?"

"I did not," Noble says, lowering her eyes to the desk and raising her palms. "Keith, my next in charge, saw the argument and filled me in after Faith left. If you'd like, I can send Keith in after you finish interviewing me."

"That would help. We need the names of the man and woman."

"Geoff and Alexandra Voss." The curl to Noble's lips speaks to her distaste for the couple. "This isn't the first time they've started trouble inside the restaurant. Get a few drinks in them, and they become abusive. Fortunately, the other patrons ushered them outside before the situation spun out of control. I'm banning them from the establishment until the end of summer."

"Have they instigated physical encounters in the past?"

"Geoff and a tourist guy got into it last summer. I don't recall the specifics, but I'm sure Geoff started it. The argument spilled into the parking lot. The police arrived and diffused the situation before someone threw a punch."

"Is there any chance Geoff and Alexandra waited outside for Faith to leave?"

Noble's eyes widen.

"Do you think they hurt Faith?"

"I'm asking you. From what you say, they're irrational after a few drinks."

"That's accurate. But I can't picture either attacking a teenage girl with Down syndrome."

"The police have eyewitness accounts of someone calling Faith a freak," Darcy says, shifting her chair to buy leg room.

"Geoff or Alexandra said that about our Faith?" Noble rubs her temples, then sets her palms on the table. "That's it. They're banned for life. I won't have anyone harassing Faith or using abusive language in my restaurant."

"Ms. Noble, have you noticed anyone paying Faith too much attention at the Veil Lake Grill? Has she ever complained about a guest?"

"No," Noble says, squinting. "The patrons are extra-friendly with Faith. Everyone is in Veil Lake."

"Because she has Down syndrome."

"And because she accomplishes so much on her own. People around here don't pity Faith. They empower her."

"We're looking at someone who seemed too friendly," says Ketchum. "A person who spends an inordinate amount of time at the restaurant."

"We have so many people coming through our doors," Noble says, motioning toward the clamor beyond the walls. "Sure, we have regulars. But we're the number one restaurant in Veil Lake, and you can't get a seat without a reservation most nights during the summer. I can't keep track of faces."

"What about security cameras?"

"Yes, I have one behind the bar near the cash register, just in case someone gets rowdy or robs the place."

"How much of the restaurant does the camera cover?"

Noble's eyes travel to the ceiling.

"Hmm. One-third of the main room, but that's a rough estimate."

"I'd like a copy of the footage from last evening and for the last week, if you have it."

"Sure. Give me one second." Noble slides a drawer open and rustles her hand under a stack of papers. When she doesn't find what she's looking for, she pulls a second drawer open and removes a USB drive. "The footage only goes back seven days. Is that okay?"

"That's perfect."

Ketchum asks Noble about her employees while the footage transfers. Darcy doesn't spot a red flag, but that doesn't mean a staff member didn't abduct Faith. Kidnappers and murderers are chameleons, blending into their surroundings. Five minutes later, Noble hands the thumb drive to Ketchum.

"I'll make a copy and get this back to you," Ketchum says.

"No rush. The original is on the computer's hard drive."

After Ketchum finishes interviewing Noble, she returns to her duties. Keith Marsella, the assistant manager for the Veil Lake Grill, sits in Noble's chair. He confirms Alexandra Voss called Faith a freak, but claims Geoff was abusive and out of control. Keith witnessed Geoff threaten a man at the bar.

"He's in here a lot," Keith says, referring to the man Geoff Voss picked a fight with. "Sorry, but I'm lousy with names."

Ketchum clicks his pen and flips to a new page on his memo pad.

"Did this guy talk to Faith?"

"Yeah, he seemed to be talking her ear off."

"Any idea what the topic of discussion was?"

"No idea. I was at the end of the bar, fighting to keep up with orders. You already know how loud this place gets when we're packed."

"Is this guy a local or a tourist?"

"Definitely a local. He pops in during the off season, but I couldn't tell you his name or what he does for a living. I'd ask Rosanna, but she didn't see the fight."

After Keith describes the man, Ketchum slips a card from his wallet and hands it to the assistant manager.

"This is my number. If you remember the guy's name, call me anytime, day or night."

Darcy and Ketchum find an unoccupied corner at the back of the restaurant. She can see the security camera near the ceiling angled toward the cash register. Ketchum leans his ear toward Darcy so they can hear each other.

"I almost forgot. We got you a rental and dropped it off at the police department. Hope you don't mind driving a Kia."

"You didn't have to do that."

"Sure we did. You need to get around, and we won't keep the same hours every day. Check with the front desk. They're holding the key for you."

A waitress carrying four seafood plates on a tray squeezes around them.

"Noble is right," Darcy says, pointing to the camera. "The camera covers a third of the room."

"You suspect our unsub came here."

"I do. He's careful and watches his victims for days. My guess is he canvassed the restaurant multiple times before he moved on Faith."

"If that's the case, we might catch his face on the security footage."

"Only if he sat at the bar. This guy would come alone if he wanted to watch Faith. I can't find a table for one in the room. Chances are he watched Faith from the back of the restaurant. Kept a safe distance."

"Unless he got bold and spoke to her."

"That's possible," Darcy says.

Because Faith has Down syndrome, the unsub might find the girl less threatening and easier to talk to than his previous victims.

"What next?"

"Do you have the key to the Lieberman house?"

"I can get it."

Darcy shifts her glare across the faces at the tables and bar, wondering if the killer is here tonight. To enter Doll Face's head and predict his next move, she needs to follow his path.

10

The police cruiser crawls half a block behind Darcy's Kia. She's still getting used to the rental's controls as she veers onto Bridge Street. She takes two sweeps down the road before she spots the Lieberman residence, yet she can't see the house from the road, only the pitched roof and two dormer windows staring lifelessly into the night.

Killing the engine, Darcy waits for her hearing to adjust. The silence overwhelms her. Did Doll Face park his vehicle along the curb and watch the Liebermans through the upstairs window? The cruiser's lights fill her mirrors before Officer Nix brings the vehicle to a stop two properties behind Darcy. He stands a few inches taller than Darcy with auburn hair and a small paunch stretching his belt. Cloaked in silhouette, the officer touches his cap, and Darcy raises a hand in acknowledgment.

She steps out of the car and pockets the keys. Her shoes make scuffing noises against the macadam. Ketchum insisted an officer follow Darcy to the Lieberman residence, but orders dictate the policeman cannot come inside the house, except in an emergency. But Darcy doesn't intend to enter the residence. Not right away.

The concrete driveway curls between trees and brush like a forgotten wilderness road. She climbs a hundred feet before the path ends in front of a three-car garage. The couple owned one vehicle—a black Ford Expedition the police can't locate. The Lieberman house is white. Darcy knows this from the police report. In the moonlight, it glows blue and silver.

The yard stretches a hundred yards toward a brush-covered ridge. Old trees, some towering twice as high as the two-story residence, circle the property. A wooden privacy fence taller than Darcy circles the backyard. The Doll Face Killer could have watched the Lieberman family for multiple nights without drawing a neighbor's attention. Darcy locates a canopy swing a stone's throw from the deck. Two garbage cans stand against the fence. The shadows run too deep for Darcy to see the property line.

She pads through the Lieberman's lawn, the dew thick and the night cool enough to produce a fog before sunrise. The moon is the lone witness as she walks from one corner of the house to the next, searching for an open window, a vantage point, any clue that puts her on the killer's track. A sliding glass door opens to the deck. Darcy climbs the steps, cringing when an old board squeals under her weight. At the glass door, she peers inside. Though the deck door is like the one she has in Genoa Cove, the Liebermans don't have a locking bar at the bottom to thwart burglars. Skilled intruders can jostle the locking mechanisms of most deck doors and break inside, but she can't find evidence of forced entry.

Fishing the house key from her pocket, she circles to the side of the house and enters through an old door that must be drafty during the winter. A hard kick would break the knob. Yet it doesn't appear anyone forced his way inside. The door opens to a landing. Stairs lead down to a cellar and up to the main living quarters. She prefers darkness when she walks through a victim's house. Murderers don't flick on the lights when they enter homes. Yet it's impossible to see into the basement without a guiding light, so she aims the flashlight down the stairs and holds her breath as she turns the corner.

The finished basement features high pile wall-to-wall carpeting. A television covers much of the far wall, and a Detroit Tigers throw pillow sits on the couch in front of the television. Past the entertainment center, a dry bar stands in the corner. She pulls one of the four stools back and sniffs the shot glass on the bar, careful not to touch the glass. The oaken coconut smell tells her someone drank a shot of whiskey in the last week.

Climbing the stairs to the main floor, Darcy shuts off the flashlight and stops. Waits for the shadows to reveal themselves again. The first floor is an open design with the living room in front of her and a sizable kitchen in the corner. Moonlight glistens off the sliding glass door to the deck as she searches for another way into the house. Something the police and FBI might have missed.

Darcy closes her eyes and regulates her breathing. In her mind, she hears muffled snores from the master bedroom on the second floor. Doll Face stood at the base of the stairway and listened. Patient. Waited until they fell asleep.

Then what?

Did he creep up the stairs, overwhelm and bind the couple, then live within these walls for three days without a neighbor or family member noticing? The CSI team found cornstarch powder in the bedroom, kitchen, and bathroom, evidence that Doll Face wore gloves as he moved about the house. But wearing gloves for three days would irritate his skin. He must have taken them off at some point and left a print.

Wearing her own pair of gloves, Darcy pulls the refrigerator open. Squints at the light. The refrigerator contains various condiments, a half-gallon of milk, three eggs, a jar of strawberry jelly, and little else. Understandable, considering the Lieber-mans were supposed to leave for vacation. The killer must have known of their plans.

A stack of bills, coupons, and junk mail sits on the kitchen counter. Darcy sifts through the mail and stops on a brochure for a luxury waterfront inn on the Gulf Coast of Florida. Opening the brochure, she reads a welcoming letter tucked inside. This is the resort the Lieberman family booked. Someone knew of their plans. Darcy starts a voice recording app and raises her phone to her lips. They need to look at family members, close friends, anyone who knew the Liebermans would be out of town. Postal workers. Who delivers mail to the Liebermans?

Nightmare images flash as Darcy climbs the carpeted stairs toward the second floor.

Flick.

A powerful hand gripping Carol Lieberman by the hair, dragging the thrashing woman up the stairs.

Flick.

The bedroom door at the top of the stairs slamming shut before the killer binds them to chairs and turns them to face the lake.

Flick.

Darrrrrcyyy. The Full Moon Killer's voice trails Darcy through an unlit house before he plunges a knife into her belly.

She stops two steps shy of the upper landing and grips the banister. Her legs wobble, eyes roll. When the stairway stops spinning, she touches her wrist and measures her pulse. She hasn't experienced a panic attack this severe since Dustin Gendron murdered two women and kidnapped Julian's niece.

I watched Michael Rivers die, she tells herself. Pictures the shock on the serial killer's face after Julian pulled the trigger. But ghosts are real. They live inside our minds and feed off the power we grant them.

Pulling herself onto the landing, Darcy stands before the open door of the master bedroom. From the hallway, she can see the glimmering lake beyond the floor-to-ceiling windows. Two chairs face the glass.

Her heart drilling into her throat, Darcy edges forward. Splintering runs down the edge of the door and the jamb. The Doll Face Killer locked the Liebermans inside their bedroom.

Her shoes swish over the gray carpet. A red spray of blood stains the walls and carpet, its coppery scent overpowering in a room that hasn't seen airflow since the police departed. The camera flash ignites the room with lightning as Darcy photographs what remains of the scene. She has access to the police and FBI pictures, but she needs to document what she sees and feels. In her mind, the Doll Face Killer swipes the blade across Jim's throat. Then Carol's. She can't prove he followed this order, but it makes sense to eliminate the male threat first. The shattered night stand on Jim's side of the bed provides additional evidence Doll Face attacked the husband on the night he slipped unheard into their bedroom.

"They don't hear him when he comes inside," she speaks into her phone. "He's quiet and careful. Wearing gloves so he doesn't leave a print. Yet something brought the husband up from sleep. A floorboard groaning. Or a sixth sense that they weren't alone in the house."

Turning away from the bloody carpet, Darcy circles the bed to the crushed nightstand. Takes another picture.

"Before Jim Lieberman reacts, Doll Face attacks him and bludgeons the husband with a blunt object. Maybe a flashlight. Jim fights back as Carol comes awake screaming. Doll Face topples Jim off the bed and onto the nightstand. Another blow to the skull to disable Jim. Then he turns his attention to Carol."

The covers lie haphazardly to Carol's side of the bed as if Jim threw them off when he spotted the psychopath looming over his wife.

"But you didn't kill them yet," Darcy says, her observations posed to the murderer. "Why do you keep them alive for three days before you slice their throats?"

One more picture, then Darcy moves back to the window, careful not to disturb the chairs. She wants the chairs positioned as Doll Face left them. Standing over the chair Carol Lieberman occupied, Darcy kneels down and faces the lake. Two moons leer back at her—the full moon in the sky, and the stretched, funhouse version on the water. The lake glimmers, black and silver. Cottages circle the lake, but there are no boats on the water this time of night.

"What is it you want them to see?"

Darcy disables the flash and shoots two photographs, one from behind Carol's chair and the other near Jim's. She examines the pictures on her phone, searching for something her human eyes missed. It's just a lake with a dark bulk of an island off to the left. A platform sits fifty yards off the island. She imagines kids leaping off the platform into the water, covered in suntan oil and lying on its sunbaked boards. Did something happen to Doll Face on this lake? A near drowning, perhaps. No, that isn't something that would drive a man to kill.

Three days.

"Need additional photographs of the lake from this vantage point. Morning, midday, and sunset. What am I missing?"

After examining the bedroom, Darcy slips the phone into her pocket and searches each room. The bathroom, the three spare rooms—two of which belonged to the Lieberman children before they grew older and moved out. Nothing appears out of place. A thought pops into her head as she walks toward the stairway. Doll Face locked them inside the residence for three days. Though she doubts he took a shower, he must have used the bathroom. Walking faster, she turns the bathroom light on and averts her eyes from the glare. Then she lowers herself to her hands and knees, examines the tub, the tile around the toilet.

"You wore the gloves, but you used the bathroom. Somewhere you left DNA. And that's how I'll find you."

Darcy grabs the sink to lift herself. Her knees make crackling and popping sounds, reminding her she isn't thirty anymore. Turning off the light, she descends the staircase to the open floor design and crosses the living room to the kitchen.

A sound comes from the basement when she reaches for the light switch. Tension locks her bones.

Darcy slides the Glock-22 from her holster. The police officer waits outside, but she can't see his vehicle from the kitchen. Moonlight draws an azure rectangle over the downstairs.

When the sound comes again, Darcy grabs the radio. The noise is familiar. Not wanting to cry wolf, Darcy moves to the landing above the side door and listens. A wall of darkness stands between her and the entrance to the cellar.

Whoosh.

Darcy releases a breath and leans her head against the wall. The water heater. One of those old models with the blue flame visible beneath the tank. She closes her eyes and knocks her head against the wall, angry with herself for jumping at shadows.

And she has less than forty-eight hours to find Faith.

11

The Lake View Inn seems misplaced and misnamed. Rather than a quaint bed-and-breakfast, the inn resembles a hotel plucked from Manhattan or Los Angeles. Glass frontage welcomes starlight inside the inn as Darcy drags a rolling suitcase across a freshly polished floor. The lobby, pool, and communal areas take up the first floor. The hotel's thirty-eight rooms sit on the second floor, accessible from an escalator climbing up from the center and elevators on the north and south walls.

A girl behind the desk covers a yawn with her hand and paints on a smile when Darcy approaches. Ketchum called ahead to inform the inn Darcy wouldn't arrive until after midnight. After the girl hands over her key card, Darcy sets her bag down on the bottom step of the escalator and lets the moving stairs drag her to her destination. Peering into the parking lot, Darcy spots the police cruiser. It's Officer Nix, the man who waited outside the Lieberman house while Darcy performed her walk through. Nix will stay until his relief arrives in the middle of the night. Interesting Ketchum wants the police to guard the entrance to the inn, if nobody knows Darcy is here.

When Darcy slips the key card into the door, one arm braced against the wall to keep her from falling, she realizes she hasn't stopped moving since she awoke at six o'clock Wednesday. The empty room wrenches free memories of home. Her heart squeezes. The door opens to a spotless, organized room with a full kitchen and a private deck overlooking the lake. With the light on, she can't see past the glass. There's a work desk in the corner with an ethernet jack for her laptop. A folder of menus lies open on the desk with a coupon for the Veil Lake Grill. Complimentary water bottles and tea packets await her on the table, along with a note from *Eustace* to enjoy her stay. She wheels her suitcase inside a long closet with an ironing board in the corner, hangs her jacket, and collapses on the bed.

Darcy snaps her eyes open a moment after they close. Images of the blood soaked carpet beneath the chairs inside the Lieberman's master bedroom assault her, send her pulse into overdrive. One night on the hunt, and she's a basket case. Groaning when she looks at the bedside clock, Darcy writes a text message to Julian and wishes him goodnight. She expects he'll find the message waiting for him at dawn when he typically rises for a morning run. She's surprised when he responds.

Can't sleep without you here.

Darcy bites her lip.

Hold on. I'm calling you now.

Julian answers on the first ring. She needs to hear his voice.

"How are the kids?"

"Jennifer crashed before midnight, if you can believe it."

"No, I can't," she laughs.

"Kaitlyn came over and watched some teen romance movie on Netflix with Jennifer. I drove Kaitlyn home after, and by the time I got back, Jennifer was sawing logs."

"I'll bet Hunter is still awake."

"You got that right. Had to tell him to keep it quiet before he woke up the neighbors. He's having a *Call of Duty* marathon with his buddies."

They share a giggle. Then an uncomfortable silence settles in.

"So how was the flight into Michigan?" he asks, coughing away from the phone.

"Bumpy. I was glad when we touched down."

Another pause.

"Darcy, I don't have a good feeling about this case. It seems too close to the Full Moon Killer murders."

"This is a different unsub with a unique motivation."

"Any idea what his motivation is?"

"He faces his victims toward the lake," she says, plucking a thread off her shirt. Darcy clenches her free hand into a fist. "Julian, I did a walk through of the Lieberman house."

"With Ketchum?"

"No."

"Shit."

"A police cruiser waited at the curb. In fact," she says, parting the curtains and surveying the parking lot. "The officer is outside the inn now."

"Good that someone has your back at the hotel. But what if Doll Face was inside the house when you did the walk through? These guys return to the scenes of their crimes."

"I don't understand how he broke inside the house without a sign of forced entry," Darcy says, diverting Julian's discomfort over her solo journey through a crime scene.

"Maybe he posed as a deliveryman. Knocked on the door and put a gun to the head of whoever answered."

"The house sits back from the curb, surrounded by trees. I'm uncertain anyone would hear a scream from the entryway." Darcy chews a nail. "The Liebermans have a large house in a wealthy neighborhood. They have a cleaning crew come into the house once per week."

"What day?"

"Every Thursday. Ketchum believes Doll Face captured the Liebermans Thursday night.

"You think one of the crew could be your killer?"

"The idea crossed my mind."

"Here's a possibility. First year on the GCPD, I responded to a burglary at a beach house two miles south of the cove. Same deal. The woman who owned the place brought a cleaning crew in once per week. No surprise, but the lead detective suspected a cleaner. But it wasn't. Turns out the thief canvassed the house for weeks, knew when the cleaners showed up, and slipped inside after they unlocked the side door. The dirt bag hid in the closet for ninety minutes while the crew worked. Then he ransacked the house, locked the place up, and drove off."

Darcy switches the phone to her other ear and props her head on the pillow.

"How did you catch him?"

"He left a print. Biggest mistake he made was locking up after himself, making it look like the cleaners robbed the house. Dumb ass left a thumb print on the knob."

"Not our unsub. The CSI team found cornstarch powder inside the Lieberman residence."

"Cornstarch powder, like they use for the old style gloves."

"They don't use it anymore?"

"No. Check with the team that conducted the search. Most law enforcement agencies switched years ago."

Darcy rubs her eyes. She needs sleep, but every second she loses brings Doll Face closer to murdering a teenage girl with Down syndrome.

"I'll look into it tomorrow. Crap."

"What?"

"I just remembered I'm supposed to present a profile at eight o'clock in the morning, and I haven't written anything down yet."

"Be confident, Darcy. If I know you, you've worked most of it out in your head. Jot down notes and wing the rest. They can't expect you to solve the case your first night on the job." Darcy covers her mouth when she yawns. "I spoke to Hunter."

"Yeah?"

"He's hanging around the house all week. No big parties. Claims he wants to chill all summer, so he's refreshed for fall semester."

"I like that plan, but why are you bringing this up now?"

"Hunter can watch Jennifer, and things are quiet at the department. The chief won't blink if I tack two days of annual leave onto my three-day break."

Sighing, Darcy shuts her eyes.

"No, Julian. You can't drop everything and fly to Michigan."

"It wouldn't be a big deal."

"I'll be home before you notice I'm gone. This case won't last more than a week or two."

"Oh, so now we're up to two weeks?"

He issues a disarming laugh, but she hears the frustration driving it.

"Never know. We might wrap the case up by evening. That is, if I get enough sleep to think straight."

"I got your hint. Sleep well, Darcy. But if you want me there..."

"I always want you with me. But I feel better, knowing you're there with the kids." A blast pulls Darcy's eyes open. "Julian? Are you still there?"

"Don't worry. Someone is shooting off fireworks at the cove."

Darcy covers her face and chuckles. She's wound too tight.

"I can't believe I'm missing the celebration. Sounds like they couldn't wait until the fourth this year."

"The fireworks start earlier every year. Ten years from now, they'll light the first bottle rockets on Christmas morning. I'd better let you go before you phone 9-1-1 about gunshots on Genoa Cove."

"Very funny. Talk to you tomorrow, Julian."

They wish each other goodnight. Darcy rests on the pillow with the phone balanced on her outstretched hand. She's tempted to call him back and ask him to grab the first flight in the morning. That isn't fair to him. He worked too hard to become a detective. Rumors around Genoa Cove hint at the chief stepping down in the next two years. Julian will be a strong candidate to win the position. No sense in ruining his chances now.

When sleep comes to Darcy, she dreams of walls sprayed with blood, and a boiling lake which matches the color of the stained carpet in the Liebermans' bedroom.

The first vestiges of morning glow against the drapes when Darcy opens her eyes. She groans. After tossing and turning through a never-ending loop of nightmare images, she managed an hour of sleep. She paws her notes, scribbled on a complimentary memo pad, off the bedside table and turns on the light. The brightness warns her she's asking for a migraine. Flicking the light off, she sets her hands behind her head and studies the ceiling. The guest in the next room runs the shower. Darcy isn't the only unlucky soul awake at this ungodly hour.

Pulling the laptop out of her carrying case, she waits for the computer to connect to the inn's WIFI. A quick check of her social media messages, then Darcy taps her nails against the touch pad. A thought occurs to her. Photographs on the serial killer website proved *FM-Kill-Her* hid in Veil Lake. The forum member always knows too much about Darcy and her family, and the fan fiction he posted suggests he fantasizes over Darcy's murder. He knew about the smiley face the Darkwater Cove murderer painted on Amy Yang's wall. Yang had been Michael Rivers's first target. But the girl escaped Rivers and fled into the night. In the coming months, as Darcy investigated the Full Moon Killer, she became close with Amy Yang. After they lost contact, Darcy learned Yang moved to neighboring Smith Town to be closer to Darcy. The girl never recovered from the abduction attempt. Wanting to save the girl, Darcy invited Amy to live with her before the Darkwater Cove killer caught the girl, avenging Michael Rivers.

FM-Kill-Her also posted updates from Georgia after another madman kidnapped Jennifer and terrorized Laurie, Darcy's cousin. Now he's in Veil Lake. Could he be the Doll Face Killer?

Darcy loads the website and scans the messages. The Veil Lake murders dominate the discussion. Locating the forum member's posts proves difficult until Darcy enters his profile name into the search bar. A second later, the screen fills with posts from *FM-Kill-Her*. Darcy clicks the first message. A photograph of the Lieberman residence fills the screen. Trees obscure all but the upper reaches of the house. The driveway glows in the moonlight. She recognizes the vantage point—he composed the picture curbside, close to where she parked last night. The Lieberman murders are public knowledge. Anyone with a search engine can find their address.

The moonlight.

Darcy enlarges the photograph. The neighbor's Subaru rests beside the opposite curb, the full moon reflecting in the windshield. Shit. He took the picture last night.

While Darcy was inside the house? That seems too brazen, even for *FM-Kill-Her*. The officer inside the police cruiser would have spotted the photographer.

Her hands trembling, Darcy clicks on the second message.

Found her.

The two words draw a hundred likes. Darcy scrolls down to an image of the Veil Lake Inn. A woman hidden in silhouette drags a rolling suitcase through the entryway. Darcy's mouth goes dry. It's her. The son-of-a-bitch knows where she is.

Shoving the computer off her lap, Darcy yanks the drapes open and stares into the parking lot. Releases a slow breath when she locates the police cruiser below her window. She can't see the officers inside the vehicle, only their shadows. The police officer in the passenger seat lifts a cup to his lips.

Darcy snatches the phone off her nightstand and calls Ketchum. He answers after three rings.

"You up?"

"I'm heading out for breakfast," he says. Ketchum stays in a chain hotel on the far side of the lake, a block from the police department. He tried to get Darcy a room, but they're booked solid with tourists. "Something is bothering you. What happened?"

Darcy tells Ketchum about the website and her history with *FM-Kill-Her*.

"The bastard posted my location," she says. "He couldn't have been more than five parking spaces from the cruiser."

Darcy hears him tear a sheet of paper off his notepad.

"Give me the URL."

Darcy reads off the website address and spells the poster's profile name. A few clicks of the mouse, and Ketchum loads the same picture Darcy has on her laptop screen.

"Dammit," he says. "Okay, I've got the picture up."

"This guy is on my list of suspects, Ketchum. He's at the top as of this morning."

"Hold on." Another click. "Darcy, I blew up the image. Look at your screen and tell me if you notice what I'm seeing."

Darcy checks the parking lot again, then swivels the laptop on the mattress. She kneels beside the bed, studying the picture.

"What are you referring to?"

"There's a ghosting aberration at the top of the screen. A

reflected light. That looks like a windshield. He must have been inside a vehicle when he took the photo."

Darcy squints. It's too early for her eyes to function after a sleepless night. She spots the imperfection and nods as if Ketchum is in the room with her.

"There's something else. See the shadow at the bottom of the picture?"

"The curved shape?"

"If I had to guess, I'd say that's the top of a steering wheel."

"Darcy, I'm calling the officers inside the cruiser. Don't leave your room until they arrive at your door. Grab something for breakfast in the lobby, then drive to the department without stopping. I'll make sure they trail you. You think this guy might be Doll Face?"

"It's possible. Hell, I don't know. Otherwise, it's an enormous coincidence he seems to always be around when a serial killer is loose on the east coast."

"After I speak with the officers, I'll check with the inn's security desk. We'll grab camera footage of the parking lot. With any luck, we'll nail this guy and get his license plate."

The shower spray works the knots out of Darcy's shoulders, yet she barely has the strength to stand. Switching the water to cold, Darcy forces herself to stand beneath the icy spray. After she towels off, her eyes fill with life. A knock on the door announces the police. Two officers, Grayson and Mathews, walk Darcy down the escalator and into the lobby where she grabs a to-go bag. She doesn't check the contents until she backs out of the parking lot with the cruiser on her bumper. One bagel, one apple, and a fruit juice composed of sugar and water.

Chewing the dry bagel, she checks the still gloomy street and turns toward the main loop around the lake. She adjusts the mirrors, spies the cruiser trailing her a quarter-mile behind. Her phone rings and connects to the Bluetooth sound system in the rental.

"The hotel security manager gets in at seven," Ketchum says over the speaker, his voice lower with the bass amplified. "He'll send the footage from last night. I half-wonder if this forum poster checked the hotel out before you arrived. Maybe he got brave and wandered inside for a look around."

Darcy shakes off a shiver. The thought of the deranged forum member stalking around the lobby and riding the escalator up to her room unsettles her. She can't deny the possibility. This guy doesn't recognize boundaries.

"How soon before you examine the footage? The profile begins at eight, and I'd like to know who we're dealing with before I take the podium."

"The Veil Lake PD runs a slick operation. Lots of money surrounding this lake. Their analysis system is state-of-the art, so we should be able to clean up the footage in house."

Darcy rounds a bend. For a moment, the cruiser's lights disappear behind the trees. Her heart thumps until they reappear. Easing off the gas, she lets the police close the distance.

"I want the CSI team to go through the Lieberman house again."

"Their report looks thorough. What concerns you?"

"Seventy-two hours is a long time to stay inside. Our unsub had to eat, use the bathroom. Hell, with the couple bound in the house, he could have taken a shower for all we know. Have them check for prints around the bathtub faucet, hair around the drain and beside the toilet. No way he wore gloves for three consecutive days."

Ketchum speaks to someone in the background.

"Darcy, I'm walking inside the department now. Let me get with the chief, and I'll meet you in ten minutes."

The call ends. Dawn creeps across the lake as wisps of fog

rise off the water. Fiddling with the radio, Darcy tunes to a sports talk show, anything to get her mind off *FM-Kill-Her*. The two hosts argue over the upcoming Detroit Lions season and whether the team has enough defense to make a run at the division championship. Darcy loses herself in the banter. Julian turns the dial to sports radio on trips around Genoa Cove. He's sound asleep back home, down the hall from Hunter and Jennifer. She'd do anything to see their faces again.

At the top of the lake, the road forks left and right. She takes the left turn and leaves the loop.

The Veil Lake Police Department sits in a brick building with two stone pillars guarding the entrance. The concrete pathway leading up to the building appears recently paved, the lawn manicured without a weed in sight. Sun peeks around the building when Darcy parks her rental and waits for the cruiser to pull alongside. The two officers climb from the vehicle, both vigilant and scanning the parking lot. They walk Darcy inside the well-lit building. It's not yet six-thirty, and the department bustles with the fervor of midday. Ketchum glances in Darcy's direction from the end of the hall. He's speaking to a bronze colored officer with salt and pepper hair. Ketchum pats the man on the shoulder and moves down the hallway to meet her.

"I trust you arrived without incident," Ketchum says as his eyes dart toward the parking lot behind the glass.

"Ours were the only vehicles on the road."

"That's a relief."

Ketchum appears rested, his eyes alert, hair combed, suit without a hint of a wrinkle. He hands Darcy a Styrofoam cup of coffee. The aroma hits her nose and knocks her senses awake.

"Just what I needed."

He sips from his cup and says, "Thought about grabbing coffees at the twenty-four-hour cafe around the block, but

Officer Nix told me about the gourmet brewing unit in the break room."

"Was that Chief Iglesias you were just talking to?"

"In the flesh." He walks Darcy through the security check point, flashing his badge. "His lead detective is on maternity leave, so he's running point on the Doll Face case."

"That's unusual."

"Not outside the big city departments. In a small department like the VLPD, everyone fills in where needed. Iglesias has two officers examining the restaurant footage, and I'm waiting on the security manager to upload the data from the hotel cameras. You don't look good. Did you sleep at all last night?"

Darcy pushes a stray hair off her brow.

"Does it show that much?"

"Knock out the profile, then we'll follow up on the camera footage. You'll have downtime this afternoon, Darcy. Take advantage of it. The VLPD will keep a cruiser outside your hotel whenever you're there, so grab some shuteye while you have the chance."

"I can't do that, Agent Ketchum," Darcy says while they pass the break room. A pair of officers inside the room, one female, one male, follow Darcy with their eyes. The male leans over and says something to the female as he nods in Darcy's direction.

"Why not?"

"Because the Doll Face Killer has Faith Fielder. I can't sleep until we bring her home."

13

She hates these moments.

Darcy stands beside the podium as Chief Iglesias addresses a packed room of officers. The chief holds their attention, but curious eyes wander to the woman FBI profiler they've read so much about. Her foot taps a nonsense beat until she forces herself to stop. Drawing in a breath, she focuses on the profile and ignores the staring officers. She presented countless profiles during her brief FBI career and has confidence in her ability. But the stakes are always higher when a young person goes missing, and this case will draw national attention until she catches the elusive murderer.

The LED lighting scours away every shadow, and a wall length LCD screen behind the podium displays an image of Faith Fielder. She wears a graduation cap and tassel on her head. The girl's infectious smile bangs off the monitor.

"A reminder that half the village will set off fireworks around the lake this evening," Iglesias says, leaning his arms on the podium. "And like every year, someone will mistake the fireworks for gunfire and call the 9-1-1 center. Also, be aware that the village is reporting record tourism this week. The hotels are booked solid, and we've heard reports of people camping on private land along the ridge. With everything else that's happened in Veil Lake, we have our work cut out for ourselves with the holiday weekend approaching."

Iglesias assigns duties and summarizes the Veil Lake murders. When he introduces Darcy, her feet turn to ice.

Clearing her throat after she shuffles to the podium, Darcy adjusts the microphone down. Feedback squeals from the speakers, drawing a laugh from somewhere in the crowd. Iglesias reaches beneath the podium with an exasperated sigh and fiddles with the volume knob. Then the room goes quiet.

"Good morning," Darcy says.

Nobody responds. At the back of the room, Ketchum stands with his arms folded. Darcy didn't have time to construct a proper presentation. She leans on pictures taken from the crime scenes and another she pulled off the Internet to keep the officers focused.

"We're looking for an intelligent killer. The unsub is an organized murderer. He has a high IQ and plans his attacks ahead of time, watching his targets for a week or more before he strikes. The way he binds his victims and holds them for three days suggests he's motivated by power and needs his victims to suffer. Terror plays an enormous role. He feeds off it. Our unsub is a white male in his forties or fifties. I base this theory on statistical evidence that most serial killers are white males, and also on the lack of diversity in Veil Lake."

Darcy's statement draws murmurs from the officers.

"Aren't most serial killers in their twenties and thirties?"

Darcy swings her gaze to the male officer in the front row.

"A study by Radford University showed a surprising number of serial killers are older than first thought. But what makes me think our killer is in his forties or fifties is the phone call Mrs. Fielder received. We believe the caller who claimed to work for the Learning Disabilities Center at North Chadwick University, is our unsub. He convinced the mother, and that tells me his voice matched that of a forty or fifty-year-old."

Darcy rests her hands on each side of the microphone and searches the faces in the crowd.

"Now I'll tell you something you don't want to hear. The Doll Face Killer is one of your own, a lifelong Veil Lake resident, someone you pass on the street and sit beside at the barbershop or corner bar."

More grumbles.

"Hell, no." The others turn to look at the heavyset, mustached officer in the back row. "This killer, he's a tourist." The crowd nods in unison. "This is some loon that came over from Detroit or flew in from New York City. We don't raise murderers around these parts. If this guy is from Veil Lake, why hasn't he killed anyone until now?"

Iglesias raises his hand to stop the mumbling. They shift their attention back to Darcy. She sees the doubt behind their eyes.

"Something set our target off and drove him to kill. A recent stressor. Could be a death in the family, job loss, divorce."

"That doesn't narrow down the suspect list," the argumentative officer says, his arms folded over his chest. "We get our share of barroom scraps after midnight, and the tourists drive like they're racing up the New Jersey Turnpike, but we don't get serial killers in Veil Lake. And anyway, if someone displayed psychotic tendencies in a village like Veil Lake, everyone would take notice."

Darcy waits for the clamor to quiet down.

"You wouldn't. Organized killers hide their secrets well. Able to hide in plain sight, they're your neighbors, your friends, the guy who helps you with the door when your arms are full of groceries. Dennis Rader, the BTK Killer, stayed married for thirty-four years. He worked as a Boy Scout leader, was the president of his church congregation, and held employment with local government. Over two decades, he murdered ten people without drawing notice."

Eyes dart around the room, the officers appraising their neighbors as though the Doll Face Killer might sit in the next chair.

"BTK remained deadly patient, only striking when his urges grew and the timing dictated he wouldn't get caught. Doll Face isn't as careful. Although he chooses his victims with care and abducts them when neighbors and family members are unaware, he's moving too fast. The unsub murdered five people in the last month, and now he's kidnapped a teenage girl. We call this escalation. He no longer controls his urges. While the danger has never been higher in Veil Lake, he's bound to slip up, and that's what will get him caught."

Confident and holding the room's attention, Darcy brings the microphone closer and runs her gaze over the officers. Two of them shift in their seats.

"The water plays an important role here. Maybe a traumatic event in the unsub's life, or it could be symbolic. He keeps his victims for seventy-two hours before he kills. Each murder took place along the lake at sunset. That means we have until sunset tomorrow to locate Faith Fielder and bring her home to her parents. You know your village better than I do. Think. Who in the village might have a relationship, personal or working, with Faith and the five victims? A common thread draws them together."

Darcy spends five minutes answering their questions. The police reach a higher level of alertness. They understand the killer is one of their own, a village local who nobody would suspect. After she finishes, she collects her bag and squeezes through the mass of officers congregating in the aisle. Iglesias disappears through the doors, bypassing Ketchum's handshake, then the FBI agent turns his attention toward Darcy.

"You did well up there. Like riding a bike?"

Darcy lifts a shoulder.

"Even when I presented profiles every month, it never felt comfortable."

"Well, you convinced them. That might be half the battle. Get them looking at their neighbors instead of the overweight guy with Connecticut plates." He holds the door open for her. "Follow me. We're getting somewhere with the restaurant footage."

The video analysis lab resides at the end of a long hall on the east end of the building. Shades cover the window, leaving the inside dusk-like. Two male police officers—an Italian-looking man in his middle twenties, and a tall black officer with dots of gray in his mustache, skim through the footage and take notes on a sheet of paper. Ketchum knocks on the open door.

"Mind if we say hello? Officers Narulla and Cross, this is Darcy Haines, the best profiler to come through the FBI in ten years."

"You're the one who caught that serial rapist down in Alabama," Cross says, pointing his pen at Darcy.

"The local PD caught him. I only drew the profile."

"That was excellent work. Don't sell yourself short."

A video monitor sits before each officer. Separate computers allow Narulla and Cross to divide the footage into manageable chunks, one interrogating the restaurant during the first half of the week, the other studying footage from the past few nights.

"Find anything on the footage?" Ketchum asks, holding his hands behind his back.

"Nothing yet," Cross says. "We spotted six regulars, but two are women, and one is a middle-aged man who needs a cane to get around. I doubt he's your target."

Narulla nods and adds, "The problem is the camera only covers part of the room. No way I can tell if someone visited the restaurant multiple times and stayed out of the camera view."

"You get eyes on the altercation Tuesday night?" Ketchum asks Narulla.

"I've got that piece of footage," Cross says, raising a hand. "Not much to see. I've got video of Geoff and Alexandra Voss teetering back and forth on the side of the frame. You can tell when the fight starts because the other patrons jump off their stools and break things up off camera."

"So you can't see the guy they went after. The good Samaritan who spent a long time chatting up Faith Fielder."

"No, just the back of his head for five seconds. I'll keep looking."

"What are we searching for?" Narulla asks, staring at Darcy. "A quiet guy who spends his time people watching, or a talkative type?"

"Concentrate on any male in his forties or fifties who watches Faith or starts a conversation. Doll Face will shift between quiet and conversational, depending on the crowd."

"So it might be the guy Geoff Voss started the fight with."

"Could be. Keep in mind the killer called Faith at the restaurant. He could have been on his cell phone, watching her the whole time."

"All right, officers," Ketchum says. "We'll leave you to it. Call me as soon as you have a suspect."

As the patrol units depart the parking lot, the bright hallway empties, leaving the reflected sun on the waxed floor. The squeaks of their shoes echo down the corridor.

"Why don't you head back to the inn and sleep through lunchtime," says Ketchum, touching her arm.

"There's too much to do, and every minute lost decreases the odds we'll find Faith alive."

"You've done everything asked of you. I was truthful with you in Genoa Cove. All I want is the profile of the killer. Let us handle the field work."

Darcy shakes her head. Though her body wants nothing more than to collapse on her bed with the drapes drawn across the window, she'll never sleep until the police save Faith.

"Let's pay the Fielders another visit. I want to know more about the messages Glen Filmore made Zoe record for Faith."

14

He watches over the garden like a scarecrow protecting the rows from scavengers.

Faith senses his glare as she wipes sweat off her brow. The sun slumbered behind the trees when Mr. Filmore rousted her out of bed, irritated she'd slept in. It's too hot. On her knees, Faith grabs two fistfuls of crumbling compost from the plastic bucket and spreads it around the roots of the heather. Yesterday, the flora invoked a sense of wonder. Now she'd be happy if she never encountered another heather plant for the rest of her life.

"How can my heather flourish if you daydream?"

Faith flinches. Mr. Filmore seemed so much nicer yesterday. He's short-fused this morning, impatient. As though a hidden clock ticks against them. She should feel grateful. Never has Faith had an opportunity like this. She's earning college credit, though she cannot understand what the gardening has to do with the awful pictures. Something about change. Becoming.

"Faith!"

"Yes, Mr. Filmore."

She works in double time, moving from one plant to the

next. The rows stretch to the back of the property. She'll be at this until nightfall. As Faith works, Mr. Filmore stomps inside and slams the door. The pane rattles.

A thought pops into Faith's head. Run. While he's inside and not paying attention. She tilts her head at the camera spying her from one corner of the cabin. He claims the camera watches over the garden, helps him keep the animals out. But her clammy skin tells her he's inside watching her now. She averts her eyes and returns to her work, her hands blackened by the rich soil.

When she shifts around a ruby colored plant to better get at its roots, she realizes the camera can't spy her anymore. The heather hides her. Faith's heart races. She parts two plants, careful not to injure the stems and draw Mr. Filmore's wrath, and spies the gate. It's too high to scale. Why does she want to leave? It's normal to miss her parents, and challenging work strengthens her. But there's something *wrong* about the photographs he forces her to study. Crime scene photographs of dead people, something she'd see in a horror movie. And the pictures of the murderers. Their eyes seem to move and follow her across the room, all knowing. Which makes no sense. They're just photographs. According to Mr. Filmore, the murderers are behind bars or dead. No reason they should frighten her.

Faith's gaze settles on the locks. Mr. Filmore carries a set of keys with him at all times. Sometimes they jingle in his pocket. If she can get a hold of the keys...

"Now what are you doing?"

She screams and spins around, finding him looming over her. The sun bleeds around his body, lighting him from behind and concealing his face. He sighs and rubs a forearm across his brow.

"My apologies. It's so hot this morning, and I fear I've let the heat get the best of me. Come into the cabin where it's cooler. I'll pour you a lemonade, and perhaps we can study more pictures."

Faith's mouth goes dry. Her eyes drop to her muddy knees. She'd rather work under the searing sunlight than view the pictures again.

"They scare you, don't they?" Mr. Filmore asks, dropping to one knee between the rows. The kindness she remembers from Tuesday night takes up residence in his eyes. "I wish there was another way. There isn't."

"But why? The pictures frighten me. They're horrible, and I never want to see them again."

He touches her chin and directs her gaze to his.

"You're the only one I trust to study these men. They're reprehensible, Faith. Murderers. Rapists. But good exists in all of us, and I believe they could have ascended to a higher purpose and brought happiness to the world. Helped people instead of hurt them. They all stopped killing. Do you understand?"

She shakes her head, swinging her hair across her face.

"Faith, please. With God as my witness, I can't believe not a single one of them embraced the goodness hidden in their hearts. Don't you understand? When we discover why they injured so many people...and why they stopped...there must be a way."

His words trail off into silence as his lips continue to move. Mr. Filmore's eyes glaze over. He gazes over the garden, past the heather, over the fence, engaging with a reality only he can see.

"I want to go home."

Her proclamation shakes him out of his trance.

"Come," he says, offering his hand and rising to his feet. "We'll look at the pictures together. I'll open the drapes, let the sunshine into the cabin so the shadows can't reach you."

Faith bites her lip and stands.

He leads her inside and sits her at the kitchen table. With a thunk, he drops the folders and books in front of her. She turns her head away. Pulling the curtains open over the sink, he assesses the brightness of the room and nods to himself. Next he throws the drapes open in the living room, inviting the steamy morning into the cabin. She has to admit the cabin appears less sinister now. But it doesn't scour away her apprehension.

"Where were we?" he asks, shuffling through the photographs. "Ah, yes."

He removes a stack of photographs from the folder and places it beside her. The book he chooses appears thicker than most dictionaries. He opens to the middle, licks his finger and thumb, and pages through the tome until he finds what he seeks. Mr. Filmore taps his index finger, still slick with spittle, on a black-and-white photograph of a burly man. A black beard curls around the man's chin and cheeks, his eyes chiseled from stone. He looks more bear than human.

"I don't want to look at him," Faith says, concentrating on the backs of her hands.

"John Brewster," Mr. Filmore says, ignoring her plea. "He wooed women in bars and slipped drugs into their drinks. After he took them home, he raped and strangled them with an extension cord." He tuts. "Not a good man, Faith. Before the police caught him, he murdered four women in rural Wisconsin."

"This makes my tummy sick. Please."

"He stopped. And not only because the authorities tracked Brewster down and threw him in a cell. Brewster's lawyer argued he wasn't mentally fit to stand trial, and the courts agreed, declaring the man insane."

Faith peeks at John Brewster. She lowers her head, swearing the murderer's eyes followed hers.

"What happened to him? He isn't still alive, is he?"

"The answers are all in these pages, Faith. I don't want to spoil the story for you. But if it makes you comfortable, John

Brewster died in a mental institution twenty-three years ago. Start reading. You'll take a quiz in one hour."

She peers at the clock on the kitchen wall. When she attempts to rise out of her chair, his hands thunder down on her shoulders. For a second, she senses an electrical current pouring off his palms.

"You're my most prized student. Do not fail me."

When she glances up at him, his face changes. He's the killer in the photograph—John Brewster. She chokes out a sob, invoking another change. The leering skull face disappears, leaving behind the kind face of Mr. Filmore.

"This is most disturbing," he says. "I understand. But there's nothing to fear, Faith. See this?" He lifts the page and lets it drift into place. "It's paper. No monsters will crawl out of the book and hurt us. And you'll have me with you the entire time. I'll work in the kitchen and the living room, close enough for you to see me. This isn't what you imagined college would be like, is it?"

Faith chews her lip. Tastes blood on her tongue.

"Fairy tale endings don't occur in the real world, and hard work is often nasty business. Take your job at the Veil Lake Grill. Do you like it?"

A smile twitches at the corner of her mouth.

"Yes. I like my boss. Her name is Rosanna, and she's pretty and kind."

"Pretty," Mr. Filmore says, stroking his thumb across her forearm. "But her job isn't fun. I'll bet sometimes she gets frustrated and worries the business will drag her to an early grave."

Faith thinks hard. He's correct. Ms. Noble couldn't keep up Tuesday night. All those customers, many from out of town and acting rudely.

"Imagine if the sewer workers decided they wouldn't do their jobs anymore. The village would be afloat in poop."

Faith snorts. She raises her eyes to his. His grin stretches from ear to ear, displaying teeth.

"That was funny, Mr. Filmore."

"Yes, it was. Crude, but funny. Do you feel better now?"

Her body no longer trembles.

"I can do this."

"I knew you could, Faith. You're the only hope this village has."

Faith quirks an eyebrow.

"I mean it," he continues. Filmore pats her shoulder. "Get back to work. You have one hour to tell me why John Brewster stopped. If you answer correctly, you'll pass your first college quiz."

Whistling to himself, Mr. Filmore tidies the kitchen. Faith draws in a long breath and closes her eyes when he turns his back. She can do this.

It's only a book.

15

THURSDAY, JULY 3RD 10:20 A.M.

Wind snaking through the valley agitates the lake waters. Countless ribbons of white caps rock boats and slosh water over the shoreline.

Ketchum drums his fingers on the steering wheel as he navigates the loop around Veil Lake. Darcy watches the cottages shoot past, wondering if Doll Face hides inside one, staring back at her through the window. Her attention moves to the mirrors, searching for a trailing vehicle. If *FM-Kill-Her* is bold enough to photograph Darcy with a police cruiser parked a few spaces away, he won't think twice about following her with Ketchum in the vehicle.

Craning her neck, Darcy spots the Fielder residence up the ridge and behind the trees.

"Here it is," Darcy says.

Ketchum hits the brakes and puts the SUV in reverse. Wes Fielder shoves a lawn mower through knee-deep grass and weeds as Ketchum stops the SUV in front of the garage. Shirtless and cooked pink by the sun, Wes slings sweat off his forehead and glares at them.

"Mr. Fielder," Ketchum says, hopping down from the cab. "We're following up on our last conversation."

"You find my girl yet, Agent?"

"We're doing everything we can. Is your wife home?"

"Zoe?"

"Yes."

He kills the engine and glances between the house and Ketchum.

"What do you want Zoe for? She answered all your questions."

"Please, Mr. Fielder. We won't take but a minute of your time."

Wes removes his sunglasses and tosses them on the porch stoop. He holds the door open as Darcy and Ketchum enter the house, the curtains closed and the room holding too many secrets. Zoe Fielder glances up at them from her place on the couch. Her eyes are red with recent tears. One leg crosses over the other, her dangling foot twirling in a circle. She clamps a cigarette between her middle finger and forefinger, holding it away as gray smoke ascends the living room. Her gaze remains vacant.

Darcy assumes this is the first cigarette Zoe has smoked in a long time. The couch and carpet held a fresh scent when Darcy and Ketchum spoke with the Fielders last evening. No evidence a smoker lived in the house. Zoe takes a long drag on the cigarette. The end lights with red fire. She crushes it in a saucer.

"Sorry to bother you again, Mrs. Fielder," Ketchum says. He points to the two chairs opposite the couch for approval. Zoe shrugs. "Tell me more about this man who phoned you from North Chadwick. Glen Filmore?"

"Yeah, what about him?"

"Do you recall the exact words he asked you to record for Faith?"

Zoe tilts her gaze to the ceiling.

"Something like, whenever you feel you can't handle college, Faith, Mr. Filmore will be there for you. You can trust him no matter how hard your coursework seems."

"What else?"

"That it was okay if he gave her a ride. I didn't like Faith relying on her friends for rides, or paying for those ride sharing services, even though she uses them here."

"It's different if she's in an unfamiliar town," Darcy says.

"That's right. I've a right to worry."

Ketchum meets Darcy's eyes. He's thinking the same thing she is. The caller could have recorded Zoe's messages and spliced them together on a computer, changing their meaning.

"Can you recall the time Mr. Filmore called?"

Zoe eyes the cigarette butt and reaches for the pack. Wes, who shuffles into the living room with a glass of water, places his hand on hers. He shakes his head.

"Sure. Around nine o'clock last Monday."

"Ten days ago."

"Yes. Faith got stuck working until eleven that night because the restaurant was down a server. We were gonna pick her up ourselves on account of how late it would be when she finished."

Darcy glances at Ketchum. He nods and excuses himself from the conversation, leaving through the front door. As Zoe continues to talk, Wes by her side and holding her hand, Darcy watches Ketchum pace the driveway with his phone pressed to his ear. After another five minutes of questions and answers, Darcy thanks Zoe for her time.

"Is that it?" Wes asks, his face reddening to match his burnt shoulders. "How does that get you closer to figuring out who took Faith?"

"I seriously doubt the man that called you worked for North Chadwick. We'll call to confirm his story."

Zoe's eyes widen.

"Mr. Filmore kidnapped Faith?"

"We'll confirm if the real Glen Filmore called your house ten days ago. In the meantime, if you receive any strange phone calls, I want you to call me." Darcy scribbles her number on her notepad and tears off the sheet. "This is my mobile number, Zoe. Anytime, no matter how late."

Zoe accepts the paper with haunted eyes. Ketchum finishes the call when Darcy steps onto the stoop. He has a hop to his step as they walk to the SUV.

"Got off the phone with the North Chadwick Learning Disabilities Center," Ketchum says after starting the engine. "Glen Filmore runs the center, but he's in Europe this week for a symposium. The college sent him a message and expects to hear from him this afternoon."

"Whoever phoned Zoe, it wasn't anyone from the Learning Disabilities Center."

Ketchum hits the brakes at the bottom of the driveway. He waits until a sports car with New Hampshire plates speeds past.

"The VLPD is checking the phone records. We'll have the caller's number soon." Ketchum backs into the road and guns the engine before another vehicle shoots around the blind curve. "You mentioned the lake during your profile. Something about the symbolism of water."

"Water holds symbolic significance in religion. Some equate water with fertility and purity. In Christianity, water symbolizes purity of the soul and admission into faith."

"So this guy could be a religious nut."

"Possibly. It's more likely he experienced trauma on Veil Lake."

Ketchum purses his lips as if he expected her reply and already knew the answer. Was this a test?

"Why do you live along the ocean?"

The question knocks her off balance. She stares through the trees toward the blue lake.

"The water draws me. Always has."

"Symbolic reasons?" he asks, cocking an eyebrow.

"I'm not religious. Yes, there's a God, though the horrors I've seen cause my faith to waver. Large bodies of water soothe me. I imagine it's the same for the people living around Veil Lake."

"You were right about the bathroom at the Lieberman house," he says. The interior of the SUV grows silent when he raises the window. "A CSI tech found a hair follicle at the base of the upstairs toilet. The lab is checking the DNA against the Liebermans."

"He slipped up," Darcy says, her gaze fixed on the road ahead.

"Doll Face?"

"It's impossible not to leave DNA at the scene after seventy-two hours. I'm shocked we haven't lifted his print yet. You can't wear gloves that long."

"Maybe he takes them elsewhere."

Darcy swings her head toward him.

"Why would he do that?"

"Think about it. This guy lives close to the village. He might have tossed Jim and Carol Lieberman into his vehicle, gagged them so they couldn't scream in the driveway."

"That's a lot of work. He'd have to bring them back to their house to murder them. But it explains the lack of DNA evidence at the scene."

The thought plays around in Darcy's head when Ketchum's phone rings. He switches the call to the SUV's speaker. An unrecognized number appears on the screen.

"Agent Ketchum."

"This is Keith Marsella, the assistant manager at the Veil Lake Grill. We met last night."

Ketchum glances at Darcy and raises the speaker volume.

"How may I help you, Mr. Marsella?"

"I ran into one of my neighbors, Kent Seebach. He was at the restaurant the night Voss started the fight."

"Go on."

"Kent says the guy Voss bullied is Trevor Funes. He's a postal worker with a route on the west side of the lake."

"This is the guy that talked Faith's ear off?"

"According to Kent, yes."

Darcy leans forward and asks, "How often does Funes visit the restaurant?"

"He's in there two or three nights a week."

"What about when Faith is working?"

Keith pauses.

"I'm sure he's visited while she was behind the bar, but I can't tell you if he only comes in when she's on shift."

Ketchum thanks Keith for the information and ends the call.

"We need to speak with Funes," he says. "I'll tell Iglesias to crosscheck the guy's phone number with whoever called the Fielders."

16

Narulla and Cross are staring at a fuzzy picture captured off the hotel's security camera when Darcy and Ketchum return to the office.

"That's an L," Narulla says, jabbing his finger at the screen while Cross shakes his head like a shaggy dog that just splashed out of a pond.

"Can you settle this?" Cross asks, glaring with mock impatience at Ketchum and Darcy.

Darcy leans close to the monitor and scrunches up her face.

"Looks like a seven to me."

"Thank you," Cross says, swinging his chair around to Narulla. "I've been trying to tell him this for the last ten minutes."

"Fine, it's a goddamn seven," Narulla says, rolling his eyes.

"Is that the plate from the parking lot?" Ketchum asks, kneeling so his face is even with the monitor.

Cross decodes the license plate number on a piece of scrap paper.

"Damn sure it is." He looks out the tops of his eyes at

Ketchum. "This guy was three parking spaces from Nix. You believe that?"

"Nix. That's the officer who accompanied Darcy to the Lieberman house."

A grin curls Cross's lips.

"Two years ago, I was making my rounds through the north end of the village. Nix radios me. Says there's a woman two blocks from my cruiser yelling *fire* at the top of her lungs. So I take the bait, hit the lights, and pull up to the curb in front of the lady's house, expecting the fire department to follow." Cross leans his head back and chuckles. "Lady had a cat named Fire. Nix set me up. So expect me to ride his ass over this screw up," he says, displaying the paper with the license plate number.

Wearing a smirk, Narulla snatches the paper and hustles down the hall. Cross makes small talk with Ketchum while Darcy struggles to keep her eyes open. She could use a booster shot of caffeine. When Narulla returns, he leans against the door frame.

"The name Phillip O'Grady mean anything to either of you?"

Ketchum looks at Darcy, who shrugs.

"He's from Xenia, Ohio," Narulla continues. "Drives a blue Chevy Cobalt. We're checking around town to see if he booked a room."

"Phillip O'Grady," Darcy says, repeating the name.

"We need to bring this guy in," Ketchum says. "It's one thing to show up at the Lieberman house when Darcy is inside. That might be coincidental. Darcy says he frequents this serial killer forum, so perhaps he wanted a picture for the website. But to follow Darcy to the inn...I don't trust his intentions."

"This guy could be our killer," Cross says, looking between Darcy and Ketchum.

Darcy gives a hesitant nod.

"It's worth putting him on our suspect list."

"Which is up to one now."

"Two. Officer, do you know a postal worker named Trevor Funes?"

Cross itches his chin.

"Funes. Fair-haired dude, about this tall?" Cross sets his hand at shoulder height. "Never met him, but I've seen him around the village."

"Has he lived here his entire life?"

"Couldn't tell you without looking up his records. What makes you believe he's a murderer?"

"An eyewitness saw Funes speaking with Faith before the abduction," says Ketchum. "He paid Faith too much attention."

"Well, it's a weekday. Funes is walking his route now. I'll call over to the post office."

"Get me the neighborhood he's delivering to. I'll swing through and strike up a conversation."

Back in the SUV, Ketchum lowers the windows and expels the midday heat. He casts a wary eye across the seat at Darcy.

"I'd offer to swing past the inn and drop you off, but I figure you'll say no."

"I'll be fine," she says, closing her eyes as she leans her head against the seat back.

"Don't burn the candle at both ends. You can't help us locate Faith if you're too tired to function."

The hum of the engine takes Darcy in. She darts awake when Ketchum stops the vehicle. Darcy blinks. How long was she asleep? Middle-class houses, built before cookie cutter neighborhoods became the norm, stretch down the tree-lined street. Two school-age boys ride their bikes down the sidewalk.

"Where are we?"

"Maple Street on the east end of the village."

Darcy scrubs the blur out of her eyes.

"How long was I out?"

Ketchum eyes the console.

"Thirty minutes."

"It doesn't take that long to drive here from the police station."

"Nope. I pulled into a parking lot a mile up the road and let you sleep."

"You didn't have to do that."

"I don't want my partner keeling over."

Partner? Darcy pictures Eric Hensel and feels a sob form in her throat. But she's not rejoining the FBI. Nothing Ketchum says will convince her to return to the Behavior Analysis Unit. Before she can argue, he hops out of the SUV and makes a beeline across the road toward the sidewalk. She looks ahead and spots his quarry. A male postal worker in shorts and a baseball cap slings his mailbag over his shoulder and crosses the front lawn of a blue Cape Cod.

"Trevor Funes?"

Funes halts and glances up at Ketchum and Darcy. When Ketchum displays his badge, Funes's eyes dart around the neighborhood.

"What's this about?"

"I'm Agent Adan Ketchum with the Federal Bureau of Investigation, and this is my partner, Darcy Haines. We'd like to talk to you about Faith Fielder."

Funes looks around, worried a neighbor is listening in.

"I read about the kidnapping. Do you think it's that guy on the news? The Doll Face Killer?"

"When is the last time you spoke with Faith?"

Funes rubs the back of his neck.

"I don't know her. She's just a teenager."

"We have eyewitnesses who saw you speaking to Faith Tuesday night at the Veil Lake Grill."

"Just making conversation. I feel bad for her, you know? Bad and proud at the same time. She's overcome so much. Not only does she work at the restaurant, she's going to college."

"You know a lot about Faith," Darcy says, taking a step forward.

Funes itches his arm. There's a red bump above the elbow. Darcy can't tell if it's a hive, or an insect stung him on his walk.

"Not really. I just see her around the village. She's almost a star. Everyone knows her name and treats her well."

Ketchum removes his sunglasses.

"Not everyone. Geoff and Alexandra Voss badgered Faith at the restaurant, and you risked a fight by stepping in to defend her. Faith must mean a lot to you, Trevor."

"I couldn't sit there while they made fun of her. Look, they were drunk and belligerent. Were it not for the alcohol, neither would have said those things."

"But they did, and you stuck up for Faith," Darcy says. "How long have you known her?"

The postman coughs into his hand and hoists the bag to his other shoulder.

"I don't know her."

"You spoke for a long time at the bar."

"Like I said, I was being friendly."

"How long have you delivered mail in Veil Lake?" Ketchum asks.

"Seven years this September. Why does that matter?"

"You deliver to the Fielders?"

"I work the west side of the lake." Funes shuffles his feet and points toward the lake waters a mile down the road. "The Fielders live on the east side of Veil Lake, three miles from the school. Not sure off the top of my head who delivers to their neighborhood. I can ask at the office."

"Your route hasn't changed in seven years? That's unusual in your line of work. You haven't delivered to the Fielders?"

"Not that I can recall. Why would it matter if I had?"

Ketchum shrugs.

"I have a hard time believing you don't have prior contact with Faith Fielder. Concentrate, Trevor. Perhaps you saw her on the porch during your rounds and spoke to her."

"I don't think so."

"You're a friendly, outgoing guy. Wouldn't be unusual for someone like you to know most of the townsfolk, especially someone like Faith."

"I told you. I stuck up for her at the restaurant because those jerks gave her a hard time. Nothing more to it than that." Funes glances at his watch. "And now I'm behind schedule."

"How often do you see her?"

Funes tries to step around Ketchum, but he shifts to block him.

"Do I need a lawyer?"

"Answer the question."

"Other than Tuesday night, hardly ever."

"You don't visit the restaurant three times per week? I spoke with one worker, and he says you're a fixture at the grill."

"So I go there for a fish sandwich and a draft beer. It's the most popular restaurant on the lake."

"Faith works twenty hours per week. You must see her a lot."

"I need to go."

When the postman appears agitated, Darcy softens her eyes and touches Funes's arm.

"You care about Faith. Would anybody in Veil Lake want to hurt her?"

Funes scowls.

"Of course not."

"During your visits to the Veil Lake Grill, have you ever noticed someone following Faith around or watching her?"

"You make it sound like I go there to check on her. I don't. I want to see her do well, but there's nothing more to it. If you have more questions, you can find me at the office. I need to finish my route before I get fired."

Ketchum hands Funes a card.

"Should you think of anything else, call me."

Funes lowers his head and hurries down the sidewalk. Ketchum sets his hands on his hips and observes the postman stuffing a magazine into the neighbor's mailbox.

"What's your opinion of Funes?" Ketchum asks.

"He's lying. No way he hasn't spoken to Faith before. He takes a strong interest in the girl."

"He's greasy. That welt on his arm. Insect bite?"

Darcy folds her arms.

"I can't be certain. Might be a scrape."

"Like someone fought back when he grabbed hold of her."

"We're jumping to conclusions. Funes doesn't strike me as a murderer, and he doesn't fit the profile. He barely held eye contact, and I wouldn't describe him as personable."

"We should monitor him. Why would he lie about knowing Faith?" Ketchum checks the time on his phone. "Dammit, it's almost one. No wonder I'm starving. There's an Italian place around the corner that sells pizza and calzones. Looks promising. You up for a slice?"

Darcy covers a yawn.

"If it's no difference to you, I'd rather grab an hour of shuteye while you go to lunch."

"No problem. I'll drop you off at the station and circle back to the pizza joint after. You know, Darcy, it's fine if you crash until dinner."

"All I need is an hour. Can you get me a key to Cassy Regan's house? I want to walk through."

"Yeah, I can get it. But I don't like you visiting these places in the dark with some wacko following you around the village."

"I have a process."

"I'll have an officer follow you over. Maybe he should accompany you inside this time."

"Please, Agent Ketchum. You requested my presence and asked me to build a profile of the killer. Let me do my job."

Ketchum presses his lips together.

"All right. But keep your phone on you at all times. You hear anyone creeping around outside or notice anything out of place, you get the hell out of there and let the police handle it."

Fifteen minutes later, Ketchum drops Darcy off at her rental. Checking her messages inside the car, she finds a recent text from Jennifer asking when she'll finish and come home. Darcy's eyes tear up as she replies. Her body melts into the seat as she twists the key in the ignition, exhaustion and loneliness claiming her.

During the ride to the inn, she studies the homes around the lake, distracting herself from the sudden bout of homesickness. Given the ample lake frontage, the tax bills must be extraordinary. Every home offers a unique view of the lake, some framed by groves, others looking out at the miniature bays and sloshing waves. She ponders the water's significance. *Tragedy* keeps popping into her mind. What drove Doll Face over the edge? To Darcy's eye, the lake appears idyllic, tranquil. A place where nature merges with heaven.

She pulls into the inn's parking lot and pats her pockets for her key card. After an anxious moment, she sighs, remembering she slipped the card into her wallet. Her feet drag across the steaming pavement. A wind gust blows hair around her face and makes her fumble her bag. The contents roll around on the blacktop. At least the phone was inside her pocket. Gathering up her supplies, she senses eyes on her.

Darcy stands erect. Phillip O'Grady could be watching her now. There's no cruiser in the parking lot, no officer standing guard. She touches the Glock-22 on her hip and pulls her hair back. Casting a look over her shoulder, she searches for a Chevy Cobalt. When she doesn't find O'Grady's car, she picks up the pace, not slowing until she's inside the lobby. Yet the sensation she's being watched won't go away.

Turning her head, her eyes pass over the man near the coffee pot. Darcy's sleep-deprived mind catches up to her vision. She swings her head back to the man.

Julian.

He doesn't realize she's staring at him until he stirs a packet of sugar into his coffee and tosses the stick into the trash. When their eyes meet, his mouth hangs open. He does a poor job of hiding something behind his back. But she already spied the flowers. She grins, and that breaks the ice between them.

"What on earth are you doing here?" she asks, setting her bag on the table and hugging him.

The flowers emerge from behind his back. It's a seasonal mix of wildflowers and pink roses.

"I wanted to give you these," he says, handing her the bouquet. "It would have been cheaper to mail them, but what the hell."

The deadpan reply gets her laughing.

"They're gorgeous, thank you. But you shouldn't have come."

Julian waves away her concern.

"Don't worry. The chief says I could use a vacation. Something about me being wound tighter than a drum."

"What about the kids?"

"Hunter promised he'd stay with Jennifer." He raises his hands to cut off her argument. "I asked the Fennels to keep an eye on the house, and I pulled a few strings and got the GCPD to swing through the neighborhood. If the kids throw a party, I'll find out. How's the case going?"

"We haven't found him yet, if that's what you're asking."

"Give it time. You just started yesterday."

"I don't have time," Darcy says, pouring scalding water into a cup. She sifts through the tea choices and settles on black tea. "This guy kills after seventy-two hours. I have until sunset tomorrow to figure out who he is."

"Any suspects?"

"Two, but neither fit the profile." Darcy sips the tea and winces at the heat. "I still can't believe you're here."

"Won't you invite me up to your room, Mrs. Haines?"

"On the first date?"

Julian rides the escalator beside Darcy, who can't suppress her giddy smile. Being apart from Julian for a day threw her into a funk as though the miles between them turned the hours into weeks. Now he's here, and though Darcy misses her kids, the uneasiness which tracked her around the lake vanishes. She forgets about Phillip O'Grady, aka *FM-Kill-Her*, until she glances over her shoulder toward the parking lot.

"Something wrong?" Julian asks, following her gaze. Darcy tells him about O'Grady. "That creep has been a thorn in your side for as long as I've known you. I've read his posts, Darcy. O'Grady could be Doll Face."

"It doesn't feel right."

"I'll never forget the story he wrote about you and the kids. O'Grady wishes he was Michael Rivers. What if he's taken up the cause now that the Full Moon Killer is dead?"

Inside the room, Darcy drops her bag on the chair and sets the tea on the nightstand.

"Will this be like Treman Mills?" Darcy asks, referring to last autumn's investigation when they rescued Julian's niece. "The VLPD won't let you muscle your way onto the case."

"I'm here to keep you company. And to watch your back."

She kisses his lips.

"Thank you so much for coming."

"There's no reason for you to be alone."

Darcy parts the curtains and scans the parking lot. A woman in a black suit loads a suitcase into her van. Turning toward the mirror, Darcy scowls at the mess of hair atop her head and combs it with her fingers. With a groan, she sits on the bed and pries her shoes off.

"Would I be a horrible guest if I dozed for a half-hour?"

"No offense, but you look like you could sleep until nightfall."

"Not that long, please. I'm walking through another house this evening, and I want to prepare."

She nestles her head on the pillow. He leans over and kisses her cheek, then pulls out his Kindle and loses himself in a book. With Julian near, Darcy falls asleep as soon as her eyes close.

17

Sunlight through the cabin's dusty window burns a hole through Richard Oswalt's bedroom floor. Faith's report lies torn and tattered on his desk, little pieces crawling to and fro with the whims of a breeze cutting through the open window. He falls into the chair and gathers the shreds into his palms. Stares at them the way he would a tiny animal after he squeezed the life out of it.

Through the wall, he hears sobs. He shouldn't have screamed. Richard expects more from her. She might as well have copied the report word for word from his books. She gleaned no additional information.

His fingers drum the desk like cobras striking. The porcelain mask rests on the edge of the desk. He runs his thumb along its smooth edges, follows the contours to the eye sockets. In the distance, thunder rolls over the lake and causes the ground to tremble. Yet the sun continues to blaze. He lowers his head and clutches his hair, realizing it wasn't thunder, but a passing truck.

He shoves the chair back and strides to the wall. Places his ear against the wood and listens. The mattress squeals as she climbs into bed. He pictures her swiping a tissue across her nose as she pulls the covers over her head. He's locked himself in the cabin for too long and needs a fresh perspective. Should he leave her alone?

Swinging his head back to the desk, he glares at the torn report and worries he made a grave error. Faith failed him today, but she has tonight and tomorrow to complete her work. He whips open the desk drawer and retrieves the keys. Jangles them in his hand before stuffing the keys into his back pocket.

Entering the hallway, he stops and stares at the closed door across the corridor. A long scratch runs down the paint-chipped door as if a beast raked a claw down the wood. His eyes follow the jagged road map until it ends at the jamb. *Hello, Mother.*

A screeching noise comes from behind the door. Like someone stepping on a loose floorboard. Sweat dots his forehead as his mouth goes dry. He reaches for the knob, then pulls his hand back as if the doorknob grew fangs. Listening for the noise, he holds his breath. Thudding sounds move through the room. Footsteps.

Impossible. His imagination plays tricks on him.

Richard tests the knob and finds it locked. Jiggles the knob, then pulls back when the noises come again. He backs away, shaking his head at the possibility someone is inside the closed bedroom. He keeps the room locked. Always. Nobody is to enter.

Shaking free of his fear, Richard moves down the hallway. Outside Faith's door, he knocks once.

"Faith? It's Richard—it's Mr. Filmore."

No reply. The quiet cleaves him.

Another knock.

"I'm sorry, Faith. I shouldn't have yelled. You're an excellent student."

"You're mean."

The reply, little more than a whisper, strikes at his heart.

"No, no. I'm not, Faith." He sighs and runs a shaking hand

over his head. "There was a teacher in high school I hated. She picked on me, graded me harder than my classmates. Yelled when I failed to complete an assignment to her specifications. It wasn't until I entered college that I appreciated her. Before then, I wondered why she never badgered the other kids. Only me. That's when I realized she expected more from me than she did my classmates. When a teacher yells, she's telling you she believes in you and expects you to do better. It's when she stops yelling that you need to worry. Do you understand why, Faith?"

"Leave me alone."

He knocks his forehead against the wall. Slaps his hand against the door jamb. She isn't being reasonable. He must give her time to recognize the error of her ways. Though they have little time left.

Quietly, so she doesn't hear him leave, he pads away from her bedroom door and steps into the garden. With a twist of the key, he locks the cabin. It's risky to leave her alone. Yet he's confident she can't escape. The gate stands too high and won't unlock without his keys. There's no reason for her to leave this paradise, regardless.

He walks into the garden and merges with the heather, arms outstretched beneath the benevolent eye of the sun, at one with the beauty surrounding him. He recalls when only a few plants dotted the barren landscape. Mother envisioned what the garden could become with patience and care. Now look at it. From humble beginnings to nature at its most extravagant. The plants survived two blizzards and zero degree temperatures last winter, only to bounce back stronger in spring.

Richard Oswalt inhales the scents before slipping through the rows. He feels powerful now. Impenetrable. Except he can't kick this runny nose. Colds are rare during summer. And why do his hands itch? At least they're not as bad as yesterday.

Putting the altercation with Faith behind him, he decides a

walk in the woods will do him good. Clear his mind so they can tackle the study this evening when she's ready.

At the gate, he glances back at the cabin, sensing someone watching from the window. Not Faith. She's too distraught to leave the bedroom. A chill ripples down his arms. There was someone inside the locked bedroom. No, they were alone in the cabin. Nobody else was inside.

He prays he's right. If he isn't, Faith is in grave danger.

18

Cracking one eye open when she comes awake, Darcy stares at the clock. She sits up and throws the covers off, frustrated she slept into the late afternoon. Outside, a pair of car doors slam. Children giggling announces new arrivals at the inn.

Julian lounges in the corner chair, the e-book still in his hand.

"Why did you let me sleep so late?"

"Because you needed it. Don't get upset. I contacted Agent Ketchum and told him you were catching up on rest. He supported the idea."

"I won't ask how you got Ketchum's number."

"I have connections."

Darcy rushes around the room, searching for a missing shoe. Pulling the bedspread up, she finds it beneath the bed. Her body surges with adrenaline. Yes, she needed rest. But she lost three hours she'll never get back, and she's no closer to catching the Doll Face Killer. Twenty-nine hours until the Fourth of July sunset. Darcy prays she'll celebrate the holiday by returning Faith Fielder to her parents.

After she splashes water on her face over the bathroom sink, Darcy grabs her belongings.

"I need to go."

"Yes, and I'm coming with you."

"Julian—"

"I'll give you all the space you want. Think of me as the silent muscle watching your back."

"I'm a profiler consulting for the FBI, not a mob boss."

Darcy hands the keys to Julian so she can fix her hair while he drives. The effort seems wasted when he lowers the window and lets the fresh air off the lake whip around the car at fifty-five mph. Directing him as she answers a text from Hunter, Darcy slows her breathing to control her racing heart. This is her last night to hunt the Doll Face Killer.

Darcy leads Julian past security as his gaze drifts with wonder over the high-tech interior of the VLPD.

"This town has money," he says, raising his eyebrows.

They locate Ketchum and Officer Nix inside the media room, standing over Narulla and Cross. The two officers continued analyzing the footage, though their shifts ended at four. Darcy makes introductions before Nix ducks out for a bite to eat. When the officer returns with a half-eaten apple in hand and his phone pressed to his ear, he motions for Darcy to follow.

Nix closes the conference room door after Julian, Darcy, and Ketchum enter.

"Thank you, Dr. Lewis. You're now on speaker phone with Agents Ketchum and Haines with the FBI, and Detective Haines with the Genoa Cove Police Department."

Darcy glances at Julian, who lifts a shoulder.

Lewis clears his throat and says, "I analyzed the hair follicle taken off the upstairs bathroom floor in the Lieberman house. It doesn't belong to Jim or Carol Lieberman."

"So it must have come from our unsub," Ketchum says, giving a thumbs up to Darcy.

"Or a cleaner. Testing the three members of the Lieberman's cleaning crew could take weeks, but you don't have much time. The hair belongs to a middle-aged male."

"How do you know?"

"It's a long enough piece that the color changed from dark brown to silver."

"Our killer is graying. Okay, Doctor. What else?"

"Narrowing the DNA down to a male is significant, because two of the three housekeepers are female."

"Who's the male cleaner?" Ketchum asks Nix.

"Oscar Bailey," the officer says, paging through his notes. "He's twenty-five."

"That makes it unlikely the hair belonged to Bailey."

"True," Doctor Lewis says. "But I've seen males in their early and middle twenties with dots of gray in their hair."

"Doctor," Darcy says, leaning over the upturned phone on the conference room desk. "Your lab identified the cornstarch powder taken from the Lieberman house, correct?"

"Yes, and that's interesting."

"How so?"

"The medical and law enforcement communities moved away from the old style gloves to non-powdered. For some, cornstarch powder acts as an irritant and causes an allergic reaction on the skin."

"We believe our unsub wore the gloves for the better part of seventy-two hours."

"Hmm. That would cause a reaction in most anyone."

"What sort of allergic reaction are we looking for?"

"Wound inflammation, hives, a runny nose. Puffiness around the eyes. It might look as if he's recovering from a cold or an insect stung him. Keep in mind, it's been three days since the

Lieberman murders. Chances are the killer recovered by now, provided he removed the gloves."

"It wouldn't hurt to check with pharmacies in town," Nix says, looking at them from the tops of his eyes. He leans forward with his arms braced against the table. "See if anyone remembers a middle-aged male with hives purchasing Benadryl."

"Or an anti-itch cream," Dr. Lewis says in agreement.

Nix thanks Lewis and ends the call. Darcy stares at Ketchum.

"Trevor Funes had a welt on his arm," Darcy says.

"Who's Trevor Funes?" asks Julian.

Darcy recounts Funes's story.

"And neither of us trusted Funes when he claimed he barely knew Faith Fielder," Ketchum adds.

"What about Geoff and Alexandra Voss?" Darcy asks.

"The chief brought them in for an interview this afternoon," Nix says. "Neither appeared to be suffering from an allergic reaction, though they were both coming off benders and hungover. Without evidence they kidnapped Faith, we let them walk. But we're keeping tabs on both."

"Have Geoff and Alexandra lived in Veil Lake a long time?"

Nix scoffs.

"Unfortunately. Like most of the village, they were born and raised on the lake. I've dealt with them for ten years."

"Would you describe them as violent?"

"You'd have to be," Julian says, interjecting himself in the conversation. "Who starts a fight with a teenage girl with Down syndrome?"

Nix blows the hair off his forehead.

"I brought both of them in for public intoxication two years ago. Geoff had a DUI last winter. But I never witnessed violent streaks in Geoff and Alexandra Voss, and they both claim alibis for the time Faith was abducted."

"That seems unlikely," Darcy says. "We found them on

camera the night Faith Fielder disappeared outside the Veil Lake Grill."

"According to the video time stamp, the altercation between Funes and Voss occurred at 8:52 p.m. Faith left the restaurant after her shift ended at nine o'clock. Geoff and Alexandra Voss claim they took a taxi and arrived home a few minutes after nine."

"Did they pay with credit card or cash?" Julian asks.

"Cash, so there isn't an electronic transaction to back up their story. I'm checking with the taxi company to see who picked them up at the restaurant."

Darcy brushes her hair back.

"The taxi driver arrived at the restaurant around the time Faith walked outside. Veil Lake doesn't get a lot of traffic that time of night."

"I like where you're going," Nix says, snapping his fingers. "Maybe the cab driver noticed a vehicle canvassing the area."

"Can you recall a lake drowning in recent years that received a lot of attention?"

Nix scrunches his face in thought.

"Nothing in particular. Veil Lake is twenty-five miles long and six hundred feet deep at the center, plus we have ninety thousand residents county wide, and that's not counting the number of tourists coming through during summer. Doesn't matter how much we stress safety. A drowning every few years is an inevitability."

"The way Doll Face positions his victims to face the lake, I assume he experienced tragedy on the water. A spouse drowning. Or a boating accident."

"No boating accidents in the last year, knock on wood. Then we have your Internet forum psycho, Phillip O'Grady. I called around. If the guy is staying in town, he didn't reserve a room under his name. Our officers know his car model and license plate. We're keeping an eye out for him."

Darcy leans against the table and taps her foot.

"Would you mind if I walked through Cassy Regan's house this evening? I'm missing something crucial to the investigation."

"I'll get you a key," Nix says, turning out of the room. "Be right back."

"You're not going alone," Julian says, not waiting for Ketchum to agree.

"I'll put another officer outside Regan's house," says Ketchum.

"This O'Grady nut followed you to your last investigation, even though you had a police escort. I don't like you walking through a vacant house without backup."

"I agree," Ketchum says, folding his arms.

Darcy glances between Julian and Ketchum, displeased they're in agreement.

"I can't do the walk through with either of you with me," Darcy says. "You understand why."

"Then I'll wait outside the door while the officer watches the street," says Julian.

"Seems I don't have a choice in the matter."

"No, you don't," Ketchum says. "Especially after what happened last night."

"In the meantime, let's check the records for drownings and boating accidents over the last ten years."

19

THURSDAY, JULY 3RD 6:15 P.M.

Wiping the sleep from her eyes, Faith squints at the checkerboard pattern of light glaring against the floor. She doesn't remember falling asleep. The cabin holds an eerie quiet that makes her wonder if she's alone. She shuffles to the bedroom door and listens. No sounds come from the living room or kitchen. After a moment of hesitation, she unlocks the door.

The unlit hallway holds a furtive hush. Shadows cloak the east side of the cabin as she slides along the wall, listening for Mr. Filmore. He isn't the man she thought he was. Mr. Filmore has a mean streak she doesn't trust. College doesn't feel safe anymore. She'd be better off staying in Veil Lake with her parents and working at the restaurant. Ms. Noble never yelled at her like that, and she wouldn't force Faith to look at horrible, bloody pictures. She wants nothing more than to call home and tell Mom to pick her up. Except she doesn't know where she is. Did Mr. Filmore give Mom his address? Yes, he must have. Otherwise, Mom would never allow Faith to accompany the professor to his house.

A groaning sound comes from behind her. Faith stops

outside the living room. A monstrous claw rakes against the window, causing her to cover her mouth. Just a tree branch. When the groan doesn't repeat, Faith slips through the down-stairs, fearing Mr. Filmore will jump out from behind a chair and scream at her again.

Her breath flies in and out of her chest. Through the living room window, she looks into the heather garden. Runs her gaze along the fence. She sees the enclosure as a cage, a cell, rather than a means of protecting the flora from outside intruders. The heather bobs and dances with the wind like children laughing. Did Mr. Filmore leave her alone?

Hope gets her pulse racing. If she can find a way past the gate, maybe she'll recognize her surroundings and find her way back to the village. Back to Mom and Dad.

Her phone. Mr. Filmore forbade Faith access to her phone until she completed her coursework. He must have hidden the phone inside the cabin. The wind pushes against the home and rattles the windows. Backing away from the glass, she turns into the kitchen and yanks open drawers and cupboards. No phone. In the living room, she drops to her hands and knees and peers under the couch and chairs, inside the coffee table drawer. Unable to locate her phone, she checks the bathroom, whipping open the medicine cabinet and sliding the drawers beneath the sink open.

Faith waits in the hallway. Two rooms remain. Mr. Filmore's bedroom and the locked room across from his. Though nobody is home, she pads light-footed toward her professor's bedroom, careful to remain quiet as though the cabin will hear Faith and alert her captor. Or perhaps the cabin is a living thing that cocoons Faith in an inescapable web.

Between the two doors, she glances from one to the other. Reaching with an unsteady hand, she tests the doorknob on the locked room. Twists. It won't open without a key. As she swerves to Mr. Filmore's room, a scratching sound comes from inside the forbidden bedroom. Faith catches her breath in her throat. It could have been the wind scraping a tree branch against the bedroom window. Or someone is inside.

Backing away from the entrance, she bumps into Mr. Filmore's door and yelps. He forgot to lock his bedroom. She whips the door open and staggers into a bedroom with a threadbare, oval throw rug covering the center of the floor. His queen size bed rests against the back wall, the white bedspread pulled military tight, each pillow propped against the headboard. A wood desk divides the room. She expects a computer and monitor but finds none. Which makes no sense. Professors need computers. Perhaps he has a laptop and took it with him when he left the house.

She opens the desk drawer and finds an assortment of pencils and pens. A memo pad and a handful of paper clips. On top of the desk, a porcelain mask with hollow eyes stares at the ceiling. The blank face reminds her of the ceramic theater masks hanging on the wall when her parents took a young Faith to see a musical in Detroit. She touches the mask. Draws her hand back from the cold surface. She can't take her eyes off the mask as she opens more drawers.

Her attention shifts to a maple wood dresser with a lamp on top. His clothes will be inside, and she knows it's wrong to sift through his private belongings. But this is the last place she can think to check.

When the first drawer whispers open, the garden gate squeals. Faith freezes in place. His footsteps trail through the heather rows as Faith begs herself to run. She's a deer caught in the headlights of an onrushing tractor trailer, knees locked, arms stuck to her sides like the rigid limbs of an animal trapped in perpetuity by taxidermy. The key jiggles in the knob. Faith forces her feet to drag her from the room. She spins into the hallway as he curses and slides the key into the lock again. Faith turns back, remembering she left his bedroom door open. She pulls it shut as the front door opens with a gust of wind. Sticking to the shadows, she hurries for her bedroom.

And finds him glaring at her at the end of the hallway.

"Ah, Faith. You've been a very bad girl."

The last sliver of sun glows Halloween-orange over the western ridges when Julian drives Darcy across the village toward Cassy Regan's neighborhood. Two headlights shine in the mirrors, and Darcy keeps ensuring the lights belong to Officer Nix's cruiser and not to a Chevy Cobalt driven by a cyber-stalker. They keep the radio off so the only sounds are the hum of the tires and the chirping crickets outside the windows.

"You're certain you don't want me to come in with you?"

She leaps at his voice and touches her chest.

"This is something I need to do alone."

He doesn't answer. Simply shakes his head. The police radio Officer Nix gave Darcy squawks in the center compartment. Someone reported teens drag racing on the north side of the lake. She releases a breath and says, "At least we know it's not Hunter."

The corner of Julian's mouth quirks up.

"Hunter and his friends like to race? Why didn't I know about this?"

"I can't say for sure. A group of juniors and seniors used to take their cars out to the coast road between Genoa Cove and Smith Town when Hunter was in high school. That kid Hunter hung out with, Squiggs, was a ringleader. But I never allowed Hunter to take my car when I suspected they were racing."

"No offense, Darcy, but your Prius wouldn't beat a lawn tractor in a drag race."

His laughter disarms her, unlocks her frozen bones. She gives his shoulder a playful smack and lets a giggle escape her mouth. Dammit, she misses Hunter and Jennifer. But she harbors no regrets for taking this case. If it were her kid missing...and she's lived that nightmare more than once...she'd want the FBI, the police, and the nation's military searching.

The radio buzzes with activity again. Iglesias's voice booms through the radio. Does the chief work twenty-four hours per day? He's been on shift since sunrise.

"I'm here, Chief Iglesias," Darcy says, lifting the radio.

"We have a problem. Agent Ketchum and I just finished interviewing Janine Harlicki. She's the Veil Lake Postmaster. Turns out Trevor Funes lied." Darcy glances at Julian, who divides his attention between Darcy and the road, now drowning in black as the light vanishes. "Funes switches his route twice per year. Harlicki mentioned a period two years ago when their office was shorthanded. For six weeks Funes walked the east side of the lake, including Faith Fielder's neighborhood."

"That changes things. Do we know if Funes had direct contact with Faith?"

"Negative. But Funes's route took him past the Fielder's residence between two-thirty and three-thirty on weekdays."

"That's about the time Faith stepped off the bus and walked back to her house."

"That's what I'm thinking," Iglesias says with a tired groan in his voice. "We're bringing Funes in for a chat. I'd like you and

Agent Ketchum to sit in on the interview. Finish up at Cassy Regan's house. I can't waste anymore time on these side trips."

Darcy grits her teeth and glances at the dashboard clock. She feels fortunate she doesn't work for Iglesias.

"I'll finish by ten o'clock at the latest."

"Let me know when you're done. Nix will escort you back to the station. The alibis for Geoff and Alexandra Voss held up. The taxi driver remembers them. Says they paid cash. He dropped them off at their house ten minutes after nine."

"Have you found Phillip O'Grady?" Darcy asks, peering into the shadows pouring off the houses as the village turns in for the night.

"We sent his photograph to every motel within a ten-mile radius. So far nobody recognizes the guy. With so many tourists choking the village, it would be easy for this guy to blend in. By the way, Glen Filmore called from his overseas conference. He's been out of the country for six days. I confirmed his travel itinerary with the airline."

"That rules Filmore out as the Doll Face Killer, and he couldn't have kidnapped Faith Fielder."

"He also stated he never called the Fielders. It took him a minute to remember Faith from the campus tour, but he swears he would never call the parents and ask them to record messages for their kid."

"That sounded fishy from the beginning. How do we find out who called Zoe Fielder?"

"The call came from a pay phone inside the shopping and restaurant district. Yes, Veil Lake still has three pay phones left in the village. CSI is dusting the phone for prints, and I'm tracking down traffic and security camera footage from last Monday evening."

Julian turns the rental onto a narrow road that climbs through the trees. Cottages crouch beneath the night sky, the black lake waters sparkling with starlight behind the houses. The car jounces over a stretch of potholes before Julian hits the brakes and glances at the map on his phone.

Comparing the mailbox with the address, he says, "This must be the house."

Nix's cruiser waits along the road as Julian turns. The driveway drops toward the lake at a sharp angle. Darcy's stomach shoots into her throat as if they're racing down the slope of a towering roller coaster. Except amusement park rides are attached to tracks, the danger a visual illusion. Should their brakes fail, the rental will careen down the slope, ramp over a cliff, and plunge into the lake after a fifty-foot drop. She holds her breath as the car bounces along, Julian riding the brakes until the driveway curls toward the house. He kills the engine in front of a garage attached to a pale blue, single-story cottage. A wrap around deck covers the front and side of the residence. Four chairs and a small table adorn the deck, a sign the widow entertained visitors. In the starlight, the chairs look like headstones.

"Look at all the trees," Darcy says, craning her neck at the window. "Regan owned a lot of acreage."

Julian shifts in his seat and studies the property. The dense woods conceal lights from nearby cottages, lending the false semblance of a house in the middle of the forest.

"What does that tell you?"

"It's similar to the Lieberman's property. Doll Face could have abducted Regan and held her inside without her neighbors knowing."

"Judging by the number of deck chairs, she gets a lot of visitors."

When Darcy opens the door, Julian grabs her arm.

"You've got your weapon," he says. It isn't a question.

Darcy pats the holster.

"I've got it."

He fishes the police radio out of the center console.

"Take it with you. And your phone."

She nods, realizing Julian won't let her leave without them. He holds her eyes, an unspoken plea to be careful. She closes the door and pats the roof of the car.

If she'd had her way, Julian would have parked at the top of the driveway and allowed her to walk the curling path to Regan's cottage. She tries to forget he's behind her, struggles to picture the cottage as the Doll Face killer had on the night he kidnapped Cassy Regan. Five windows line the front of the house, including a casement window open a crack. Another brazen move by the psychopath. He knew no one would hear Regan scream.

Fifty feet in front of the house and behind another row of trees, the lake sloshes against the shore. A soothing sound. Hard to believe someone died a violent death with the lake as a backdrop to this macabre theater. Striated moonlight dances on the waves.

She circles the house, stepping over brush spreading along the rear. When she reaches the side of the house, she looks into the kitchen. Darcy is the Doll Face Killer, watching Cassy Regan move through the kitchen, plating a late evening dessert. Careful to watch the ground while she walks, Darcy searches for a shoe print the police might have missed. Then she passes the rental, avoiding Julian's gaze as she treks up the incline and stands among the trees. From this standpoint, she's invisible to anyone inside the house. Even Julian can't see her. A tingle moves through her body. In moments like this, she gets too close to the killer. In the past, she pictured the murder from a killer's perspective. During the hunt for the Full Moon Killer, Darcy hunkered down in a field near the Virginia border. As she studied the home where Rivers butchered a teenage girl, Darcy felt an overwhelming sensation of viewing the home through the serial killer's eyes. A moment later, she discovered a thumb print in the muddy terrain where Rivers knelt. The police hadn't found the print.

Now she's certain the Doll Face Killer stalked Cassy Regan and watched her from the woods. A perfect location. He could have come here for weeks without drawing notice. Why Cassy Regan, a widow who lost her husband to a heart attack? There has to be more to the equation than Regan being an easy target.

Not looking at the car, Darcy remains razor focused on the cottage as she descends the ridge. She sticks to the weedy undergrowth and tree line, follows the path the killer most likely traveled. The front door provides the only entrance to the house. It's possible Doll Face slipped through a window, but the police didn't find evidence of a break in. He must have entered through the front door after studying Regan for weeks. He knew she didn't lock the door until she turned in for the night. Crime is a rarity in a wealthy lake community like this one. A village resident knows her neighbor on a first name basis.

Wearing gloves, Darcy slips the key into the lock. Feels the click in her palms when the locking mechanism springs open. The door whispers forward on silent hinges.

She stands at the threshold of a living room with a television in the corner, a recliner facing the entertainment center, and a couch against the wall. The bookcase on the far end of the room holds a variety of tomes, covering artwork, wealth building, and fiction classics. Unwilling to shine the flashlight, Darcy waits until her eyes adjust to the gloom before crossing the floor toward the kitchen. The power is on. The microwave clock glows green and reflects on the floor. She tugs on the refrigerator door. It pops open with bright light. Regan had enough food in the stocked refrigerator to last another week. The sour stench of spoiled milk hits Darcy's nostrils. Four cups are missing from a twelve-pack of Greek yogurt. Did Doll Face eat Cassy Regan's food?

She steps down a narrow hallway. Pictures of a younger Cassy Regan and her husband hang on the walls, reminders of happier times. Here they are in the Keys, the husband displaying a swordfish. Next, they pose before Cinderella's castle in Disney World. Darcy pushes the first door open and steps into a tiny bathroom with a stand-up shower, sink, and toilet. Though she promised herself she wouldn't use the flashlight, she flicks it on and runs the beam around the sink, toilet, and shower, searching for that elusive print or hair follicle the CSI team missed. It doesn't appear they overlooked anything.

The spare bedroom holds a twin bed with a pink bedspread. Mauve curtains cover the windows, and a pair of over-sized stuffed animals sit in the corner, one perched on a child's rocking chair. Regan had a granddaughter in Ohio. This room must be for her.

Darcy slides the closet door open. The walk-in closet holds enough space for a large man to stand upright. Except for a pair of hangers, the closet is empty. The killer could have concealed himself inside the closet for hours, watching Cassy Regan move down the hallway, fantasizing over the murder. She breaks the deafening silence and speaks into her phone.

"Have the CSI team dust for fingerprints on the inside of the spare room closet."

Darcy's last stop is the master bedroom. It's a quaint room with a woman's touch, from the palm rose Amelia bedspread to the vase of wildflowers on the dresser. But it's the chair before the long window that pulls Darcy's gaze. The dried splash of blood stains the bare wood floor beneath the chair. She approaches the chair and looks through the glass. The bedroom window offers an unobstructed view of the lake. Someone clipped the branches back, framing a perfect picture of Veil Lake while maintaining the forest's privacy. An aluminum dock juts off the shore. A rowboat tied to the dock bobs in the water, and a kayak lies on the shore. Cassy Regan remained active. She would have put up a fight when the intruder crashed out of the darkness.

Darcy backtracks through the house, swinging doors open. She's missing something critical and can't put her finger on it. But there's nowhere else to search.

The basement.

A door off the kitchen opens to a stairway. She pulls the string on the bulb, swipes at a spiderweb, and descends the stair-case. Turning on the LED light over the washer and dryer, Darcy turns in a circle, eyes flicking from the water heater to the Rubbermaid box of cleaning supplies. Cassy Regan's cellar is nothing like The Lieberman's finished basement. Except for the lake view, everything about Regan's house seems opposite to the Lieberman's residence.

A thump draws her out of the basement. Darcy rushes up the stairs as the shadowed bulk of a large man lumbers through the front door. Darcy reaches for her gun before Julian shouts.

"Shit. You scared me. I told you to stay in the car."

Julian turns on the foyer light.

"I saw the lights come on inside the basement and thought you were in trouble."

A snapping branch stops Darcy from responding. Her eyes dart to Julian's before she raises the police radio to her lips.

"Officer Nix," Darcy says. "Are you on Cassy Regan's property?"

Silence.

"Nix?"

The radio bursts with static.

"Negative. I'm inside the cruiser. Do you require backup?"

"There's someone outside the cottage, moving through the trees."

"I'll check it out."

Julian draws his weapon. Darcy turns off the light so she can see outside. Moving from the kitchen to the living room, she interrogates the darkness pooling around Cassy Regan's cottage. The trees stand sentry, black against the sky. The noise comes again, this time followed by the crunch of footsteps on dried leaves.

Julian holds Darcy's wide-eyed stare.

"Don't serial killers return to the scenes of their crimes?"

"To relive the murders, yes."

"Jesus."

Julian pulls Darcy away from the window. Together, they slide along the wall and move toward the front door. Peeking around the jamb, Julian shakes his head.

"I can't find Nix."

Darcy hopes the officer is moving with stealth. She can't hear Nix, only the intruder edging closer to the cottage.

"What should we do?" Darcy asks, searching Julian's face.

"Without a back door, there's no way to circle around this guy and close him in. We need to—"

"Freeze, police!"

Nix's shout brings Darcy and Julian out of their crouches. They shove the door open as a shadow pinwheels out of the trees, rushing at the house. Darcy slips the Glock from her holster and cuts in front of the silhouette, aiming the gun at his chest.

"Stop, FBI!"

Julian aims his flashlight. The beam picks out a bespectacled man with a shocked expression.

"Hands in the air where I can see them," Nix says,

approaching the man from behind. "You all right, Agent Haines?"

"We're fine."

Nix pats the man down, stopping on his coat pocket. He retrieves the man's car keys and holds them up for Darcy and Julian.

"He's clean," Nix says, exhaling. The officer speaks into the police radio and informs dispatch he has the trespasser in custody. "You want to tell me your name and what you're doing on Mrs. Regan's property?"

The man's lips quiver, a drip of spittle extending to his chin. When Julian adjusts his position, allowing the intruder to see around the beam, his eyes stop on Darcy.

"You," the man says, drawing out the word with surprise and fury.

"I asked you your name," Nix repeats.

"That's Phillip O'Grady," Darcy says, recognizing the creep from the circulated photograph. "*FM-Kill-Her.*"

O'Grady sneers.

"This is the guy who photographed you at the inn?" Nix grins. "We've been searching for you, O'Grady."

After Nix reads O'Grady his rights, he walks him up the driveway to the cruiser. Before Darcy and Julian turn away, she spots a rectangular object glowing in the grass. Kneeling down, Darcy draws in a breath.

"O'Grady dropped his phone, and the screen is unlocked."

"Tough luck for him."

Darcy opens the camera app and scrolls through dozens of photographs of her taken across the village.

"Good God, Julian. How long did this guy follow me?"

21

The gray sky that hangs over the Veil Lake cemetery is a suffocating blanket. It lowers with each breath Richard takes, traps him.

He stares at the black and gold casket, not comprehending. Relatives he hasn't met before and will never see again stream past the casket, placing one hand on top and whispering secrets Richard can't discern. When they finish their loops, they shake his eleven-year-old hand as though doing so helps him draw reason from tragedy.

"I'm so sorry, Genevieve," Uncle Hal says, leaning over to kiss Richard's mother through the black veil draped over her cheek. "Why was Mason on the water during the storm? Didn't someone tell him to come ashore?"

Genevieve Oswalt glares straight ahead as if she didn't hear a word Uncle Hal said. Hal gives Richard's mother a nervous nod and a pat on the shoulder before moving on. The group seems to teleport across the cemetery. One second they're paying respects. The next they congregate in a circle full of whispers, anxious glances thrown back at Genevieve, who stands statuesque amid the whipping wind. Raindrops plunk her shoulder and face. She doesn't notice.

The priest leaves now. He's a fat man with black hair and eyes Richard doesn't trust. Thunder groans.

"Aren't they going to put him in the ground?" Richard asks. When Genevieve doesn't answer, Richard tugs at her shirtsleeve and asks again.

"After we leave," she says.

Richard feels the eyes of his extended family following them to the car. There's a strange brew of pity and fear in their stares.

"Someone needs to help the boy," a woman Richard thinks might be a second aunt says. "Genevieve needs help."

The first tear crawls down Richard's face as Genevieve turns the Volvo onto the lake road. He can't see the casket and the rows of lonely headstones anymore. It's real now. Daddy isn't coming home. His throat constricts, the tears threatening to drown him if he doesn't release them. Yet he holds them back, sensing in the way a boy his age does that there's something fragile inside his mother. One slip, and it will shatter into a million pieces.

The Volvo takes the turn off and climbs the gravel road to the cabin in the trees. She kills the motor in the driveway, sits in silence and stares at the streaks of water trickling down the windshield. Releasing heat, the engine ticks. And ticks. A time bomb.

Mother leads him inside and closes the door. Sets her purse down on the end table and falls into the recliner, opposite where Dad sat, and lowers her head into her hands. Richard shuffles his feet forward, reaches out to touch her shoulder and pulls back, no idea how to fix what's broken inside her. He expects she'll tug him into her arms, and they'll cry together. Perhaps share stories and laugh over funny memories. Instead, her sniffles grow into great gulping sobs, the clamor growing until it pushes him from the room.

That night, a black rain too cold for the second week of June hammers the house, taps upon his bedroom window with slimy fingers, and carves streams through the backyard. Richard springs awake after midnight to his mother's cursing. The basement flooded. They work until sunrise, bailing water through an open window.

When the storm ends the next day and the sun peeks out from behind tattered storm clouds, gurgling trenches of mud water flow where the garden once stood. The tomato plants lie on their sides, the lettuce and kale drowned.

"This won't do," Genevieve says, hands on her hips as she looks over the wreckage. "We'll make something better, Richard. We have to. Your father will know if we don't."

He doesn't understand the meaning behind her words. But he will learn.

Mother brings the first heather plants home that afternoon. They're stubby little things, bursting with more color than a plant this size should. Under Mother's supervision, Richard rakes the soil until he turns it over, burying the flood beneath. Blisters mar his hands. They tear and bleed as he swipes sweat off his forehead. She kneels in the garden's center and plants the first heather. Patting down the soil, she sprinkles compost over the roots.

"For Mason," she says, smiling for the first time since the boating accident.

But it's a hard smile. Teeth hide behind that grin.

"For Daddy," says Richard as he sets the second plant down.

By nightfall, Genevieve inserts sixteen heather plants into the garden. They stare back at Richard with concealed intelligence that sets his nerves on edge.

"Shouldn't we plant something we can eat?"

She pushes past him with an odd glow in her eyes. After fixing spaghetti and meatballs, Mother sends Richard to sleep. Tells him tomorrow will be a hard day. It will make him a man.

Richard tosses and turns all night. Images of sinking boats and acres of blood-colored heather disrupt his sleep and tangle him in the blankets. When he drags himself out of bed, Mother is waiting for him in the kitchen. She doesn't cook Richard eggs and bacon as she does most mornings. He fends for himself, toasting a slice of bread before she ushers him outside.

The sun slumbers below the horizon, an orange bubble crawling up from the earth when he steps into the garden. The trunk full of heather plants pull his gaze. Where did she get the plants? Aren't the nurseries closed at this hour? He itches his forehead, slaps at a mosquito.

"I don't understand," he says, staring up at Mother, taller than he remembered her yesterday.

She's a black shadow looming over his shoulder.

"Heather represents change," she says. "We should aspire to grow as the heather does. To one day flourish and become more than anyone expected."

Richard spends his summer laboring in the fields of heather, drawing protest from a boy who wants to ride his bicycle and spend vacation time with friends.

That's when Mother begins to beat Richard.

22

Darcy stares through the glass at Phillip O'Grady. Under the bright LED lights, the wiry, bug-eyed message board poster appears less intimidating than he did in the dark. Cuffs lock his wrists behind his back as he sits ramrod straight before a long table. An imposing male officer Darcy hasn't met stands at the door.

"What do you think?" Iglesias asks, peeking at O'Grady over Darcy's shoulder.

"I can't get a gauge on him. On one hand, he seems like an ordinary guy, more frightened than dangerous. But he wouldn't be the first unassuming serial killer."

Iglesias pats the notebook under his arm.

"We'll learn why O'Grady is in Veil Lake and if he's the Doll Face Killer. I want you to sit in on the interview. It's time the FBI pulled its weight and found this killer."

"Absolutely."

Iglesias squints at O'Grady.

"He hasn't lawyered up yet. I'll let him stew a while longer."

Straight out of the playbook. It's common practice to hold a suspect inside the interrogation room for as long as possible.

The longer O'Grady sits, the more anxious he'll become. And the easier it will be to catch him in a lie.

When the door closes behind Iglesias, Julian enters the observation room.

"Iglesias hasn't told O'Grady we found his phone. We went through the pictures. Darcy, he photographed you at the inn when you peeked out the window. The scumbag must have waited a long time to get that shot."

"What do the police have on him?"

"I overheard the chief speaking with Officer Nix. O'Grady works for a cleaning company. They're determining when he arrived in Veil Lake so they can compare the time line with the murders. It's a good thing we caught him, Darcy. Judging by the pictures, he's obsessed with you."

"Or obsessed with the case. *FM-Kill-Her* is the first to post whenever a new serial killer becomes active."

"Don't forget the Michael Rivers fan fiction. The Full Moon Killer butchered you, Amy Yang, and your kids in O'Grady's story."

"Can't arrest him for being deranged."

"Maybe not. But I printed a copy of the story for Iglesias. They'll throw it in O'Grady's face during the interrogation. By the way, where the hell is Agent Ketchum?"

Last Darcy heard, Ketchum was en route to the police station after following up at the restaurant where Faith Fielder worked. Iglesias won't interview O'Grady until Ketchum arrives. A knock on the door brings Darcy's head around. As if summoned, Ketchum pokes his head inside the room. The agent nods at Julian.

"I spoke with Keith Marsella again at the restaurant. Between all the commotion Tuesday night, someone at the bar ordered wings and a drink and left without paying. Guess who the deadbeat is? Trevor Funes."

"So he lied about his postal route, and he stiffed the restaurant on his bill," Darcy says, narrowing her eyes in confusion. "What's going on with Funes?"

"A waitress claims she saw Funes make a beeline for the restroom after the argument. But after she set her tray down, she noticed Funes on the other side of the restaurant, slipping outside like he was in a hurry and didn't want anyone to notice him leaving."

"The bill couldn't have been more than ten or fifteen bucks. That's not the reason he blew out of there."

"That was five minutes before Faith Fielder left for the night."

"Interesting."

Ketchum glares through the glass at O'Grady. The man tilts his head at the window. He knows they're watching.

"Let's get this over with." Iglesias glowers in the doorway. "Wait outside, Detective Haines. I can't have off-duty cops from North Carolina sitting in on my interrogation."

"Understood." Julian presses his lips to Darcy's forehead. "I'll be in the lobby when you finish."

"Thank you for being here," she says, giving his hand a squeeze.

O'Grady swivels his head when Iglesias leads Ketchum and Darcy inside the interview room. His gaze stops on Darcy. The sicko holds her with the same penetrating stare he used outside Cassy Regan's house. Iglesias makes introductions. O'Grady isn't interested in anyone but Darcy. His fixation leaves her with a sick feeling, as if a greasy film coats her throat.

"You dropped your phone in Cassy Regan's front yard," Iglesias says, tossing a stack of printed photographs in front of O'Grady.

"You had no right to look through my phone," O'Grady says,

thumbing through the images as though he hasn't seen them before. "Where is it?"

"We have it in safe keeping. You'll get your phone back when you leave."

"I want to leave now."

"Not until we discuss your whereabouts the last several days. Mr. O'Grady, where were you Tuesday, July first, at nine o'clock."

"Working."

"Where do you work?"

"I'm a cleaner for Ricardo's Cleaning Services."

"I'm unfamiliar with the business. Is this in Veil Lake?"

"No, sir. Ohio. Xenia, Ohio."

Iglesias makes a note on his pad.

"Go, Bengals," Iglesias says with a wolf's grin.

O'Grady nods his head.

"Yes, sir. Go, Bengals."

"Can anyone verify your whereabouts Tuesday night?"

"Sure, Janice can."

"Who's Janice?"

"Janice Stoulter. We're a two-person crew. That was the night we worked at the First National Bank." O'Grady shakes his head. "You'd think bankers would be clean, but they're slobs. Someone left a dump in the men's bathroom and never flushed. Whole place stunk like sewage."

Iglesias lifts his brow.

"We'll check with Ms. Stoulter. Or is it Mrs?"

Though the forum poster claims an alibi, he might be lying. And the pictures he took of the lake prove he's been to Veil Lake before.

"Uh, Ms. I think. So what's this about?"

"You don't know?"

O'Grady bites his thumbnail and stares down at the desk.

"You think I killed that couple. Jim and Carol Lieberman."

"We haven't accused you of murder, Mr. O'Grady."

"Well, I can prove I wasn't here."

Iglesias leans forward and clasps his hands on the desk.

"Yet you're here now. Why are you in my village?"

O'Grady's eyes move from Darcy to a window which looks out at the hallway. Two uniformed officers stride past.

"Answer the question. You're in Veil Lake because of the murders. Right, Mr. O'Grady?"

He shrugs and chews on his nail again.

"It's not a crime if I am."

"When did you arrive in the village?"

"I drove up from Ohio yesterday morning and arrived midday."

"But you've been here before."

"Last week, yes."

"What was your purpose for visiting my village then?"

O'Grady grins.

"Just enjoying the lake, sir."

"Where are you staying?"

"Nowhere in particular."

"Sleeping in your car is illegal inside the village."

"There's a rest stop on Highway 2. Nothing wrong if I sleep there."

Iglesias leans over the table and taps his index finger on the pictures spread before O'Grady.

"After you arrived in Veil Lake, you followed Agent Haines."

O'Grady glances between Ketchum and Darcy, perplexed.

"You mean Agent Gellar?"

"Agent Haines," Darcy says, displaying her wedding ring. "I thought you kept up on me, *FM-Kill-Her*."

O'Grady cringes as if slapped.

"I...no, I didn't hear you married."

"Why are you following Agent Haines?" Iglesias asks, the

amiable smile gone from his face. "Don't bullshit me. We've already got you for trespassing on private property and interfering with a police investigation."

The bugeyed man opens his mouth, closes it, and wrings his hands.

"All I did was take pictures. I didn't mean to hurt anybody."

Ketchum pulls a laptop out of his bag and turns it to face O'Grady. Darcy cranes her head. The screen displays the familiar serial killer fan site. An open thread discusses the Doll Face Killer murders. *FM-Kill-Her* uploaded the photos he took of Darcy.

Please don't let my kids see the pictures, Darcy prays.

"You take quite the macabre interest in tragedy," Ketchum says. "This is you, correct?"

O'Grady's face grapples with indecision. He concedes with a quick nod.

Ketchum scrolls through the pictures, stopping on a photograph of Darcy exiting the Lieberman house. The picture garnered forty-seven likes.

"How did you find out Agent Haines would be at the Lieberman house last night?"

"I didn't. I was surprised to see her."

"You just happened to be at a murder site after sunset the moment Agent Haines arrived to investigate the house."

O'Grady turns his head toward Iglesias.

"Should...should I get a lawyer?"

"No reason to ask for a lawyer, Mr. O'Grady," Iglesias says, opening his arms. "We're only talking."

"You're sure about that?"

"Yes. But it's important you remain truthful and tell Agent Ketchum why you photographed the Lieberman house last evening."

O'Grady scratches his scalp.

"It's just because of the news. The murders. All I wanted was a picture for the website. To keep everyone up to date with what's going on here."

"Can't they watch the news like everyone else?" Ketchum asks, wincing when he takes a sip of hot coffee.

"It's not the same," O'Grady says, animated. "The national news doesn't understand what's happening here."

"Fill me in."

"You get a serial killer like Doll Face once every decade. We'll study the Doll Face Killer for the next hundred years. He's another Bundy, another Rivers."

Ketchum sets his arms on the table.

"So this interest of yours is academic. You're fascinated by serial killers."

"Yes, that's all it is."

"Then explain what you were doing outside Agent Haines's hotel in the dead of night, photographing her through the window."

O'Grady's mouth freezes open.

"Start talking," Iglesias says.

The forum poster scrubs his hands over his face and fidgets in the chair.

"Because she's a celebrity."

"She's a private investigator consulting with the FBI, not a pop star."

"In our circle, she is. She tracked the Full Moon Killer, and now she's close to catching Doll Face. Like I said, this is history."

Ketchum slides the laptop to Darcy, who loads the sick piece of fiction *FM-Kill-Her* uploaded during the Darkwater Cove murders.

"Recognize this?" Darcy zooms in so the letters are large enough to see from across the table.

"That's not...how did you find my story? The forum admins deleted it."

"So you admit you wrote a story, depicting the brutal murders of me, my children, and Amy Yang."

O'Grady lifts two pleading hands and searches the room for an ally.

"It's just a story. Like *Halloween* or *Silence of the Lambs*."

"The violence seems real," Ketchum says. "You fancy yourself a screenwriter or something?"

"A horror magazine published one of my short stories last year."

"Ah. A regular Stephen King."

"That's all it is," O'Grady says, lowering his eyes and scratching above his ear. "I wouldn't wish harm on Agent Gellar—uh, Agent Haines—or her children. Nobody wants to see people die."

"Suddenly you're a humanitarian. Yet you're in Veil Lake to witness the bloodshed firsthand. Isn't that right?"

"I'd like my phone back now."

Ketchum glances at the chief. Iglesias leans back and locks his fingers behind his head.

"When you leave, Mr. O'Grady. You're an interesting fellow, and I'd hate to see you walk out that door and leave us so soon."

"You're arresting me?"

"For trespassing, yes."

O'Grady forms a protest before the beefy officer at the door circles the table and leads him from the room. The sicko shoots a glance back at Darcy. He'd love to see his story come to fruition, and she'll sleep easier knowing O'Grady is in a cell. For now, at least.

"Damn it all," Iglesias says. "I can't hold him long on a trespassing charge. The minute he calls a lawyer, we'll have to let him go. Give me your honest opinions. Is this creep the Doll Face Killer?"

Darcy and Ketchum share a glance.

"I doubt it," Darcy says. "Fantasizing about murder isn't the same as putting a knife to someone's throat. Besides, he says he has an alibi for the Lieberman murders."

"I'll confirm with the cleaning service."

"But O'Grady worries me. He could morph into a killer, if he becomes bolder. I don't sense a rudimentary understanding of good and evil with this guy."

Ketchum thumbs through photographs on O'Grady's phone, shaking his head at each image.

"How the hell did he follow Darcy from the Lieberman house to the inn without Nix noticing?"

"The inn sold out," Darcy says. "I heard the manager turning a couple away. With all those vehicles in the parking lot, you can't blame Nix. O'Grady never left his vehicle."

"Some of these pictures..." Ketchum sighs and turns the screen around. "They look like random shots. As if he took them accidentally."

"Let me see," Iglesias says, lowering his reading glasses from atop his head. He holds the phone at arm's length as he pages from one photograph to the next. "Here's one of the blacktop. Blurry traffic. A van of some sort. A bush next to a sidewalk that needs paving. I'd swear he tried to photograph someone and worried about getting caught."

"Like he lowered the camera at the last second," Darcy says.

"Right," says Iglesias, handing Darcy the phone.

She scrolls through the images, squints at a blurred photograph of a silver minivan, then sifts through another dozen images.

"Wait," Darcy says, tapping the screen with her nail. "Isn't that the same minivan?"

Ketchum looks over Darcy's shoulder.

"Check if he took more pictures of the van," Ketchum says, resting his hands on the back of Darcy's chair. "Can you read the license plate?"

Shaking her head, Darcy flips from one picture to the next, cringing when she comes across O'Grady's photograph of Darcy peering out her hotel room window. There it is again. A silver van, this time blocked by a train of traffic lining up at a red light.

"What are the chances this guy knows more about the Doll Face Killer than he's letting on?" Darcy asks, shivering at the chill running down her spine.

23

In the humid and lonesome night, Faith huddles beneath the scratchy, weathered blanket and faces the wall. Lumps in the mattress make the bed uncomfortable. Like sleeping on a cushioned bag of rocks and marbles. A tear trickles down her face. Faith flicks it away with her thumb and sniffles. She's a fool. Mr. Filmore isn't a professor. That might not even be his real name. He's a sick, angry, mean man. Why did she believe him?

Faith thinks back to the phone call at the restaurant. Her mother's voice, telling her it was okay to accept a ride from Mr. Filmore. Mom and Dad keep Faith safe. Why would they trust a man like Mr. Filmore?

For the past two hours, her brain echoed with the memories of his screaming. She'd made it back to her bedroom door when he found her in the hallway. Yet somehow he knew Faith entered his bedroom. He's dangerous. He might hurt her. As the scarlet sunlight crept down her windowpane and bedroom pooled with darkness, she planned her escape. Th has to be a y out of here. Wherever *here* is. The fence towe r th and offers no purchase for he But if she

Mr. Filmore uses for carrying compost, she can stand on the bucket and pull herself over the wall.

The silence inside the cabin has its own heartbeat. He slammed doors and cursed an hour ago. Nothing since. As she edges the blanket off her shoulder and extends one leg off the bed, the floorboards groan outside her door. Quickly, she draws her leg under the covers and pulls the blanket over her head. Her fingers grip the blanket. Body trembles as the door creaks open.

Faith can't see the shadow sliding over the bed. Yet she feels it. It's icy, sharp, like the icicles that hang off the roof in January. She brings her knees toward her chest, moving at a snail's pace so he won't see.

"Faith," he whispers.

Breath hot against her neck. The stench of his body sweat sour.

She wills him to leave, yet he stands above the bed, waiting for her to pull the blanket down and acknowledge him. His hand rests on her hip. Fingers curl and uncurl upon the blanket.

"I shouldn't have yelled. If you'll forgive me, I'll make it up to you. Promise. I'll give the magazine back to you."

What magazine? After a long while, she doesn't hear him anymore. She refuses to emerge from beneath the blanket, fearing she'll find him staring down at her, wild eyed with a knife held above his head. When his bedroom door clicks shut, she throws the blanket off and inhales the fresh air through the open window. She needs to stay calm, slow her heartbeat. Form an escape plan.

The bedside clock ticks past eleven. She waits him out. Mr. Filmore can't stay wake all night. For several minutes, he pads around his opening and closing drawers. When the bed under his we night, she glances at the clock and to remain still for fifteen minutes. If no sounds come from his bedroom before then, she'll sneak out of the house. During the wait, she busies herself with happy thoughts, picturing her parents, the lake at sunrise, and the North Chadwick campus. In less than two months, her time spent with Mr. Filmore will become a forgotten nightmare. Her eyes drift shut, and she's surprised when they pop open. It's almost midnight.

Edging the covers off her body, Faith lowers one leg to the floor. Then the next. Careful. Don't make a sound. She stops in the center of the bedroom and listens. When she reaches for the doorknob, she imagines him standing outside her room. The spider catches the fly.

Faith twists the doorknob and winces when the hinges creak. The door opens to a night shrouded hallway. A slice of moonlight on the living room floor congeals at the end of the corrridor. Every step down the hall sounds loud inside her head. Yet her movements don't rouse her captor.

Then she stands before the front door. The entrance to the heather garden. Faith glances over her shoulder and watches the closed doors at the end of the hallway. She recalls the sounds she heard inside the locked, forbidden bedroom. Nobody is inside the room, she tells herself. It's her imagination.

She flips the deadbolt and opens the door, surprised he didn't set a trap. Moonlight washes over the garden and makes it appear barren and alien. As she closes the door, she can't shake the feeling that the heather watches her. Hundreds of plants standing guard, frozen in the windless night. Casting a glance behind her, Faith forces her legs to move. She hurries down the pathway to the gate, aware of the cameras' eyes. Tugging on the handle, she finds the gate locked. She must scale the fence.

Standing on tiptoes, her fingertips curl over the top of the gate. She leaps and grabs the top of the fence. Scoots her body up the barricade. It's too tall, and she isn't strong enough to pull herself over. When the splintered wood cuts into her fingers, she yelps and drops to the ground, landing on her butt. Her eyes glaze over, but she refuses to cry.

Faith expected she wouldn't be able to climb the fence. Scanning the garden, she searches for the bucket. Anything she can stand upon. Remembering where she last saw the bucket, she cuts across the rows, through the heather, the dew covered plants caressing her skin with greasy digits. The plants grab her, shift to block her escape. But this too must be her imagination playing tricks on her. She locates the bucket beside the compost bin. It appears smaller than she remembered. Her heart sinks.

Then she spots the wheelbarrow beside the cabin. It rests beneath a camera. She'll be in full view if Mr. Filmore awakens and checks the security monitors. Grabbing the handles, she bulldozes a path to the main walkway. Now she runs faster, the wheels jouncing over dirt mounds. At the fence, Faith puts one foot inside the bed, testing the wheelbarrow's sturdiness. The wheelbarrow wobbles. One slip, and she'll topple against the fence and bring hell down upon her.

But the bed holds her weight when she steadies herself. Both hands press against the fence. Her head peeks over the top. A forest towers along a hill. The driveway, overrun by weeds and saplings, curls to the right and disappears into the wilderness. The road must be in that direction.

Faith's tongue protrudes between her lips as she places one foot on top of the fence. The wheelbarrow shimmies beneath her weight, her plant leg trembling as she fights to maintain balance. She can do this. Ignoring the sharp edges cutting into her fingers, Faith pulls herself up. She sees freedom. If she can lift herself an inch higher.

The hand clasps around her ankle. Faith cries out and falls backward. Mr. Filmore catches her as the wheelbarrow crashes onto its side.

She collapses to her back. The sobs come hard as she stares into his crazed face.

"I'll teach you to never leave me again. Never in my wildest dreams did I believe it would come to this. You're no better than the others. Now you must pay as they did."

No one hears Faith scream as Mr. Filmore drags her to the cabin.

24

THURSDAY, JULY 3RD 11:10 P.M.

"Trevor Funes should arrive anytime now," Ketchum says after hanging up the phone. "We've got him cornered. He found out his boss spoke with the VLPD. She blew holes in his claim he never delivered mail to the Fielders."

"Why would he lie?" Darcy asks just as Iglesias flicks his eyes to the front desk.

Trevor Funes stands in line behind a fifty-something man in a tank top. The burly man swings his arms around as he yells at the rookie working the front desk. Something about finding his tires slashed. Iglesias points at Funes and motions for the man to follow him around the desk. They reenter the interview room. Iglesias nods to the chair where O'Grady sat. Funes slides into the seat and fiddles with his hands in his lap.

"You lied to the FBI about your postal route," Iglesias says. "I spoke to your boss. She tells me you delivered to the Fielder residence for six weeks two years ago. You want to tell us the truth for once?"

Funes pinches the bridge of his nose.

"Our routes change every year, sometimes more often than that. It's impossible to remember everywhere we deliver."

Iglesias shifts his chair forward. The intensity in the chief's gaze warns Funes he won't tolerate another lie.

"Cut the shit, Funes. No way you don't recall the six weeks you spent delivering mail to Faith Fielder's house. The patrons at the restaurant say you acted as though you've always known Faith."

The postal worker glances toward the door. He's not under arrest and can walk out if he chooses, but their glares lock him in place.

"Yes, I lied. Only because I knew you'd consider me a suspect."

"If you're innocent, I can't see a reason."

"I liked Faith. She was just a high school sophomore, and my kid sister knew Faith from class. Everyone in Veil Lake looked past her...disability."

"Faith has Down syndrome," Darcy says. "It's okay to say it aloud."

"Yeah, well. She doesn't act like it. Faith is smarter than most people in the village."

Shifting forward on her chair, Darcy peers into Funes's eyes. Searches for a lie, but finds none.

"You spoke to Faith often during your route, didn't you?"

Funes pauses, considering his answer. He nods.

"She'd get home from the bus ride and plop down on the front porch with her books." He shakes his head in wonder. "Always studying, that one. I didn't want to bother her. Because, you know, I might break her concentration. I wasn't sure how easy studying came to..." Funes scratches his head. "I'm saying the wrong thing again. Aren't I?"

"Not at all. So you struck up conversations with Faith. What did you talk about?"

"Not much initially. She asked me what it was like to deliver mail, and if I met everyone in Veil Lake. She wanted to work my job, but I told her she was smart and should aim higher. Not that there's anything wrong with working for the postal service. Government work is good work if you can get it. Most of the time, I asked her about her classes and what she wanted to do after she graduated."

"Did she mention college to you back then?"

Funes smiles, remembering.

"Yeah. Faith was dead set on college. I didn't think it was possible. But my cousin has a son with Down syndrome, and he graduated from Michigan. That got me thinking about Faith, so I'd bring her college catalogs."

"From the post office?"

"No, I'd get into trouble if I gave Faith people's mail. The high school is three blocks from my house. I'd stop in and grab a handful of catalogs from the guidance department. Never told them they were for Faith. Figured that was between me and her."

Darcy glances at Iglesias. The chief is a bulldog ready to pounce, not buying the nice guy act. She continues her line of questioning, keeping Iglesias at bay.

"Tell me about Tuesday night at the restaurant."

"It's like I said. That asshole, Geoff Voss, and his wife started in on Faith. It wasn't her fault the barkeeper cut Voss off from alcohol. Faith answers the phones and tidies up the place. She isn't a server."

"You spoke to Faith at length. What about?"

Funes shrugs.

"College. I didn't want to embarrass her with a bunch of praise." Tears glisten in his eyes. "But I remembered those talks on the porch. Now look at her. Honestly, she didn't remember me."

"Because you weren't in uniform."

He waves her theory away.

"It doesn't matter. Who am I?"

"You brought her college catalogs and built her up, Mr. Funes. It's possible you played a larger role in her success than you're considering."

His cheeks turn rosy as he fiddles with the zipper on his jacket.

"You spoke to Faith, then the altercation occurred," Ketchum says, tapping a pen on the table. "What happened next?"

"I couldn't tell you. A few guys wrestled Voss out of the restaurant. I got the hell away from the bar, figuring I should get out of her hair, and headed for the men's room."

"And all this time you noticed no one following Faith around or watching her from the back."

"Never."

"So you used the restroom. The assistant manager claims you stiffed the restaurant and didn't pay your bill. Did you speak to Faith before you left?"

Funes massages a knot from the back of his neck and squints in concentration.

"No, and I thought I paid. The argument threw me off. I'm happy to settle my debt, if everyone will stop blaming me for Faith disappearing. She looked busy when I returned. Someone had her on the phone. I waited a minute so I could say goodbye, not wanting to be rude. But the call went on and on, so I took off."

Ketchum's eyes move to Darcy's.

"This phone call," Darcy says, feeling her pulse quicken. "Did Faith appear upset or frightened?"

"Just the opposite. I'd never seen Faith happier, which makes me think it wasn't work related. More of a personal call, like her Mom or Dad."

Wes Fielder was on his way to the restaurant, and Zoe never mentioned contacting Faith. Did the fake Glen Filmore call Faith at work?

Ketchum concludes the interview after another question. When Funes strolls out the door, Iglesias lifts his palms.

"Why are we letting this guy walk? He's our number one suspect."

"Trevor Funes is harmless," says Darcy, drawing a dagger-filled glare from the chief. "But he gave us an important clue. Grab the phone records for the Veil Lake Grill between 8:50 and 9:00 p.m. I'll bet the same guy that called Zoe Fielder phoned Faith at the restaurant."

"And talked her into accepting a ride home," Ketchum says, putting the pieces together.

Darcy bobs her head in agreement.

"Let's hope someone saw our unsub's vehicle."

25

The clock hands turn in double time as Darcy sits on the edge of a vacated desk. Five minutes until midnight. Five minutes until the final countdown begins. She's running out of time to find Faith Fielder alive when Julian hands Darcy a cup of coffee. A door slams, bringing their heads up. Iglesias stomps across the bullpen, his gaze razor sharp and locked on Darcy and Ketchum. Darcy ignores him, understanding the overworked chief needs rest.

"Funes claims Faith answered the phone after the fight with Geoff and Alexandra Voss," Darcy says. "That's right before Faith left the restaurant and vanished. The time line makes sense."

"So you're suggesting the kidnapper called the restaurant, betting Faith would answer, and talked her into his vehicle," Julian says.

"We can't ignore the possibility," says Ketchum, tapping his notepad against his leg. "The chief is waiting on the phone company. We need the phone number of the person who called the restaurant."

"What about the pay phone the fake Glen Filmore used to call Zoe Fielder?" Darcy asks.

"It's located beside Wilmington's Hardware on Lake Ave," says Iglesias, towering over Darcy. She jumps, not realizing he stood behind them. "The owner has security cameras over the door and inside the store, but none of them cover the pay phone."

As Iglesias speaks, the phone rings. He answers, glances between Ketchum and Darcy, and closes his eyes in frustration.

"Same pay phone," Darcy says after Iglesias hangs up.

"The phone in front of the hardware store. The bastard is using ancient technology to stay a step ahead of us."

Julian props himself on the corner of the desk beside Darcy.

"There has to be a traffic or security camera that caught this guy. We know when he used the pay phone. It's just a matter of gathering the recordings and sifting through each one."

"Or finding a witness," Iglesias huffs. "A village this choked with tourists, you assume someone saw this guy. I'll grab two of my officers and interrogate the traffic cams, then we'll go door to door with the store owners first thing in the morning. If we're lucky, someone has an angle on the pay phone." Iglesias glares at Darcy and Ketchum. "The two of you are dragging your feet. Sleep is laziness leaving the body. There's a fresh pot of coffee in the break room if you need fuel." The chief plants his hands on the small of his back and stretches. "Damn back is acting up. No excuses, not when lives are on the line."

When Iglesias wades deeper into the bullpen and pulls Officer Nix aside, Julian touches Darcy's shoulder.

"Don't listen to that idiot. You should rest while you can and come back fresh in the morning."

Darcy blinks the weariness out of her eyes and studies the room. These officers will work through the night to find Faith Fielder. She owes them another hour or two.

"Just a little longer," says Darcy, drawing an exasperated look from Julian. "We're closing in on Doll Face. God willing, we'll catch him on camera."

"If you insist on staying, we might as well make ourselves useful. They don't have enough bodies on the floor to scan several hours of camera footage. Let's take the grunt work off their hands."

Darcy smiles at Julian. Since they traveled to New York to rescue Julian's niece last year, this is the first time they've worked side by side during an investigation. Overwhelmed by the amount of footage waiting for him in the cloud, Nix is happy to hand some burden to Julian and Darcy. The three of them work inside the media room, one desk lamp angled over Nix's workstation providing the only light.

"You've got the Oak Avenue footage from Tuesday night," Nix says, leaning over Julian's shoulder as he demonstrates how to fast-forward through the recording. "Oak runs perpendicular to Lake, where the pay phone is located. I'll check the traffic cam on Lake for the same time period. If we come up empty, I'll load the recordings from last Monday."

Julian nods politely. After Nix sits down, Julian scans the footage, reverses, and freezes the picture when a shadow moves across the road. It's just a bird. It's obvious Julian knows his way around the controls better than Nix. Darcy sips her coffee, unconcerned the caffeine will keep her up all night. She'll work straight through sunset Friday, if it means bringing Faith Fielder home to her parents. The traffic camera focuses on the intersection but catches the sidewalk leading toward the hardware store. A plant shop sits on the corner of Oak and Lake, a display of potted wildflowers on the sidewalk. The owner must trust nobody will steal the pots in view of the camera. A young couple holding hands strolls across the crosswalk as Julian runs the video at double speed. A Corvette pulls up to the red light. The driver glances both ways before turning right on Oak Avenue.

A digital clock in the upper right corner of the screen reads 8:52 p.m. The kidnapper called the restaurant at 8:54 p.m. She can't see the pay phone from this angle, yet her body tenses with the expectation he'll cross through the frame on his way to the hardware store. Julian glances over his shoulder at Nix. He's a minute behind.

"See anything yet?"

Nix grumbles.

"Some kid on a skateboard took a leak against a garbage can. Jesus, I can't wait until tourist season ends."

"Do we have other traffic cams, if the kidnapper came from the opposite direction?" Darcy asks.

"Negative. Our only hope is another store camera caught him."

That's what Darcy fears. The Doll Face Killer knows the locations of the traffic cams.Nix reaches the 8:53 p.m. time marker as Darcy looks back and forth between the camera angles. The traffic light turns green at the intersection, but no vehicles pass. It's quiet. Like the moment before thunder growls. Darcy is about to utter a curse when a silhouette passes through the corner of Julian's frame.

"Stop the footage," she says. "Go back ten seconds."

Nix's chair squeals as he turns around for a peek. Julian steps frame by frame through the footage when the shadow reappears. A man wearing a gray, hooded sweatshirt cuts across the road, skipping the walkway as though he knows the camera's radius. He buries his hands in his pockets, head lowered with the hood pulled down to his eyes. Darcy's skin prickles.

"That's him. That's Doll Face."

Julian scrolls back to the beginning. Though the picture appears clear, bright, and free of obstructions, post-processing and video enhancement won't bring them closer to identifying the man. He's avoiding the traffic cam. Julian swings his chair around and reads the time code to Nix.

"Thirty-two seconds after 8:53 p.m. Tell me he crosses through your footage."

Nix fast-forwards, then reverses when he overshoots his target. He squints at the screen. There. A black shadow crawls across the Wilmington Hardware storefront. It vanishes when the killer swerves toward the pay phone.

"Hold on," Nix says, pulling the footage back until the silhouette appears against the glass.

The officer leans forward in his chair, studying the picture. Julian and Darcy crowd beside him. That's all there is. A shadow. No reflection of the man's face. Five minutes later, the man reverses course and disappears, avoiding the cameras again.

"Where the hell did he go?" Julian asks. "He's not crossing at the intersection."

Nix's eyes light. The officer claps his hands together.

"He cut through the alleyway."

Darcy glances between the two monitors.

"Is there another intersection at the end of the alley?"

"No. The alleyway opens to Municipal Park. The park is eighteen acres, mostly monuments, a water fountain, and a few pathways leading to City Hall."

"Any cameras in the park?"

"There should be one near City Hall, but I assume our target steered clear."

"He's crossing through parks and alleyways because he's aware of the traffic cams," Darcy says. "And he doesn't want any witnesses. But his vehicle must be close to the park unless he lives nearby."

Nix pulls out a dogeared village map and spreads it on the desk. Following the route through the park, Nix taps his finger on Grant Street.

"He might have parked here. Lots of trees. The canopy blocks out the street lights, makes it easy to hide." Nix shivers. "I hate patrolling Grant Street after dark, and this is one of the safest villages in Michigan. Well, it used to be. You think the Doll Face Killer lives in this neighborhood?"

"Unlikely. He'll want something more secluded. A place he can take Faith Fielder with no one noticing."

"Like Cassy Regan's house," Julian says. "Or the Lieberman's."

Darcy shakes her head.

"Both residences were perfect for committing a murder inside the village, but our unsub wants more privacy. A house close to the village, but more rural. He wouldn't want a neighbor close by."

"Can you think of any places that fit the bill?" Julian asks, sliding his chair over to the map.

Nix draws an invisible radius outside the village center.

"Tons of places," the officer says. "Once you get into the hills above the lake, you can take a leak in your backyard, and no one calls the cops. My Uncle Tom called it the piss test." Nix clears his throat. "Uncle Tom didn't like having neighbors."

Too much ground to cover in one day, Darcy thinks as she looks over the map.

"Let's find his vehicle," Darcy says to Nix. "He should be easy to recognize. Not too many people abandon their cars and sneak into the park."

"We'll canvas Grant Street in the morning. See if anyone noticed an unfamiliar vehicle parked along the curb."

Darcy eyes the clock. It's after midnight.

26

His body simmers with anger and hate.

Richard Oswalt sits in the living room and stares through the window overlooking the garden. The moonlight chills his skin. Like diving into a pond after the water thaws. When he looks upon the heather, he sees his mother in every row, toiling. Even when the cancer turned her insides black and hunched her shoulders, she was out in the garden every day, caring for the plants. Her children.

Faith. She shows so much promise. Why must it be this way? He rests his head against the cushion, curls his legs into a ball, and cups his elbows with his hands. Why is it so damn cold in the living room when the garden steams like a sauna?

When his eyes drift shut, he's a boy again.

HE PLAYS at Charlie's house all afternoon, a rare day when Mother doesn't force him to work in the garden. He can't explain his blistered hands to Charlie, or the farmer's tan that turns pink on his neck. After they ride bikes to the lake, Vanessa, Charlie's mother, makes them tuna sandwiches with potato chips. Richard likes to wedge the chips inside the sandwich, giving each bite a salty crunch. When they finish, Vanessa gives each of them a bowl of vanilla ice cream. This is the way it used to be, Richard thinks. Before the boating accident. Before Daddy died.

Vanessa's eyes hold pity when they flick to Richard. A month ago, her kindness might have touched him. But there's an emptiness gathering inside him, growing each day in ways he can't explain. His eyes move to Vanessa's backside as she stands on tiptoe and shoves the dishes into the cupboard. A week over forty, Charlie's mother still looks like a teenager. Tanned, shapely legs poking out from a pair of cutoff jean shorts. A tight yellow t-shirt that hugs every curve. Her light brown hair teased into a bun.

Richard's face fills with heat as he grows hard inside his shorts. What he wouldn't give for five minutes with Charlie's mother. While most boys his age would fantasize over taking Vanessa into her bedroom, his thoughts skitter down a darker corridor. In his mind, he pictures Charlie's mother on her back, hands bound and tied to the bedpost. When he thrusts his hips upon hers, her legs writhe and quiver as she stares up at him with helpless eyes. When she tries to scream, he suffocates her mouth with his hand and grinds harder.

"Can I get you anything else?"

Vanessa's voice knocks Richard out of his daydream. His mouth feels like sandpaper. He's thankful for the table hiding his erection as the family cat purrs around his ankle.

"Richard, are you okay?"

"Yes, Mrs. Gordon."

"You don't look good. Are you getting too much sun?"

He bites the inside of his cheek to prevent his smile from creeping out.

Charlie takes Richard to his room. Not blessed with his

mother's good looks, Charlie's face drowns beneath an ocean of freckles. Somehow, his hair turned out to be clown red despite neither parent being a redhead.

"Guess what I stole from my Dad?"

Richard raises an uncaring eyebrow at Charlie, expecting some stupid baseball card from an era he doesn't care about. Charlie slips a key into a padlocked chest. Instead of a baseball card or a pack of cigarettes, Charlie slips a crime investigation magazine out of the chest. Sliding the magazine from the paper bag, Charlie sets it between them while they sit cross-legged on the carpeted floor.

Richard's eyes lock on an image of a college age girl dressed in a schoolgirl uniform. Her hands are tied to a post, much as Richard imagined Vanessa's, and a gag stretches her mouth into a terrified rictus. Her eyes plead with the silhouetted captor standing above her.

The bold font reads, *"You're not a serial killer, are you?"* Her question directed at her captor.

Which strikes Richard as funny. How can the girl question her kidnapper with her mouth gagged? Yet he can't drag his gaze from the image. It's as if a light turned on inside his head, urging him to act upon his desires. He grows hot inside his shorts again as the girl's face morphs into Vanessa's.

"How did you get a hold of the magazine without your dad knowing?"

Charlie waves a hand in the air.

"It was easy. He puts all his magazines and newspapers in a paper bag on trash day and leaves them beside the curb. I snagged it before the garbage truck arrived."

"And he won't know you took it?"

The boy shrugs.

"How would he, and why should he care?"

Richard can't look away. He's transfixed by the magazine cover as if he's waited for this moment his entire life.

"Let me borrow it," he says, unable to prevent the demand from spilling out of his mouth. "I'll take good care of it and bring it back in a few days."

"I don't know," Charlie says, dragging out the words. He shifts his eyes between the magazine and Richard. "What if your mom catches you with it? She'll tell my parents, and all hell will break loose."

"Don't be a pussy. I wouldn't rat you out. Besides, she'll never find it."

"I'll think about it."

"Come on, man. You plucked it out of the garbage. How much is it worth to you? I'll trade you my bike for the rest of summer."

"Your bike is trash, asshole."

Charlie stops laughing when Richard doesn't join in, his face twisting with concern.

"How about twenty bucks? I've got money stashed in my room."

"Dude, it's five dollars at the newsstand. Don't be crazy."

"Like they'd let me buy it. Come on, Charlie. Just this one time."

Charlie hems and haws for the next half-hour. In the end, he tells Richard he'll sleep on it and let him know tomorrow. Not willing to leave without the magazine, Richard fishes it out of the chest and slips it under his shirt while Charlie uses the bathroom. Later, while they play in the backyard, Charlie spots the magazine tucked inside the hem of Richard's shorts and tries to take it back. Richard had never been in a fight before. Scuffles and grappling matches in the backyard, sure, but never a true fistfight. No way he'll relent and give the magazine back to Charlie, so when his friend attempts to steal it back, Richard fights him tooth and nail. Fists strike flesh, blood spurts from noses. By the time Vanessa realizes what is happening in the yard, Richard sits astride her son's chest, pummeling his face while the boy begs him to stop.

"What the hell are you doing to Charlie?" she screams, yanking Richard off the boy. "For Christ's sake, Richard. What's gotten into you?"

Richard's frigid, vacant glare causes Vanessa to step backward, her arms wrapped around her bleeding son. Charlie's face puffs and swells, black and purple bruises amid all that blood.

"You're not welcome here. Never again. Do you understand?"

Richard turns and leaves without saying a word. Hops on his bike with the rolled-up magazine jutting from the back of his shorts like a misplaced limb. He rides home, giddy with excitement rather than concern for his friend. Fuck Charlie. It wasn't his magazine, anyway.

That night he waits until Mother closes her bedroom door across the hall. Keeping the lights off, he pads through absolute darkness and pops the lock in place on his door. From his desk, he removes the flashlight. A permanent grin on his face, he slips into bed and fixes the beam on the magazine.

The contents cause Richard to grimace with discontent. Where are the pictures of the college girl in bondage? Thumbing through the pages, he finds nothing but stories. Even the back of the magazine disappoints. It depicts wraparound art from the front cover with a smattering of lurid text.

Unwilling to accept failure, Richard opens to the story featured on the cover. The prose isn't as provocative as the picture, but it draws him in. Soon he pictures each scene in vivid detail, the co-ed replaced by Charlie's mom.

"What the hell are you doing to Charlie?" he mocks in falsetto. "The same thing I'll do to you, if you don't give me what I want."

Before he knows what he's doing, Richard slides his hand inside his shorts. For the next hour, he orgasms to images of Vanessa cuffed and bound like the girl in the story. He becomes the kidnapper, the one holding all the power. What will it take to make the dream a reality? If he apologizes and gets on Charlie's good side again—

The door flies open. Smashes against the wall. Richard turns off the flashlight and shoves the magazine beneath the bed sheet. Too late. She sees what he's up to. Disdain contorting her face, Mother drops the hairpin on the desk. It makes a clinking noise. Richard holds his breath. He didn't know she could pick the lock.

"Give it to me."

Richard drags the sheet up to his chin and uses his foot to push the magazine across the mattress.

"I said, 'give it to me.'"

"I don't have anything."

"Don't lie to your mother. I know what you're hiding."

She whips the sheet back, exposing his erection. Tears crawl down his face as she snatches the magazine and tears it in half.

"*This* is what you look at every night when you're supposed to be sleeping?" Her eyes light with wicked amusement as she shreds the magazine in front of him. "What did you see in that whore, Richard? Answer me."

His lips quiver. Mother towers over the bed and glares down at his exposed body.

"I'll teach you right from wrong. So help me, God, I will."

When her eyes pass over the stained sheet, her mouth falls open.

"It was an accident. I didn't mean to."

"You dirty, dirty boy."

Richard cries out when Mother digs her nails into his scalp.

She rips him from the bed by his hair, drags his flailing body across the floor and into the hallway.

"Stop, Mother. You're hurting me."

"Oh, you don't understand the first thing about pain. But you will. I'll see to it."

He reaches out and grabs hold of the jamb outside the bathroom. With one tug, she hauls him past the doorway and into the living room, where his kicking legs smash the coffee table and shatter a vase of heather.

Mother freezes in place. Horror fills her eyes as she glances between the broken vase and her sobbing son.

"What have you done?"

A blood-curdling scream tears from her lungs and pierces his eardrums. Tugging him into the kitchen, she throws him onto a chair. Slaps his face when he tries to run. Stars sparkle, obscuring his vision. When his eyes clear, Mother stands before him with a steak knife.

"Give it to me," she says.

"What? I don't have anything."

She grips the waistband of his underwear and pulls them down his thighs. Gripping his penis, she places the blade edge against his flesh.

"No, Mother! I'm sorry...I won't do it again."

"Dirty boys must pay, Richard. You'll thank me one day."

27

Darcy's eyes pop open when someone sets a coffee mug upon the break room table. She rubs the blur away and sits up, feeling as though her muscles turned into mud while she dozed. Iglesias pours black coffee into the mug, picks it up and slams it in front of her. His lips pull tight, making him appear two decades older.

"Up and at 'em," he says, chugging from his own mug. "You won't find Faith Fielder inside your dreams."

Darcy curls her fingers around the mug's handle and lifts the coffee to her lips. It's bitter and scalding, but it knocks the weariness out of her bones. Julian comes awake in the chair beside her. He tests his breath against his palm and pinches his nose shut.

"Well, that was pleasant," Julian says, nodding toward the doorway where Chief Iglesias disappeared.

"He's worried about Faith and understands we don't have time to rest."

"You can't force people to work nonstop."

Ketchum turns the corner and stops upon seeing Darcy and Julian.

"You're awake."

"How long was I out?" Darcy asks, scratching behind her head.

"An hour at most. Not long enough."

"What about you?" Julian asks, directing his gaze at Ketchum. "You're ready to drop."

"I grabbed thirty minutes in the media room. I'm running on fumes, but it should get me through the day. Iglesias let O'Grady go. The chief couldn't hold him after he lawyered up. Wouldn't be surprised if the psycho caught the first flight home." Ketchum drops two manila folders on the table. "The Regan and Lieberman photos. You wanted to study them again?"

"Yes, thank you," she says, dragging the folder in front of her. She opens the two folders and places crime scene photographs taken inside the bedrooms side by side. She draws in a breath. "I can't believe I missed it. It's the island."

"Your theory is the killer turned Cassy Regan and the Liebermans toward the island, not just the water?"

"See the way he placed the chairs? Follow a direct line through the picture. If you examine the photos, you'll find the island in each."

"It could be a coincidence," Julian says, stealing a sip from her mug.

"That's why I want to return to the scenes. The Lieberman's house, Cassy Regan's, and the first murder site."

Ketchum leans an elbow on the table and turns the photographs toward him.

"I'll grab the keys. But you aren't going inside alone."

"That's fine. I already walked through the two houses. This shouldn't take long."

A knock on the break room door brings their heads around. Officer Narulla leans in the doorway.

"I found something on the traffic cam footage."

"Did you catch his face, Officer?" Ketchum asks, sliding the chair back from the table.

"No, a jogger. I'll show you."

They follow Narulla to the media room. Officer Cross sits before the monitor, shifting the footage frame by frame.

"Wonder boy thinks he found something," Cross says, rolling his eyes.

Ignoring the rib, Narulla rests one hand on the back of Cross's chair and jabs his finger at the monitor.

"See that color blur on the window across from the hardware store? Someone jogged by Tuesday night while the kidnapper used the phone. It only shows up on the traffic camera at the intersection. That's why I missed it."

"All I see is a splotch of blue and green," Cross says. "I can't tell if that's a car driving by or Godzilla attacking."

Julian leans his face close to the monitor.

"Move it forward a frame."

Cross fumbles with the controls and draws a snicker out of Narulla.

"Let me handle it, old man."

Narulla takes Cross's place in front of the monitors. When he steps the footage forward, the colorful shape moves across the glass. It could be someone running by, or a car speeding toward the light. But if the reflected color comes from a vehicle, it should show up on the camera when it moves past the intersection.

"Take it back to the beginning," Darcy says, pulling up a chair. Julian and Ketchum crowd behind her. "Now play it back at full speed."

Chewing his lip, Narulla reverses the footage and plays it back. There. The speed and bounce of the reflection convinces Darcy a jogger ran past the window across the street from the pay phone.

"The kid's right," Cross says, folding his arms. "He'll boast about his hero status for the next month."

"Little good it does us," says the younger officer, ignoring Cross. "I can't make out a face."

"Blow it up," Julian says, pointing at the frozen image of the jogger's reflection.

"Do it," says Ketchum with a nod. "Send me a digital copy, and I'll have my lab clean up the image."

When Narulla zooms in on the reflection, all Darcy sees is a kaleidoscope of colors. There's a hint of a face in the window pane. Is that an African-American woman? No way they can ID the jogger from the image. Recalling the wizardry the tech team displayed during her years with the FBI, Darcy grasps a glimmer of hope.

Leaving the two officers to their work, Darcy follows Ketchum and Julian back to the lobby.

"What's the plan?" Ketchum asks, checking his watch.

"Recheck the Lieberman and Regan houses, then drive to the shore where the Doll Face Killer murdered Forsythe and Vassallo." Darcy sighs. "And if it keeps the two of you from rolling your eyes, yes, you can come with me."

At that moment, Iglesias's voice careens down the corridor. The chief is berating Cross. Something about misfiling paperwork.

"We'd better go before Iglesias focuses on us," says Ketchum.

Darcy glances at the clock on the way out the door. They're running out of time.

28

A firetruck blocks the main road through the village center when Ketchum takes the SUV around the corner. Peering beneath the visor to see what the holdup is, Darcy watches a fireman standing inside a bucket drape a banner over the lines. The sign welcomes visitors to beautiful Veil Lake and wishes everyone a happy and safe Independence Day.

"I should have taken the long way around the water," Ketchum groans. "Nix warned me about the Fourth of July festivities, but I figured downtown would be fine until midday."

"Don't worry about it. They'll move soon," says Darcy.

She drums her legs, belying her patience. Realizing the job will take another five minutes, Ketchum looks over his shoulder and reverses the SUV.

"It's a one-way street," Julian says, worried about other vehicles.

"Yup," Ketchum says, grinning.

When the SUV is even with the turn, the FBI agent swings the vehicle onto a side road and kicks the accelerator. Watching the houses whip past on the loop around the lake, Darcy searches the water until her eyes land on the island. Perhaps she's grasping at straws. Most cottages around Veil Lake offer a view of the island, but she'd sworn the Doll Face Killer positioned the chairs to face the lump of land jutting out of the water.

Ketchum stops along the curb in front of Jim and Carol Lieberman's house. Even in the light of day, Darcy can only see the top of the home peeking over the trees, one cyclops eye for a window staring back at her. Julian climbs out first and scans the street. A hatchback backs out of a driveway at the end of the road and cruises toward the village. Otherwise, the secluded street looks like a ghost town.

After Ketchum shuts the door, he radios their position back to headquarters. By now, the FBI's tech lab is manipulating the jogger image, sharpening the facial details and removing blur and artifacts.

"I'll watch the street," Ketchum says, lifting his chin at the deep shadows beneath the trees. "Phillip O'Grady won't show his face."

Julian glances at the FBI agent.

"You sure of that?"

"Iglesias put the fear of God into him last night. Either way, there's no need for three of us trudging through the house. I'll keep my phone and radio on. If you see anything out of place—"

"I'll let you know," Darcy says.

Ketchum hands Darcy the folder of crime scene photographs.

"I take it you'll want these."

"We'll be back in fifteen minutes."

With Julian at her side, she crosses the road and climbs the winding driveway.

"Now I get why the Doll Face Killer chose this place," Julian says, swinging his gaze from tree to tree.

"The property line extends a hundred feet past the garage," Darcy says, pointing toward a strip of grass between the garage and trees. "He could have held them for a week without the neighbors figuring out something was wrong."

Though the looming two-story appears less threatening in the soft light of morning, Darcy spies movement in every shadow and a face in every window. She digs into her pocket for the key, panics until she finds it wedged inside a fold. Sliding the key into the door, she unlocks the house and releases the pent up silence. Darcy isn't the only one jumping at her own shadow. Julian's gaze darts from the basement at the bottom of the stairs to the open landing at the top. Though he doesn't draw his weapon, Julian's hand slides toward the pistol.

One eye on the open basement door, Darcy grips the banister and ascends the stairs with Julian watching her back. As she steps into the main living area, her gaze falls over the familiar open floor plan, connecting the living room, dining area, and kitchen.

Not noticing she stopped, Julian bumps into her from behind.

"What's wrong?" he whispers as if the house can hear him.

The hair stands on the back of Darcy's neck. Something is different about the room. She focuses on the couch facing the wall-mounted television, then the kitchen. Darcy shakes her head.

"It's nothing. Let's go."

Julian gives her an unconvinced look as he follows her up the carpeted stairs to the upper floor. Darcy pauses outside the bathroom and gives the door a push. The shower door stands open, shoved to the right as it had been when she searched inside. In the master bedroom, Darcy stops in the doorway. The blood splatter appears darker now, taking on a brownish coloration against the walls and rug.

"What is it you're looking for again?"

Without answering, Darcy opens the folder and sifts through the photographs until she finds the pictures of Jim and Carol Lieberman tied to the chairs. Porcelain masks cover their faces. Ropes bind their wrists and ankles and pull their heads against the chair backs. She averts her eyes from the gaping slashes across their necks and concentrates on the chairs. After she lines up the pictures with her view out the window, she shuts the folder.

"He forced them to look at the island."

Julian shifts his body and touches his chin.

"Maybe. One could argue they're looking at the cottages across the water. I wouldn't draw a conclusion without examining the other murder sites."

Julian possesses a sharp mind and has the instinct of a high profile detective. But he isn't a profiler and never entered the mind of a killer. Darcy can't convince Julian, Ketchum, or Iglesias of her theory, but the voice whispering behind her ears tells her the island plays an important role. She snaps three photographs with her phone, though she's documented every inch of the bedroom between her two trips to the Lieberman house.

They descend the stairs to the living room, the same trepidation that something changed eating at Darcy. Her eyes land on the couch and bring Darcy to a halt.

The stack of mail, including the resort brochure. It lies on the arm of the couch, not on the table where she'd found it Wednesday night.

"He came back to the house."

"Are you sure?"

"The mail. It was on the table next to the refrigerator when I did the walk through."

"And you didn't move it."

"No."

Julian grabs the pistol and steps around Darcy. After he clears the first floor, Darcy calls Ketchum on the radio.

"What's the hold up?"

"Ketchum, Doll Face came back to the house."

The radio squelches with static.

"Did you find signs of a break in?"

"The killer returned to relive the crime. Then he made himself at home and went through their mail. He's getting careless."

After a pause, Ketchum says, "I'll send the team to dust for prints."

"Have them focus on the couch and letters." The television remote lies beside the brochure. "For all I know, he might have turned on the television. Dust everything. We need to catch him before nightfall."

The crime scene investigators are en route to the Lieberman house when Ketchum's SUV jounces down Cassy Regan's steep and treacherous driveway. Darcy's heart rests in her throat until the vehicle stops in front of the house. As they did at the Lieberman house, Darcy and Julian don gloves before investigating the cottage. Vigilant to the possibility the killer returned to the scene of the murder, Darcy moves through the house and touches nothing. When they reach the bedroom, she lines up her camera with the chair at the window, comparing the position to the crime scene photographs.

"The island again," Darcy says, extending her arm over the chair top.

His mouth pulled tight and grim, Julian groans in agreement.

"See anything out of place?"

She scans the bedroom, then walks through the living room and kitchen. If Doll Face returned, he didn't disturb the house.

The last stop on their journey convinces Julian. While Ketchum keeps watch beside the vehicle, Darcy pulls back the bushes and searches for a way down to the water. A worn footpath on the northwest end of the lake cuts down a hill between two property lines. The path ends at a clearing on the shore of Veil Lake. Rusted beer cans, crushed cigarettes, and assorted garbage rot amid the trees where generations of careless teens and party-goers tossed their trash aside.

Julian opens the folder and points at two elm trees sprouting out of the ground along the shoreline.

"The police found Paul Forsythe seated against the tree on the right, Tracy Vassallo on the left. Killer slashed their throats after bashing the male in the back of his head with a blunt object."

Darcy glances over his shoulder at the pictures. Though the police couldn't have predicted the island's importance, the first photograph aligns the trees with the lake and land mass. Taken from behind the victims, the picture reveals a confusion of shoe prints covering the ground. Forsythe's legs splay in front of him as if he's resting peacefully, his gory wound hidden by the tree.

"He's facing the island," Darcy says.

"So is Vassallo," Julian says in agreement, kneeling so his viewpoint is identical to the photographer's.

"I'll phone Iglesias."

Darcy reads the time. Twelve hours until the sun begins its descent.

As Darcy and Julian climb back to the vehicle, Agent Ketchum finishes his conversation and pockets his phone.

"Good news. The tech crew cleaned up the freeze frame and sent it to the VLPD. There's an identifiable face in the window."

29

Richard Oswalt awakens with a gasp. In his dream, he watched his father's boat sink a hundred yards off the island, the torrents of rain roiling the water and obscuring the lake in a gray morass. He didn't witness the accident, didn't see his father lose visibility in the thunderstorm and smash the boat against a rock jetty. But his mind fills in the horrific details. At the burial service, he heard the stories uttered from Mother and relatives he barely knew. Why didn't anyone help?

He unclasps his fingers from the blanket and wipes the grogginess off his face. Opening the girl's bedroom, he finds Faith as he left her. Wrists bound behind her head and fastened to the bedpost. She'd kicked the covers off during the night. Her pale legs lie akimbo across the mattress as though she dropped from the ceiling and crashed into the bed. Richard isn't sure she's breathing until the girl mutters in her sleep and twists over, moaning when the zip tie digs into her flesh.

He'll kill her tonight. Frustration ripples through his shoulders. She was the one he sought, the girl who wasn't like the villagers who ignored Daddy's cries for help.

He shuffles to the kitchen and pours cereal into a bowl. Shovels the food into his mouth before he realizes he forgot the milk. It doesn't matter. Everything tastes like cardboard in the harsh morning light. When he tosses the bowl into the sink and turns on the faucet, he hears Faith stir in the bedroom. She's sitting up when he returns to her doorway, cheeks pink and chapped from old tears.

"Good morning, Faith."

She turns her head away and glares at the wall.

"Don't be angry with me. You brought this upon yourself when you climbed the fence. I had no choice."

Faith tugs at the zip tie, cries out when it pinches her skin.

"It hurts. I want my mom and dad."

"Now, now. Your parents know you're here, Faith. Remember the recording? This is what Mother wanted. For me to teach you."

"You aren't teaching me anything, just making me look at awful pictures."

"As we discussed, life can be scary sometimes. If we never face our fears, we can't grow." He sighs. "I need to clean up. In the meantime, I'll take the zip tie off your wrists."

Her face turns toward his.

"You're...letting me go?"

"I'll allow you to move about the cabin. You may eat breakfast, wash your body, or work in the garden. My home is yours, Faith. As it always has been. But I'm watching you. Should you run off again, I'll have no choice but to punish your parents."

Faith's eyes widen and flash with panic.

"Don't hurt Mom and Dad."

"Your actions reflect how they raised you. Should you disobey my orders, I'll hold them accountable. Understand? You don't live in a vacuum. Misbehave, and you'll hurt the ones you love."

Distant thunder rumbles. Richard's head swims, knees buckle. When he rights himself, his arms brace against the jamb while spittle crawls down his lip. The girl's face blurs and morphs. Is it Faith or Mother in the bed?

"A storm is coming," he says. "Someone needs to tell Daddy."

A rain drop plunks the window. Richard shakes his head and rubs his eyes. Why is a girl lying in Mother's bed?

"What did you do with Mother?"

Faith shakes her head, sweeping her hair across her face.

Richard pulls a knife from his pocket and approaches the bed. She squirms, unable to pull her gaze from the knife. In that moment, he remembers Charlie's mother, Vanessa. He'd pictured her in this position, bound to his bed, fear gripping her face as he brandished a knife.

He pauses over Faith's body. How easy it would be to plunge the blade through her exposed neck. Rip her shirt off and jam the knife into her stomach.

Richard saws the zip tie until it snaps in half. Her arms collapse.

"You see, Faith? You can trust me."

But can he trust her? He needs to. He has a loose thread threatening to unravel his plans. The black woman saw him. Richard must deal with the issue later this morning. Then he'll bring Faith to the lake at sunset and end the nightmares for good.

30

FRIDAY, JULY 4TH 9:05 A.M.

Ketchum hasn't shifted the SUV into park before Officer Nix jogs to the vehicle. Julian and Darcy hop out first, the officer short of breath as he waits for Ketchum to join them.

"We found the woman, the jogger Narulla saw in the footage."

"That was fast. Damn good work, Officer," Ketchum says, patting Nix's shoulder.

"Thank Narulla and your tech crew."

"Who's the woman?" Darcy asks, tugging on the handle to ensure they locked the SUV.

"Kashana Dorney. She lives three blocks from the hardware store. Sometimes I see her running when I'm on patrol, but I didn't think of it before."

"When can we speak with her?"

"In ten minutes. She's on her way to the office now."

Smoke puffing from his ears, Iglesias stomps through the lobby and slaps a paper on the bewildered secretary's desk.

"Fix this," he says.

"Keep your head down and keep walking," Nix says as they give Iglesias a wide berth.

Too late.

"While you were out sightseeing, I looked up boating accidents and drownings off your island. Guess what? Not a goddamn one in the last decade. You have a better theory before we lose another life?"

They sweep around the corner with Iglesias still shouting from the lobby. As they pass the media room, Cross peeks his head around the corner and gives a relieved sigh.

"I'm glad to see the four of you. Well, maybe not you, Nix."

Nix rolls his eyes and sends Cross a mock kiss.

"Chief is on the warpath this morning, I take it."

"If we don't find this girl before sunset, he'll throw the entire department out on its ear." Cross lifts his chin at Darcy. "Find anything useful?"

"Look up deaths on Veil Lake near the island," says Darcy, working a knot out of her shoulder.

"Isn't that what Iglesias just did? He's been cursing up a storm about time wasted."

"Go back further. Concentrate on events between 1990 and 2000."

"Why that far back?"

"If I'm correct about the Doll Face Killer's age, he would have been a child during that decade."

"So you're angling toward childhood trauma."

"Exactly."

A door slams at the end of the hall. Lowering his shoulders, Cross gives Darcy a nod.

"I'm on it. But if the chief asks where I am, you haven't seen me."

While Cross descends the stairs to research old cases, Darcy,

Ketchum, and Julian follow Nix into the interview room. Julian questions Nix with his eyes.

"You're welcome to sit in, Detective," says Nix. "It's always good to have an extra set of eyes and ears."

They don't wait long. Nix's radio squawks when Kashana Dorney arrives in the lobby. A minute later, Nix returns with the woman trailing behind.

Dorney is an African-American woman in her late twenties, runner's legs accented by purple yoga pants. She wears a white hooded sweatshirt. Black braids extend halfway down her back. Dorney rubs her arms as though fighting off a chill, her eyes moving between Nix and the three people seated at the table.

"Thank you for coming over on short notice," Nix says as Dorney slides her chair toward the table.

Nix makes introductions.

"What's all this about? I'm not in trouble, am I?"

"Nothing like that, ma'am. Can you verify your address for me?"

"Twenty-nine Grant Street."

Grant Street. That's the street perpendicular to Monument Park.

"Did you jog through the village Monday night around nine o'clock?" Nix asks.

Dorney clasps her hands together to keep them still.

"I jog most nights. How did you know I ran Monday night?"

"Your face showed up in the boutique shop window across from the hardware store."

The runner straightens her back.

"Was there a robbery? I'm not a thief. If you're looking for the perpetrator, start with the tourists rampaging through the village."

"You're not a suspect, Ms. Dorney, and there wasn't a robbery."

Dorney's shoulders relax.

"Then why am I here?"

"There's a pay phone beside the hardware store. A man in a hooded sweatshirt used the phone as you ran past on the opposite side of the street."

She screws her face up in thought.

"Right. I remember the guy."

"Did you recognize his face?"

Dorney thinks for a moment and shakes her head.

"I saw him, but he isn't anyone I've met. But you have to consider I moved to Veil Lake from Grand Rapids eight months ago. Besides my neighbors and the people at my gym, I don't know anybody here."

Darcy sits forward.

"Can you describe the man?"

The woman lifts her shoulders.

"Caucasian. Tough to gauge height from across the street, but he was taller than me. Lean guy, long face."

"Young or old?"

"Middle-age. In his forties or fifties."

"Any distinguishing marks?" Ketchum asks, cutting in. "Tattoos, scars."

"No way to tell. As you mentioned, he wore a hooded sweatshirt, and it was after sunset."

"Have you ever seen the man around town?"

Dorney considers her answer.

"There was something familiar about the guy. Could be I passed him on the street. I wouldn't know his name, though."

"If I showed you a set of pictures, could you pick him out?"

"What did he do? When I ran past, he was just talking on the phone." Dorney's eyes widen. "Don't tell me he's the murderer on the news, the Doll Face Killer."

Dorney catches Nix shifting in his seat, betraying the others' poker faces.

"Oh, snap. It was him, wasn't it? God." Dorney rolls a shiver off her spine. "There was something creepy about the guy. Shit, did he see me? Am I in danger?"

Nix raises his hands.

"We don't know who the man was, and there's no reason to believe you're in danger."

Lost in her thoughts and not listening to Nix, Dorney drops her face into her hands. Her eyes emerge haunted.

"After I ran past the boutique, I tripped on the sidewalk and caught myself before I fell. That's when he put the phone down and walked off in the other direction. Like he hadn't seen me until then. What if he knows where I live?"

Darcy reaches across the table and takes Dorney's hands in hers.

"We won't let anyone hurt you, Ms. Dorney. But I need you to tell me everything you remember about the man."

The runner repeats her description, giving them nothing new. Dammit. Everyone in Veil Lake knows each other, but the one person who spotted the Doll Face Killer isn't from the village.

"You have a sketch artist on call?" Julian asks Nix.

"I can get him here quick." Nix turns to Dorney. "Did you notice any unfamiliar vehicles parked on Grant Street Monday night?"

"Not that I can...wait. There was a silver minivan outside the park entrance when I jogged through. I remember it now because it was in a no-parking zone."

"You recall the license plate number?"

"Well, no. But the minivan had Michigan plates. I thought about calling it in, but I don't like stirring up trouble. That's all I remember. Sorry."

After another five minutes of questioning, Nix turns Dorney over to Narulla while she waits for the sketch artist to arrive.

"Don't answer the door for anyone you don't recognize when you get home," Darcy tells Dorney before she leaves. "We'll call if we have additional questions."

After the door closes, Ketchum looks from Darcy and Julian to Nix.

"This sounds like our guy."

"The age fits," says Darcy. "Let's hope Cross's search bears fruit."

"I don't like this," Julian says, watching the woman cross the parking lot toward a Toyota Highlander. "After everything she said, I'm afraid the killer recognized Dorney. He might go after her next. Eliminate the only witness."

"Can't rule it out," Nix says. He lowers his head and itches his neck. "But I won't be the one to ask Iglesias. We're stretched to the point of snapping. If I put surveillance on Dorney, Iglesias will lose his mind."

"I'll go," Julian says as Darcy turns her head. "Why not? As long as Darcy stays with either of you, I'm comfortable with it."

Ketchum gives a *why-not* shrug.

"This is unofficial," says Nix. "As far as the chief is concerned—"

"I got it. He won't find out."

Nix holds up a finger and exits the interview room. A minute later, he returns with a police radio and slaps it on Julian's palm.

"And I didn't give you this, either."

Julian winks.

When Julian rises from the table, Darcy grabs his arm.

"Promise me you'll be careful, Julian."

"Don't worry about me. Tell me when you I.D. Doll Face."

Darcy stands at the window and watches Julian drive off. A sick feeling rests in the pit of her stomach. This is a mistake.

31

The folder slaps against the kitchen table with a gunshot sound. Faith sets her hands in her lap and stares at the window.

"Open the folder," Mr. Filmore growls.

When she doesn't obey, he snatches her wrist and forces her to pull the folder open. His grip makes her wrist crack.

"No more pictures. They're horrible."

"Do as your professor instructs."

"You're not my professor. I bet Filmore isn't your actual name."

He huffs and spreads the photographs before her.

"All these killers stopped. I need to know why. You'll tell me."

Faith picks up a photograph of Ted Bundy. Stares at his lifeless eyes and tosses it down.

"They only stopped because the police caught them. Don't you understand? They were terrible people and couldn't stop."

He opens his mouth as if to argue. Clamps it shut.

Digging through the stack of photographs with the textbook balanced on the edge of the table, the man who calls himself Mr.

Filmore pulls a dozen pictures from the bottom of the pile and thrusts them into Faith's hands.

She identifies a new photograph. One he slipped into the pile since her last lesson. The woman in the picture stares at the water, her throat gashed, blood drenching her shirt. Faith looks away, but the image catches her attention from the corner of her eye. The water. That's Veil Lake. She recognizes the shrub and tree-covered island poking out of its depths.

The truth slams into Faith's chest. Mr. Filmore killed this woman. The stories her parents told her about a criminal at large in Veil Lake concealed the truth. A murderer stalks the lake, and he's hovering over Faith, breathing down the back of her neck like a thirsty vampire.

"You'll study until I return and give me a better answer. Not all serial killers murder forever. Some stop. You will tell me how."

He turns on his heels and stomps across the kitchen. Then he stops and looks back at Faith. Yanks a phone from his pocket and shoves it in her face.

"See this? It's a security display of all the cameras circling the cabin. If you try to escape while I'm gone, I'll see. Instead of punishing you, I'll pay your parents a visit. How would you like that?"

Faith's gaze drifts to the table.

"I'm sorry it has to be this way, but I have business to attend to. You're free to roam the grounds and work in the garden while I'm away. Understand the consequences, if you betray me again.

His footsteps crash through the living room a moment before the door slams. After, she can't hear him anymore. Just rain dripping off the eaves and the pounding of her heart.

She needs to get out of here before Mr. Filmore hurts Mom and Dad.

32

Kashana Dorney's house is a quaint English Tudor, painted white with aqua trim. Either she has a green thumb or knows a terrific landscaper. The yard appears plucked from an HGTV episode, with multicolored flowers of ascending heights guarding the porch. She installed planters outside the upstairs window where annuals bloom. Patriotic colors swim through the neighborhood on flags, pennants, and wreaths.

Julian sits low in the seat of Darcy's rental, sipping from a fruit smoothie as he scans the neighborhood with a pair of binoculars. He'd come to Veil Lake, intending to watch Darcy's back. Iglesias locked him out of the case, but the detective's instincts pull him into the action. He has an emotional stake in locating Faith Fielder.

Down the block, five boys and a girl play stick ball. The pitcher bounces a racket ball on the street. The hitter connects with a broomstick handle and sends a fly ball to the outfield which is just two Honda cars parked curbside. A girl makes a running catch in the street, eliciting a whoop from the pitcher while the batter tosses the broomstick in disgust.

Caught up in the game and remembering his younger days on the streets of Newark, Julian doesn't notice the woman walking past his vehicle until she crosses the street in front of the rental. Julian lets out a curse. He's supposed to keep his eyes on Dorney's place. But an hour has passed since he began his surveillance, and nobody has approached the house. In fact, he hasn't witnessed a vehicle come or go since a station wagon scattered the players a half-hour ago. The wagon turned into a Greek Revival home down the block, and a woman opened the trunk and carried her groceries into the house.

Taking another sip from the smoothie, Julian lifts the radio to his ear when static overwhelms the message from dispatch. He waits until the male dispatcher repeats the message, hoping the VLPD has a bead on the Doll Face Killer. False alarm. It's a domestic dispute on the other side of the lake.

Anything yet from Cross? Julian types to Darcy.

A slight pause, then—

He's still looking. How are things in Dorney's neighborhood?

Boring. My instincts are way off base. Except for a few neighbors and kids playing down the street, I haven't seen a soul.

After fifteen minutes, the kids run off with the racket ball and makeshift bat and vanish around the corner. Now the street turns quiet. No lawn mowers buzzing, no residents out for a stroll.

He considers sticking the key in the ignition and driving back to the station. Even with an FBI agent and a station full of cops to guard Darcy, Julian's skin tingles with unseen danger. Stakeout experience warns him the action always picks up when you're about to call it a day. Or a night. Most of Julian's surveillance missions occurred when normal people were sound asleep. No sooner does the thought cross his mind than movement catches his eye. He swings his head and spots a postal worker crossing the yard with a mail bag thrown over his shoulder. It's Trevor Funes. Iglesias didn't allow Julian into the interview room, but Funes must have seen him hanging around the department.

The postman's isn't the only recognizable face in the neighborhood. Julian might have considered it a coincidence that Funes delivered to Kashana Dorney's house—his route covers this side of the lake—but it isn't happenstance when the off duty detective spies Phillip O'Grady strolling down the sidewalk from the opposite direction. Darcy's stalker keeps close to a hedgerow, but Julian sees the man as he nears Dorney's house. Is O'Grady the Doll Face Killer? He has an alibi for the Lieberman murders, but maybe the police botched the time line or O'Grady's workmate lied.

Julian edges the door open and grips the radio, weighing whether he should call back to the station. If Iglesias is listening, Julian will get Nix into hot water. Neither suspect has done anything to raise suspicion. Yet. Stepping from the rental, Julian stands behind a weeping willow. Funes ascends the steps to Dorney's Tudor, stuffs an envelope in the mailbox, and rockets toward the neighbor's house, whistling as he walks. With the postman's back to him, Julian lets out a breath. Where did O'Grady go?

Julian's heart skips a beat when a shadow drifts along the side of Dorney's house, moving toward the backyard. He lifts the radio to his lips and follows the unknown figure. A gate opens and closes.

"Nix, I've got movement outside Kashana Dorney's house. Someone just sneaked down the driveway to the backyard."

Nix takes a second to respond.

"Stay where you are, Detective. I'm sending a patrol vehicle."

"Trevor Funes delivered mail to Dorney a minute ago, and Phillip O'Grady is in the neighborhood. He might be the person in the backyard."

"O'Grady?" Nix's voice rises with alarm. "Dammit, I thought we ran that creep out of the village. Watch O'Grady. Two officers will join you in five minutes."

Standing with his back against the wall, Julian peers around the corner of the house. The backyard appears empty. A concrete walkway leads off the deck and circles an in-ground pool. Dorney has money. A gazebo slumbers beside the fence.

The doors stand closed on Dorney's garage. Julian looks inside and finds the Highlander parked on the left. Then he spots a silver minivan on the right. O'Grady photographed a silver minivan. Darcy showed him the pictures. Though Julian couldn't read the license plate, and the make and model weren't obvious from the blurry pictures, he's certain this is the same vehicle.

"Nix."

No reply.

"Nix, come in."

"I got you, Haines."

Julian opens his mouth to reply when electric wasp stings pierce his back. He has a split-second to register the Taser before the voltage clenches his muscles and takes him to the ground. His body convulses, teeth clamped against his tongue as a cold shadow passes over his body.

"This won't do," a woman's voice says. "I'm afraid you must come with me, Officer."

The boot stomps his head and knocks him unconscious.

33

The minivan door slams. Faith rushes to the living room window. The gate swings open, and she draws a breath when Mr. Filmore drags a body inside the garden and locks the gate behind him. Judging by the size of the body, Faith can tell it's a man. His shoes bounce along the path as Filmore strains to drag him toward the house.

She fears the man is her father until she notices the dark hair and broad shoulders.

"Faith, open the door!"

Torn by indecision, she eyes the open door of her bedroom and considers retreating inside, barricading the door. It's no use. He'll break inside. She shivers at the prospect of more punishment. She spent most of the night tied to the bed. Her wrists remain raw and chafed from the zip tie.

"Damn you, Faith!"

He fishes inside his pockets for the key when Faith opens the door.

"How many times do I need to ask? When I tell you to do something, you obey."

Filmore grunts and hauls the man inside. The large man's shoes catch on the threshold, forcing Filmore to lug him higher as he drags him through the entryway.

"Is he…"

"Dead? Not yet."

"Who is he? Why did you hurt him?"

Filmore drops the man in the center of the living room. His mouth twists as if he bit something sour.

"He could have ruined everything, but I stopped him. I stopped them both."

The prisoner's physique marks him as law enforcement. Faith lowers her head. Even the police aren't safe from Mr. Filmore.

"What are you going to do now?" Faith asks as Filmore catches his breath and lifts the man by the shoulders.

He releases a frustrated breath. Faith cringes as Mr. Filmore speaks in a higher pitch. In a woman's voice.

"Did you work on your studies? Because the garden looks no different from when I left. Don't tell me you wasted the entire morning. You're no better than the rest of them. Lazy, slovenly. You'd watch a man drown and not lend a helping hand."

He plants his feet and groans. The man's legs disappear around the hallway corner. A door opens as Faith chews a nail. As Filmore strains to position the man inside the bedroom, she glances at the recliner. The fake professor placed his keys on the arm while he rested. If she grabs the keys and sprints for the gate, he'll see her on the cameras. Her hand drifts toward the key chain. More grunts and curses from the bedroom. The house goes quiet. He's coming.

Faith snatches the keys and slips through the open doorway. Aware of the camera's watchful eye, she keeps the keys concealed beneath her shirt. Stumbling through the heather, she hears him yelling for her. He's in the hallway, searching.

Faith falls to her knees and drops the keys beside a thick-stalked plant.

"Answer me, Faith!"

Grabbing a clump of dirt, she spreads soil over the keys and tears a leaf off the heather, wincing when the plant quivers. As though she tore a limb off an animal.

He bursts into the garden as she stumbles out of the rows. His face relaxes.

"There you are. I knew you wouldn't leave me, dear Faith. Why didn't you answer when I called?"

"I wanted to work in the garden."

Confusion skews his brow before he nods.

"Very good. You appreciate the garden and its significance."

"So it will grow. And change," she says, repeating his words.

"Yes, Faith. So it will change."

There it is. That female voice again. Faith edges into the garden. It takes all of her willpower not to rush the fence.

Mr. Filmore places his hands on his hips and tilts his head toward the sky.

"Faith, have you seen my keys?"

Is he asking because he suspects she took them? He pulls out his pockets, turns in a circle, then paces to the house and back.

For the next hour, they work together in the garden, the keys forgotten. Mr. Filmore slaves over the heather on hands and knees, not bothering to wipe the sweat off his forehead as he rushes between the compost bin and the plants. Faith weeds around the heather and tosses the intruders into the wheelbarrow she tried to stand upon. As she works, her ears tune to the bedroom at the end of the hall. She hears knocks and moans as the prisoner awakens. She imagines him tied to a chair, the legs clomping down on the hardwood floor as he struggles to escape.

As the afternoon sun burns her shoulders red, she keeps one

eye on the clump of dirt beneath the tallest heather plant in the row. She must remember where she hid the keys.

34

Darcy pushes past a group of officers pawing around the garage behind Kashana Dorney's house. Her rental rests beside the curb two houses down, while the ambulance lights whirl in front of the Tudor. The CSI team works inside the house. The responding officers found Dorney on the kitchen floor, her body a pincushion of stab wounds. Lights ignite the windows as flashbulbs fire. Where is Julian?

Ketchum touches her shoulder as she kneels beside the garage. No blood. But Julian had been here. She senses the ghost of his presence.

"No sign of O'Grady," Iglesias says, stomping out of the yard.

Darcy's head spins. She'd convinced herself O'Grady couldn't be the Doll Face Killer. Yet Julian witnessed the deranged forum poster stalking toward Dorney's house a moment before his radio went dead. Now there's a dead body in the house, and it belongs to the only person who can identify the Doll Face Killer.

"Don't worry," Ketchum says, ushering Darcy away from Iglesias before the chief turns his wrath on her. "We'll find

Julian. That O'Grady didn't kill Julian gives me hope he's using your husband as leverage."

"A kidnapping."

"Right."

Darcy reads Ketchum's fear. Doll Face will keep Julian alive until tonight and sacrifice Julian and Faith Fielder on the lake shore at sunset. Force them to face the island and live the killer's nightmare.

"Yet he didn't abduct Dorney," Ketchum adds, batting away a fly. "He shut her up."

"Exactly. It's not a break in the pattern. Doll Face murdered Kashana Dorney because she's the only person in Veil Lake who can identify him."

She turns when Iglesias's shadow passes over her.

"Will either of you explain why Detective Haines camped outside Kashana Dorney's house? He doesn't work for the VLPD and shouldn't be in the field. Was this your decision, Agent Ketchum?"

Darcy looks over the chief's shoulder. Nix opens his mouth, intending to throw himself on the sword.

"It was my decision," says Darcy.

"Your decision? You're not even full time FBI. Who gave you jurisdiction to place off-duty officers from other departments in the field?"

"Julian wasn't on official duty."

"But now he's my problem."

Nix forces himself between Iglesias and Darcy and draws an icy glare from the chief.

"We need to stay focused. The lady next door didn't hear any commotion, but she claims a silver minivan backed out of Kashana Dorney's driveway an hour ago and headed north."

"She didn't get the license plate number?" asks Ketchum.

"No. She had no reason to believe anything out of the ordinary had occurred."

"That scumbag, O'Grady," Iglesias says. "And we let him walk."

"You said yourself you couldn't hold him," says Darcy. "But none of the evidence adds up."

"How do you figure?"

"O'Grady drives a blue Chevy Cobalt, not a silver minivan. And how did he take pictures of the van, if he was behind the wheel?"

"Are you suggesting I have two psychopaths running around Veil Lake on the busiest weekend of the summer? I don't give a shit about FBI theories. I want O'Grady found. Now."

Iglesias shoves Nix aside and barks orders at the female crime scene investigator working in the backyard.

Darcy glares at the parked rental. Where are you, Julian?

35

Julian raises his head and regrets it. It feels as if someone clubbed him with a hammer. Eyes drifting open, he takes in his surroundings. He's inside a cabin, arms and feet bound to a chair. A bed stands three paces away. A desk beside the wall holds a textbook and two folders choked with photographs.

What happened?

He recalls standing beside Kashana Dorney's garage and noticing the silver minivan inside. Did he radio headquarters about the minivan? Interrogating his memory makes his head spin. Blood cakes his nose and drenches his shirt. The killer beat him, though Julian has no memory of the attack.

Something obstructs his vision. He stares around the room through two holes, feels the cold porcelain mask pressed against his face. An elastic band wraps around his head and holds the mask in place. Two bobs of the head slide the band off his ears. The mask falls off his face and shatters on the floor.

Tugging at the zip tie, he notices the chair back rattling. If he can generate enough force, he should be able to break the chair back and free his arms. That won't be easy. The zip ties around his ankles and wrists make it impossible to stand. While he struggles, a floorboard creaks outside the bedroom door. He stops and listens. When the noise comes again, he closes his eyes and drops his head to his chest. Make his abductor believe he's unconscious, then throw his shoulder into the killer's belly when he least suspects an attack.

The door slides open. A puff of fresh air touches his face and awakens his senses. Something unexpected is happening. He squints one eye open and finds a girl standing in the doorway. Dust motes sparkle. Now he lifts his head and opens both eyes. She edges the door shut behind her and pops the lock in place.

"Who are you?" she asks, her mouth quivering.

He swallows to wet his throat. Tastes copper.

"My name is Julian Haines. I'm a police officer."

"A policeman? Thank goodness."

He grits his teeth and wipes his bloody mouth on his shoulder.

"We're looking for you, Faith. Everyone in the village is."

Faith touches her lips.

"You know my name."

"I do.Where is he? Where's the Doll Face Killer?"

She frowns.

"What are you talking about?"

"The man who kidnapped us and locked us inside the cabin. Do you know his name?"

"He told me his name is Mr. Filmore, that we met during college orientation. But I don't believe him. He's an awful person, and I think he killed people."

She glances behind her as if expecting the murderer to crash through the door. A distant, frustrated grunt tells Julian the Doll Face Killer is outside the cabin.

.   .   .

"He forces me to look at pictures. Famous serial killers, murder scenes. Some pictures are from Veil Lake. I recognize the island in the water."

Julian's eyes narrow. Darcy was right about the island. The son-of-a-bitch even photographed it.

"Where is he now?"

Faith crosses the room and parts the curtain.

"He's in the heather."

"The heather?"

"His garden. It's all he cares about. If you could see him now, his clothes are drenched with sweat, and his face looks like a big red beet. He needs to rest, but he won't stop working."

With any luck, the Doll Face Killer will give himself a heart attack.

"Faith, you need to break the zip ties and get me out of this chair. Can you do that?"

Faith circles back to Julian, assesses his bindings, and gives an uncertain nod.

"You can't break the ties with your hands," Julian says, tugging his wrists as a way of demonstration. "They're too strong. You'll need a knife or a pair of wire cutters. Can you find either of those things and bring them to me?"

Another cry from the garden. The man who calls himself Glen Filmore sounds unhinged.

"He'll catch me if I try."

"Sounds like he's preoccupied. This is our best chance."

She shifts her feet.

"I'll try. Oh, I almost forgot. I have his keys."

"The keys to his minivan?"

"The keys to the gate," Faith says, bobbing her head. "He built a fence around the cabin. It's too tall for me to climb over, but you could probably make it. The key unlocks the gate. I stole the key chain while he dragged you into the house. Then I hid them in the garden. He's looking for the keys, but he doesn't know I took them."

"Outstanding work, Faith. Listen, if he gives you the chance, you open that gate and run. The police and FBI are searching for you. Find your way back to the village, and contact the Veil Lake Police Department. Ask for Officer Nix, Agent Ketchum, or Agent Haines. They'll take care of you."

"I can't leave you here. It wouldn't be right."

The Doll Face Killer curses outside the window. He's close now. If he peeks inside and sees Faith...

"Go now. Before he loses interest in the garden and comes looking for you." When she unlocks the door, his voice stops her in the entryway. "Faith, do you have a phone?"

"He took mine away and promised to return it after I finished my studies."

Her studies?

"Never mind. Get me out of this chair, and I swear I'll bring you back to your parents before nightfall."

Faith bites her lip and closes the door.

As Julian tests the zip ties for a weak point, her footsteps move through the house. A wheelbarrow squeaks around the cabin, circling toward the front door. Hurry, Faith. A drawer opens and closes. Then another.

"Why aren't you working in the garden?"

The killer's voice echoes down the hallway. A loud slap follows the shout, then Faith sobs. Julian's head drops to his chest. If the Doll Face Killer caught Faith searching for a tool to break the zip ties, he'll hurt the girl.

"Don't hit me anymore."

Another slap.

"You deserve this, you filthy boy."

The killer's voice sends chills through Julian. It's shrill, a woman's voice. Almost enough to convince him there's a second person inside the cabin. Did he refer to Faith as a boy? White-hot rage washes away the chill. He'll kill Doll Face with his bare hands for striking Faith.

The shouting continues before the killer demands Faith labor in the garden. The front door slams, shaking the cabin walls.

Silence fills the cabin. Faith did her best. Now he must escape on his own.

As Julian sighs, a steak knife slides beneath the threshold and stops beneath his feet. Good girl, Faith.

36

How long have they driven around Veil Lake? Darcy reads the time and bites a nail. Less than three hours until sunset, and the only person who saw the Doll Face Killer lies in the county morgue. Ketchum turns the SUV down a cul-de-sac that resembles every side street they've investigated over the last two hours. They can't locate a silver minivan matching the vehicle in Phillip O'Grady's pictures.

She drums her legs, reads over her notes, and slaps the folder shut.

"You're making yourself crazy," says Ketchum, taking the folder off her lap and jamming it into the center compartment.

"This is my fault. I'm not the profiler I was during the Rivers case. I should have found Doll Face by now."

"Stop. Your profile is dead on. You gave the VLPD everything they needed. It's up to them to dig up a clue for once."

That won't happen. Iglesias has the department walking on eggshells, afraid to take a risk. She's resigned to handle the case on her own. Ketchum's radio comes alive. It's Officer Cross, and his voice rings with excitement.

"We found the bastard."

Ketchum pulls the SUV to a stop in front of a white Cape Cod with a brick driveway and grabs the radio. The woman in front of the house narrows her eyes at the SUV, settles on Ketchum, and hurries inside. No one trusts a stranger these days.

"You know who Doll Face is?"

"Richard Oswalt. CSI pulled his print off the brochure. Get this. There was a boating accident off the island in Veil Lake. Mason Oswalt drowned after his boat struck the rocks during a severe thunderstorm. He left behind a wife, Genevieve, and a son, Richard. I searched the archives like Agent Haines suggested. The reason it took so long is the accident took place in 1989, not between 1990 and 2000. Once I expanded the search, I found the case."

"That has to be him," Darcy says, leaning over the console so Cross can hear her.

"Sounds like it was horrible for the wife and kid. The search crews found the boat, but it took days before they fished Mason Oswalt out of the lake."

"Let me guess. Three days."

"Correct. I asked the vets around the station if they recalled the accident. Iglesias remembers. He was a beat cop then. Says Genevieve blamed the village because no one helped. My guess is nobody saw the accident in the storm. Veil Lake isn't a callous place. We help our neighbors during times of trouble."

"What about the mother?" asks Darcy. "Is she still alive?"

"Negative. Genevieve Oswalt passed nine weeks ago."

"There's your stressor," Darcy says to Ketchum. He nods in agreement.

Cross sets the radio aside and speaks to another officer.

"I'm sending you two pictures," Cross says, returning. "The

sketch artist's rendition of the man Kashana Dorney spotted at the pay phone, and Richard Oswalt's driver's license. And I'll save you from asking your next question. Richard Oswalt drives a silver 2010 Dodge Caravan. According to Iglesias, there were rumors of abuse. Child services paid the Oswalts a visit, but they never found abuse, and Richard continued to live with his mother."

"What have we learned about Richard Oswalt?"

"He's well thought of around the village. Soft spoken. He's a botanist at the community college."

A botanist? Darcy wouldn't have pegged a serial killer as a botanist, but his work at the community college might have led to connections with North Chadwick University. She wouldn't be surprised to learn he crossed paths with the real Glen Filmore. Ketchum's phone hums when the photographs finish downloading. Pausing the conversation, he opens the sketch artist's picture and compares it with Oswalt's driver's license. It's him. There's no mistaking the resemblance. Kashana Dorney led them to the Doll Face Killer.

"Give us the address," Ketchum says.

"Fourteen Crestview Hill. But you're not to approach the house. Chief Iglesias is running the show and putting together the siege team. As soon as we get the warrant, we'll go in together."

Ketchum ends the call and slams the radio into the cup holder.

"Iglesias wants to be the bull in the pasture. In the meantime, the sun is halfway to the tree line."

"Crestview Hill is only four miles from us," Darcy says, checking the map on her phone. "If we cut across Pine Ridge—"

"You know I can't do that," Ketchum says, reversing the SUV. "I'm not happy about the situation. But a coordinated plan of attack gives us our best chance to bring Faith and Julian out alive."

As Ketchum races back to the station, Darcy feels tempted to shove the door open, leap from the moving vehicle, and break into Oswalt's residence on her own. She can't lose Julian.

37

Darkness seeps into the bedroom, close enough to touch Julian's ankles. His head swims from the beating the Doll Face Killer gave him while he was unconscious, and sweat stings his eyes as he shifts the chair. The knife lies at his feet. Little good it does him. If he could free his legs, he could clamp his feet against the knife and lift it into his lap. Then what? His wrists remain bound behind his back. There has to be a way to use the knife to cut away the zip ties.

The Doll Face Killer raves inside the cabin. Twice he approached the bedroom door. Julian dropped his head and feigned sleep when the killer poked his head inside. Both times he covered the steak knife with his shoe.

"Prepare yourself, Faith," the killer says in the hallway. "We leave for the water at sunset. Then you will see."

Julian tugs his wrists until his arms tremble. He's out of time. In a moment, the madman will transport Julian and Faith to the lake and force them to face the island. No, he won't let the girl die.

An idea occurs to him. A desperate measure to give Faith a chance to run, even if it means sacrificing himself. He slides the chair forward, careful to make as little noise as possible. With the knife behind him now, he swings his body left and right, building up enough momentum to fall over. The chair legs fight him, as if the damn furniture conspires with the killer. Finally, the chair topples over. His shoulder takes the brunt of the fall, shooting pain down his arm. Holding his breath, he expects the murderer to break through the door. But he's distracted and screaming at the girl about the keys.

Straining against the zip ties, Julian's fingers search for the knife. Where the hell is it? His hands brush over the rough floorboards until his pinkie clinks against the hilt. Scooting the chair backward, he shifts his body until he reaches the knife. He grasps it in one hand, temporary victory achieved. If the killer comes for him, he'll have a weapon to defend himself with. Three times he fumbles the knife before he's able to slip the blade into his back pocket. The hilt sticks out of his pocket, visible should the killer turn him over.

Julian closes his eyes. Catches his breath. He hopes Faith takes advantage of his distraction, unlocks the gate, and flees while she has the chance.

A shadow drifts across the room. Julian swings his head around and spots a face in the bedroom window. It ducks below the sill before he can identify the person. Maybe the police are here. All the more reason to pull the murderer's attention to the bedroom.

Lifting his legs, Julian slams the chair against the floor. He can't generate enough force to break the chair, but he's causing enough racket to scatter birds from the trees outside his window.

"Hey, let me out of here!"

Julian keeps shouting and smashing the chair until the door flies open. A tall man with a long face stares down at him. He looks more like a scientist than a serial killer. It's the eyes that open a window to his madness.

"Shut up, or I'll tear your throat out and feed it to the girl."

Julian hoists his legs higher, wrenching his back. The chair bashes against the floor.

"I'm a police officer. Don't you realize the entire force will come after you, if you harm me? Let me go, and I promise the courts will show lenience."

The Doll Face Killer glares at him, red faced. A vein pulses in his neck. Then his lips curl into a grin, and he leans his head back and laughs at the ceiling.

"You're a funny man, Officer. It's a shame I need to—"

A thump against the cabin pulls the murderer's eyes to the window. Someone is outside.

"It appears we have a visitor," Doll Face says, stepping over Julian, who covers the knife hilt with his hands.

"Don't leave me here. If the police are outside, let me go. I'll negotiate on your behalf."

"It's not the police," Doll Face says, standing beside the window.

The murderer's eyes light with fear.

"Is that you, Mother?"

The Doll Face Killer leaps over Julian's prone body. He has just enough strength to lift the chair and trip the murderer. The man's feet fly out from under him a moment before his body slaps against the bare floor, the murderer's knees slamming down on the chair legs.

Moaning, the killer drags himself up. He leans in the doorway until air fills his lungs. As Julian struggles to pull the zip ties apart, he realizes the chair back snapped during impact.

"No need to wait for sunset. I'll kill both of you now."

The Doll Face Killer draws a knife from his pocket and stalks toward Julian.

38

FRIDAY, JULY 4TH 7:35 P.M.

The setting sun bleeds deep reds over the land, curling around the ridges and reflecting off the water. Iglesias and a team of five officers park behind a tree grove at the base of Crestview Hill. Agent Ketchum tightens the Velcro straps to his Kevlar vest and checks his weapon. Darcy dons an FBI vest that feels a size too large and unwieldy.

"You remember the plan," Ketchum says. "Stay with the vehicle and let us handle the extraction."

"That's Julian in there," Darcy says, lifting her chin toward a shadowed cabin above the tree line.

"All the more reason for you to stay with the vehicle. You're too emotional, Darcy. Besides, we had an agreement. Your rules, remember?"

Darcy chews the inside of her cheek. True, she forced Ketchum to promise her she wouldn't risk her life in the field. But the stakes grew. She wants to get Faith and Julian out of that cabin, and she doubts Iglesias's instincts.

"This isn't up for discussion," Ketchum says, fixing her with a hard stare. "Wait with the vehicle."

Lightning flashes over the ridge as a cool breeze snakes

down the hillside. Darcy looks over Chief Iglesias's shoulder. His tablet displays a satellite photograph of Richard Oswalt's property. A tall, wooden fence circles the cabin. Plants she doesn't recognize sprout from the earth like a vigilant army. For unknown reasons, the plants send a chill through Darcy. Narulla appears barely old enough to hold a driver's license. His head pokes above the vest as his eyes dart between the tablet and the spreading shadows. Something skitters through the bushes, probably a raccoon, and Narulla draws a breath.

"We'll position my men here," Iglesias says, pointing toward the gate entrance. He eyes Ketchum. "You take Narulla and Cross around the side. The drop off behind the cabin is too steep for Oswalt to make a run for it."

"You need to go in quiet," Darcy says with a warning in her glare. "He'll kill Faith and Julian, if he hears you coming."

"There's no time for subtle approaches. We go in fast and take him down before he hurts anyone."

Darcy starts to argue and stops when Ketchum shakes his head behind Iglesias. Ketchum doesn't agree with the chief's tactics, but nothing they say will change the man's mind. Better to execute his plan to the best of their abilities.

Putting the tablet aside, Iglesias and Ketchum lead their teams through the trees. Before the forest swallows the officers, Narulla looks over his shoulder at Darcy. She reads his fear. He's never done anything like this. None of them have, including Iglesias.

Then she can't see or hear them anymore. Waiting inside Ketchum's SUV, Darcy sets her radio in her lap and scrubs her hands across her face. The light fades, the forest darkening around her. Turning the radio volume higher, she jumps when the chief's voice comes through. They're closing in on the property. Another four minutes until they're in position.

Darcy leans her head back and closes her eyes. Prays Iglesias knows what he's doing.

Overcome by anxiousness, she snatches the radio and leaps out of the SUV. She wears a groove in the soil as she paces from the vehicle to the woods and back. Thunder brings her head up. The sky over Veil Lake appears ready to burst. Crickets shrill through the grass, the sound of peepers ringing off a pond. As she leans against the rear bumper of the SUV, her eyes stop on a splash of blue hidden behind the trees further down the ridge. It's a blue Chevy Cobalt. Phillip O'Grady's car.

She raises Ketchum on the radio. An unexpected danger hides in the forest.

39

A crash inside Mr. Filmore's bedroom stops Faith in the kitchen entryway. She'd sneaked inside the kitchen for another knife, worried the madman stormed into the bedroom to kill Julian. Now she hears them fighting down the hall. She's torn between helping Julian and running while she has the chance. When she peeks her head into the hallway, a shadow grows against the wall. A heavy grunt as one man climbs to his feet.

She backs toward the front door when Julian staggers out of the bedroom and slumps down in the hallway. Somehow, he freed himself. Where is Mr. Filmore? Julian's eyes shift to Faith in the doorway.

"Run," he growls.

Faith turns to leave as the killer lunges out of the bedroom and wraps his hands around Julian's throat. Screaming, Faith bolts into the humid night and stumbles through the garden. A sudden wind gust whips her hair across her face. Trees above the fence dance and sway, their limbs making cracking noises as a rain drop plunks the back of her neck.

A heather plant reaches out and grabs Faith's ankle. She

yells as the wind whips the plants into a frenzy. Just her imagination playing tricks on her. Don't panic.

Another yell from inside the house gets her moving. If Mr. Filmore killed Julian, she'll be next. The locked gate blocks her passage at the end of the row. Dropping onto all fours, she paws at the dirt, searching for Filmore's keys. They were here. Swiping the dirt away from the roots, she digs deeper, utters a frustrated moan.

Taunts assault her from the back of her mind. Unwanted memories of a cruel childhood when the mean kids in class called her stupid for being different. Maybe they were right. All she needs to do is dig the keys out of the ground and escape. But she can't find them. Can't recall where she buried the keys.

The wind topples her when she rises. Back on all fours, she crawls beneath the building storm. Every time the heather slaps against her, she fears it's the killer's hand snatching her out of the darkness. He murdered Julian. She senses it.

Her frantic eyes stop on a heather plant towering above the others. A mound rises at its base with a torn leaf to mark the lump. The keys. Now she remembers.

Faith dives at the plant as thunder peels across the sky. The rain falls harder, soaking her to the bone. She claws at the dirt, panics when she doesn't locate her quarry. Digging deeper, her fingers close over the key ring. Thank God.

She lowers her shoulder against the storm and struggles toward the gate. Maniacal screams follow her from the house.

40

Ketchum parts the flora masking the edge of the trees and points his binoculars at the cabin. One light shines at the front of the residence, the other rooms black as night. His team members, Narulla and Cross, flank him, their bodies at one with the black belly of the forest.

Keeping the volume low on his radio, Ketchum grits his teeth when Iglesias announces he's in position outside the front gate. Fool. Oswalt must have cameras covering all entry points. The madman is probably watching Iglesias's team approach the gate now. So much for the element of surprise.

A loud crash inside the house pulls Ketchum back to the cabin. It came from a room toward the back.

"You hear that?" Narulla whispers. "Sounds like a fight."

The rookie's eyes are twin moons in the night.

Ketchum nods and brings the radio to his lips when movement along the back corner of the cabin grabs his eye. He redirects the binoculars. Focuses. Shadows run deep along the back of Oswalt's home. Ketchum swore someone moved around the corner, but he doesn't see anyone now.

Narulla moves as if he means to pursue the intruder. Ketchum places a hand against the rookie's chest.

"I'll take the corner of the cabin," Ketchum whispers. "Cross, move along the other side. Narulla, watch our backs."

A protest forms on the rookie's face, but he doesn't fight the FBI agent. After Ketchum radios his intentions to Iglesias, he motions Cross forward. At the fence, Ketchum hoists himself over the barrier in one smooth motion. Landing on his feet, he's surprised when the older officer ascends the fence and drops feather-light to the grass. Ketchum's senses are on full alert now. Taking a quick peek at the roof as he angles toward the back corner, he spies a security camera. Shit.

Another thud rocks the cabin. When he places his ear against the wall, he hears a scuffle inside the room. Worried Julian is fighting Oswalt and losing the battle, he speaks into the radio. They need to move in while Oswalt is detained. No reply comes from Iglesias. Ketchum glances over his shoulder. Cross stares back at him in confusion. If Iglesias entered radio silence, he didn't inform the other team members.

Darcy's voice comes over the radio and warns them Phillip O'Grady parked his car in the woods at the bottom of Crestview Hill. Ketchum's eyes narrow in contemplation. Did *FM-Kill-Her* learn Oswalt's identity? That explains how the forum poster photographed the Doll Face Killer's minivan before the police knew Oswalt was the murderer. But is O'Grady here to document the Doll Face Killer or aid the psychopath?

"Iglesias."

Still no answer.

No time to figure out why Iglesias won't respond, Ketchum motions for Cross to go around the opposite side of the cabin. Crouching low, Ketchum spins around the corner and spots a window. The fight sounds grow louder. Ketchum's heart pounds inside his ears.

When he positions himself below the bedroom window, a horrible scream rises out of the forest. The sound of a man gutted. Narulla.

Scrambling back to the fence, Ketchum calls the rookie's name over the radio. No response. As he grabs the top of the fence and hoists himself over, he looks for Cross. Can't find him. It's as if the night swooped down and swallowed the team members. Gun raised, he edges toward the forest. Rain pelts his face and blurs his vision, the wind shoving him from each side as though he stumbles through an angry mob.

Pulling back the weeds and tall grass, Ketchum searches for Narulla. He's gone. Black speckles dot the leaves, a larger splash pooling at his feet. Blood. He can't find Narulla's body anywhere.

"Ketchum, I'm here."

Cross's voice. Ketchum fills Cross in on the scream from the edge of the forest. He hears the concern in Cross's voice. But they don't have time to search for the missing officer, and nobody knows where Iglesias is.

"There's a fight inside the cabin," Ketchum says. "I think Detective Haines escaped and attacked Oswalt. I'm going in."

When a girl cries out, Ketchum spins and searches the night. It came from outside the cabin. Somewhere inside the fence line.

He sprints toward the barrier, shielding his face from the storm. Throwing himself over the fence, he races past the window toward the front of the property.

When he turns the corner, his eyes whip around in confusion. A mass of strange plants choke the front of the cabin and stretch to the fence line, snagging his shoes. Rows extend in every direction. A psychopath's labyrinth.

He cups a hand over his eyes and searches for the girl. Rain lashes his face.

As he leaps the heather, a shovel crashes down on the top of his head. Ketchum's eyes roll back.

He drops to his knees as footsteps race past. The garden goes black.

41

Blood pours from Julian's nose and mouth as he crawls down the dark hallway. One light shines inside the kitchen, a beacon of false hope.

Floorboards groan as the Doll Face Killer stalks behind him. A boot to the ribs lifts Julian off the floor. When he lands on his side, the murderer falls on top of him.

"You can't have the magazine, Charlie," Oswalt says, his eyes crazed and lit like Christmas trees by the distant lamplight.

His voice wavers between male and female as though two souls wage war inside the man.

"After I finish with you, I'll fuck your mommy and make you watch. How would you like that, Charlie?"

Julian's head spins. Oswalt's weight pins him to the floor. The killer's fist lifts and bashes his face. Again and again. Julian wavers on the edge of consciousness. Oswalt means to beat him to death. But every second he focuses his hate on Julian, Oswalt loses a step on Faith. Hopefully, she retrieved the keys and fled this house of horrors.

Oswalt rises to his feet and looms over Julian, looking impossibly large in the failing light.

"Get up. I'll kill you for what you did to Daddy."

Though the Doll Face Killer is stronger than Julian expected, the detective doesn't doubt he'd best the man under different circumstances. The beatings left Julian weak and groggy, his arms rubbery and useless.

A boot to the face whips Julian's neck sideways. Blood splatters the hallway. The killer reaches down and grasps him by the shirt, hauling him up. Julian's knees buckle. Oswalt prevents him from falling and tosses Julian against the wall. The detective's eyes cross.

By now, Faith should be off the property and searching for a road back to civilization. A smile creeps across Julian's lips. She's free. Faith Fielder will survive and live her dream as a college student.

"What are you smiling about?" Oswalt's voice shifts to a woman's again. He bends low as Julian slumps against the wall. When Oswalt rises, he holds a knife in his hands. "You dirty, dirty boy. Mommy has a special punishment for you. I'll cut it off so you never look at whores again."

Julian bashes his head against Oswalt's. The killer staggers back and blinks. A cut opens along his brow and trickles red rain down his face. The murderer bellows and lunges across the hallway with the knife raised. Tapping the last of his strength reserves, fighting on pure adrenaline, Julian ducks the wild slice of the knife and barrels his shoulder into Oswalt's midsection. Momentum carries them across the corridor where Oswalt's back smashes against the wall.

Outside the cabin, lightning cuts a white hole in the sky. Rain pours off the roof and floods the open entryway.

Oswalt stabs Julian's shoulder. Gritting his teeth, Julian clasps his hand around Oswalt's wrist and squeezes until the psychopath releases the knife. The blade clangs against the floor as the two men struggle toward the living room. Oswalt wraps his hands around Julian's throat. Picturing Darcy and the kids, Julian refuses to close the book on his life. Not at this man's hands. He thrusts his arms between Oswalt's elbows and breaks the stranglehold. Before the killer can raise his hands in defense, Julian slams a fist against Oswalt's face and sends the killer reeling.

Julian blinks away the grogginess and braces an arm against the wall. Oswalt rises. He's too strong for Julian to overcome in his weakened state. As the killer leaps at Julian, a shape materializes in the darkness. Before Julian realizes the silhouette belongs to Faith, the girl swings the lamp base and strikes Oswalt. The Doll Face Killer clutches his head. He topples over the recliner and sprawls on the living room floor, eyes blinking in confusion as Julian leaps over the fallen piece of furniture.

"Get out of here, Faith!"

The girl wipes rain off her face.

"You helped me, so I helped you."

"It's not safe. Run for the road. Bring the police back to the cabin."

Faith's eyes shift between Julian and her stunned abductor.

"Go!"

Faith holds Julian's eyes for a moment before she turns and flees.

The Doll Face Killer crawls toward the open door, now banging against the cabin wall as the wind drives rain through the entryway. Before he reaches the exit, Julian grabs Oswalt by the ankle and drags him back into the living room. Julian registers the panic in Oswalt's eyes. The killer's plans are falling apart. Faith is free and running toward safety.

"You're not going anywhere," Julian yells over the wind.

A punch rocks Oswalt's head back and draws another gush

of blood from his nose. Grabbing the killer by his shirt, Julian hurls Oswalt across the living room, where he slams into the wall and crumples. Julian stalks toward the Doll Face Killer. The fallen knife ignites with light with each flash of lightning.

"You ruined everything," Oswalt says, spitting blood. "It was meant to be."

Throwing his gaze to the window when a shadow moves across the pane, Julian wonders if the police are here. He expects Darcy gave them the clues they needed to identify the Doll Face Killer and led them to the cabin in the woods. Oswalt raises a pleading hand. Julian slaps it aside and kicks Oswalt's chin. The killer's eyes cross as he gasps.

"Mother! Where are you? Mother!"

As the killer crawls down the hallway, Julian follows. Instead of retreating to the bedroom where he'd imprisoned Julian, the psychopath veers left and jiggles the handle on a locked door at the end of the hallway. Unable to unlock the door, the killer grasps the doorknob and pulls, cursing over the storm.

Julian stops in his tracks when the doorknob turns on its own. Lightning tears over the cabin.

"Mother, save me. Charlie's hurting me!"

The door bursts open. An elderly woman lunges across the threshold with a knife and plunges the blade into Julian's stomach. His eyes go wide. Stumbling across the hall, Julian feels his legs give out. The woman holds the dripping blade, a wicked smile on her lips. Julian covers the wound with one hand and pushes against the floor with the other.

Oswalt stares with wide-eyed wonder at the old woman.

"I knew you wouldn't abandon me," Oswalt says, laughing as joyful tears spill from his eyes.

The woman pulls the gray haired wig from her head and lets the nightgown fall to the floor. It's not a woman at all, but a man. He grabs Oswalt by the arm and helps him to his feet.

"Who are you?" Oswalt asks.

His mouth hangs open.

"Your truest fan," Phillip O'Grady says a moment before Julian's eyes flutter shut.

42

Darcy pounds the dashboard and glares at the radio. Neither Ketchum nor Iglesias has uttered a word since she warned them about Phillip O'Grady. If the police delayed the siege, she should have heard about it by now. Meanwhile, she's relegated to hiding inside Ketchum's SUV while a murderer holds her husband and Faith captive.

She decides. Darcy won't stay with the vehicle when the police need her help. Checking the Glock after removing it from her holster, Darcy slides the radio into her pocket and steps into the rain. Lightning flashes disorient her, steal her sight as the storm soaks her clothes. Already the dirt road turns slick with mud. A drainage creek along the road overflows and spills rushing water down the hill, reminding her of the flood she rescued Hunter from on the night Julian shot and killed the Full Moon Killer.

Shielding her eyes with her forearm, Darcy struggles against the wind and climbs the hill. Her shoes slip. She grabs hold of a tree branch and fights to stay upright.

The radio bursts with frantic yells. Somebody is attempting to make contact, but she can't make out the voice.

"Ketchum, did you call me?"

Nothing. Darcy shoves the radio into her pocket and fights through the storm. A yell pulls Darcy's attention to the trees. There, a hundred feet inside the forest. Eyeing the desolate road for movement, Darcy races for the forest and leaps the choked drainage ditch. Her foot plunges shin-deep into the water. The flood tries to tug her downstream before she grabs a tree trunk and hoists herself out of danger.

The yell comes again. This time Darcy recognizes the girl's scream. Faith escaped. Estimating the girl's position, Darcy pushes through the trees and angles across the hillside. The ground becomes a quagmire. It's as if she's pursuing Faith through a marsh.

"Faith? Come to my voice. I'm with the FBI."

Darcy pauses and catches her breath beneath a thick canopy. Listens. Faith yells out from below Darcy's position. From the sound of the girl's voice, Darcy fears Faith injured herself. She hurdles a fallen limb and stumbles down the hill-side. Losing balance when the ground becomes too slick, Darcy falls backward and slams against the hill. The breath rushes from her lungs. A branch snaps. They're not alone in the forest.

Darcy crawls to her feet and races toward Faith.

"Faith Fielder? Tell me where you are. I'm Agent Darcy Haines with the FBI. I'll keep you safe."

As Darcy dodges trees and bramble, she pictures Faith, lost in the woods after a killer held her captive for three days. The girl doesn't trust anyone. Why should she trust Darcy? Everyone let Faith down.

When she rounds a creek bed, Darcy spots Faith sprawled in a clearing, both hands clutching her ankle. Releasing a sigh, Darcy rushes to the girl's side. Faith throws her hands up in defense.

"It's all right, Faith. I'm an FBI agent. I've been looking for you."

Faith glares at Darcy. Displaying her temporary badge and ID, Darcy waits until Faith lowers her hands.

"Are the police here? The man at the cabin made me promise to find the police and bring them to the cabin."

Darcy touches Faith's shoulder.

"Who was the man, Faith? Was his name Julian?"

The girl nods. Darcy closes her eyes and touches her speeding heart. Thank God, Julian is alive. But why haven't Ketchum, Iglesias, or the other members of the siege team answered her calls? They must have the Doll Face Killer in custody by now, since Julian broke free and Faith escaped. Who is following them through the forest?

Footsteps move through the darkness. Just up the hill. Darcy shifts in front of Faith and grips the Glock-22, aiming it toward an enemy she can't see.

43

The storm huffs against his face. Rain drops plunk his skin and rouse him awake.

Agent Ketchum tries to sit up and grabs the back of his head. Agony throbs from his skull to his shoulders, the strange garden spinning around him as he leans over and vomits. Wiping his lips, he remembers rounding the cabin in search of Faith Fielder when someone came out of the night and slammed him in the back of his head. The metallic clang of the weapon convinces Ketchum his assailant struck him with a shovel. He gropes inside his pocket and finds it empty. The FBI agent spots the radio beneath a plant inches away. Pulling the radio out of the mud, he's surprised to find his weapon on his hip. The man who knocked Ketchum unconscious must have assumed he'd killed the agent.

Or he was in a rush.

Worrying the Doll Face Killer ran after Faith Fielder, Ketchum pushes himself into a crouch. His body protests. The spinning begins anew. He gives the vertigo a moment to pass before he struggles into a standing position. Off to the east, lightning strokes across the heavens. The sky lies black and low, ragged clouds churning over the cabin as rain continues to spit in his eye. He pushes aside the plants and finds an endless expanse of garden. No lettuce or chard or cucumbers. Only the bizarre jungle that seems to watch his every move.

Trudging through the jungle, he stumbles toward the open doorway. The living room appears as if a freight train rolled through its center. Two chairs lie on their sides, and the couch is shoved off the wall and into the middle of the room. A table lamp rolls past his feet. Directing the Glock across the overturned furniture, he steps through the gloom. To his left, he spies a kitchen. The drawers hang open, and two hollow slots in the knife rack suggest someone grabbed a couple of weapons.

A moan pulls his attention toward the hallway. Reaching for his flashlight, he realizes he lost it in the garden. At least he has his gun.

Senses on full alert, he slips around the corner and aims the Glock at a man sprawled at the end of the hallway. Both doors at the end of the corridor hang open, the door on the left groaning and creaking as it gyrates with the wind. Ketchum licks his lips and edges closer to the man.

"FBI. Show me your hands."

The man doesn't respond. His chest rises and falls in slow, ragged breaths.

Ketchum repeats his order and steps closer. Recognizing Detective Haines, he hurries to the man's side and sweeps the gun toward the open doorways.

"Julian, it's Agent Ketchum. Where are you injured? Are we alone in the cabin?"

The detective's eyes blink and flutter shut. One hand clutches his belly. Blood slicks his fingers. Ketchum speaks into the radio and requests an ambulance for an injured officer. He's relieved when dispatch answers. None of the siege team members reply.

"Have you heard from Chief Iglesias?" Ketchum asks the dispatcher.

"Nothing."

Ketchum bites off a curse and sets a hand on Julian's shoulder. Where is everyone?

"Help is on the way," he tells Julian.

The detective doesn't acknowledge Ketchum. Julian's breathing sounds worse as blood trickles off his lower lip.

"Ketchum? Are you with Julian?"

Recognizing Darcy's voice, Ketchum lifts the radio and peers into both open doorways. It's too dark to see the back walls. He feels exposed.

"I'm here, Darcy."

"What happened to Julian?"

Panic tinges the woman's voice. He doesn't want to tell her the truth, but she'll find out before long.

"Someone stabbed Julian. He's alive, Darcy, but he lost a lot of blood. An ambulance is on the way. I can't find Iglesias or any of the siege team. It's like they vanished off the face of the earth."

Silence.

"Darcy? You with me?"

The radio crackles.

"Someone is following us," Darcy replies. "I'm with Faith Fielder in the forest off Crestview Hill. She's alive, but I think she broke her ankle."

Ketchum's skin tingles. They're not alone in the cabin. Muddled memories come back to him. He'd heard Narulla scream a moment before the officer disappeared at the forest's edge. Darcy had warned them she'd spotted Phillip O'Grady's car hidden amid the trees. Two killers in the night.

Removing his soaked jacket, Ketchum folds it and presses the fabric against Julian's stomach. The detective's eyes open to slits, and one hand slips over the jacket to hold it in place.

Ketchum perceives a slight nod, a good sign. As long as Julian remains semiconscious, he has a fighting chance to survive. But the growing puddle of blood on the hallway floor warns Ketchum they're running short on time.

"Hold your position," Ketchum tells Darcy a split-second before a floorboard groans behind him.

Throwing himself in front of Detective Haines, Ketchum aims the Glock through the open doorway on the left side of the hallway. Darkness spills over the threshold. Enough gray light exists for Ketchum to make out a queen size bed with a feminine, flowery bed cover. Frilled drapes dance over an open window. An army of porcelain dolls watch him from the dresser.

"FBI. Put down your weapon and show yourself."

Ketchum swallows.

Haines lays a hand on Ketchum's back when the floor creaks again. Then a shriek pierces the agent's ears.

Phillip O'Grady lunges through the doorway with a knife in his hand. Ketchum squeezes off two shots. Both puncture the man's chest and throw him backward. O'Grady collapses over the threshold. His legs writhe as he grips his chest, growls escaping his throat.

Ketchum darts across the hallway. O'Grady picks up the knife and drops it. His hand trembles. Hate spills from the man's eyes as he stares up at Ketchum. Using his foot, Ketchum slides the knife into the hallway and holds O'Grady with the gun. The shots won't kill O'Grady immediately. He'll hang on for several minutes, requiring Ketchum to keep the gun on him while he attends to Detective Haines.

He radios dispatch and fills the officer in on O'Grady. As Ketchum questions why the ambulance is taking so long to arrive, he hears the siren screaming over the wind.

"They're coming now, Detective. Stay with me."

Julian's eyes close.

44

He's unstoppable. Nothing can stand in his way.

Richard Oswalt, the Doll Face Killer, a name teenagers will forever whisper about beside late night campfires, bounds through the doorway and into the garden. Now among the heather, strength and untapped energy surge through his body. His work isn't finished. Fate must be on his side, for she sent a man into his mother's bedroom to defend Richard.

Faith has a head start, but she's slow, and she doesn't know the woods like Richard does. Sniffing, he smells her beneath the rain. Blown by the storm, the heather leans toward the exit, pointing Richard toward Faith.

The knife clutched in his hand and the sweet taste of blood in his mouth, Richard smashes into the wheelbarrow and feels no pain. The obstacle spins and falls in his wake. How stupid he was for wanting to stop killing. He doesn't need Faith to save him. The village deserves its fate.

Unstoppable. Invincible. The Doll Face Killer will murder Faith beside the water and kill again and again.

Just as he reaches the open gate, a shape flies out of the night and blocks his path. Gun raised, the police officer shouts at him to stop. Richard leaps into the air, becomes weightless as though he grew wings. The officer's cap flies off as his eyes widen. Richard drives the knife into the man's throat. Leaves him dying in the mud and sputtering lifeblood.

Landing on his feet, Richard never breaks stride. He races through the entrance and past the van. A gunshot explodes. Fate diverts the bullet which whistles over his head and buries itself into a tree. More gunfire. Not running from the shooter, the Doll Face Killer bursts through a thorn bush and rushes the gunman. Having lost sight of the killer, the officer is unprepared when Richard bounds into view and buries the knife into his chest with a guttural scream.

Another enemy fallen, Richard breaks out of the trees and hits Crestview Hill running. Somewhere ahead, Faith yells out in pain after she stumbles.

Richard smiles.

"I'm coming, Faith."

45

Shivers wrack Darcy's body as she huddles beside Faith Fielder. The remnants of the storm drape a premature nightfall over the hills outside Veil Lake, every shadow a potential threat. She hasn't heard the man pursuing them for five minutes. But she senses eyes watching her every movement.

A moment earlier, an ambulance motored up the hill toward the cabin. Darcy bites back a sob and prays the medical team reached Julian in time. If Darcy loses Julian as she lost her first husband, Darcy won't be able to face life alone. Ketchum radioed Darcy to tell her he shot Phillip O'Grady inside the cabin. No sign of the Doll Face Killer. Now Darcy knows who follows her through the night.

Tears stream down Faith's cheeks. Darcy strokes the hair away from the girl's eyes and wraps an arm around Faith's shoulders. The girl trembles so much that Darcy fears she'll succumb to hypothermia.

"You'll be fine, Faith. I won't let anyone hurt you."

"He'll keep coming after me," Faith says through chattering teeth. "You can't stop him. He's the devil."

A branch snaps, bringing Darcy's head up. The Doll Face Killer is close. A hundred feet up the ridge.

"He's just a man," Darcy says. "His name is Richard Oswalt. Does that name mean anything to you?"

Faith shakes her head.

"He grew up in Veil Lake, just like you."

"Why does he want to kill me?"

"Because he's sick, and—"

Footsteps approach in the darkness. Darcy searches her surroundings as she hunkers beside Faith. As she aims the gun into the night, battling to keep her arms steady, the footsteps stop.

Faith opens her mouth. Darcy places a finger to her lips. Night sounds ring through the forest.

The roar comes without warning when the Doll Face Killer crashes out of the brush ten paces in front of Darcy.

She fires the Glock. The bullet strikes Oswalt's shoulder and spins him around.

He rights himself and lunges for Faith as the girl's screams deafen Darcy. Darcy squeezes the trigger.

The shot blasts through the Doll Face Killer's forehead. Blood splashes out the back of Oswalt's skull.

The blade falls from the killer's hands as he stands upright. The message he's been shot hasn't made it through his body. Finally, he collapses before Darcy and Faith. Mud splatters. Darcy kneels beside Oswalt with the gun trained on the killer. Checking his pulse, she finds it fluttering on death's edge. His chest stops moving.

"Grab my arm, Faith. Let's get you back to your parents."

46

FRIDAY, JULY 4TH 9:50 P.M.

Muddy water drenches Darcy's pants to her knees when the police hear her cries inside the thicket. Cross and Ketchum trudge through the swampy terrain and support Faith, who can't put weight on her ankle. Worry creases the girl's brow before Darcy tells her she's safe and can trust the men. Agent Ketchum hoists Faith into his arms and forces his way through the forest as Cross knocks aside limbs to clear a path. Darcy slogs beside him.

"Julian is at the hospital," Ketchum says. The pale coloration to the agent's face warns Darcy the news isn't good. "He lost a lot of blood and wasn't conscious when the medical team laid him on the stretcher. I'll take you to the hospital."

The knot in her chest is too tight for Darcy to answer. She thanks Ketchum with a glance and parts Faith's hair.

"You're such a brave girl," Darcy says, sniffling. "Looking at you, I can tell you helped Julian."

Faith's cheeks color.

"It was nothing. He saved me, so I came back to help him. Is he going to be all right?"

Darcy glances at Ketchum, who turns his head away.

An ambulance waits at the bottom of Crestview Hill when they break out of the forest. Ketchum's SUV rests beside the ambulance. Trembling in sodden clothing, Darcy can't wait until she's inside the vehicle with the heat blasting.

Darcy holds Faith's hand as the paramedics roll the gurney into the ambulance.

"You're in good hands, Faith. The police contacted your parents. They'll meet you at the hospital."

"Will you be there too?"

"Yes. I'll come to see you."

After the doors slam shut, Darcy watches the ambulance pull away. Somehow, being close to Faith strengthened her belief that Julian would pull through. She closes her eyes as an unexplainable warmth moves through her body, taking away the chill.

"Don't you leave me," Darcy says to the night. "We have so much left to do, so many dreams."

Blinking away a tear, Darcy accepts Ketchum's arm. During the drive to the hospital, the FBI agent avoids discussing what occurred inside Oswalt's property until Darcy coaxes the truth out of him. Together, O'Grady and Oswalt murdered three police officers. A fourth, Chief Iglesias, is in critical condition. Ketchum refused to go to the hospital until they located Darcy and Faith. He keeps clutching the back of his head.

Two news crews block the hospital entryway. A woman Darcy recognizes from the national news shoves a microphone in her face as Ketchum and Cross push through the mob.

"Is Richard Oswalt the Doll Face Killer? Did he target you because you captured the Full Moon Killer?"

They don't know about Phillip O'Grady. But they'll learn soon.

Though Ketchum requires medical attention, he accompanies Darcy to the emergency room check-in window and waits until a gray-haired doctor in a white lab coat briefs them.

"Your husband is in surgery and needs a blood transfusion."

"Please tell me Julian will make it."

"He's strong, Mrs. Haines. A fighter. The next two hours are critical. There's a worship center on the second floor."

The waiting room chairs are too uncomfortable to sit in. Despite Darcy's exhaustion, she paces the room with her arms folded over her chest as Ketchum sits with his head in his hands.

"Will you get your head checked? O'Grady slammed the back of your head with a shovel."

Ketchum rubs his eyes.

"You don't mind waiting alone? I won't be gone long."

The glare she gives him gets him moving. Then Darcy stands alone in the waiting room, one eye trained to the window, looking out on the parking lot. The throng of news vehicles tripled in the last thirty minutes. Tragedy attracts people like flies to carrion.

A woman with tattered clothes curls on the couch. It's after one in the morning when the gray-haired doctor returns. Darcy rises from her chair when the doctor pushes through the double doors.

"He did well in surgery," the doctor says, working a crick out of his neck. "Vital signs are better, but he hasn't regained consciousness."

"Can I see him?"

"Only for a minute. It's important Julian rest. We'll know more in the morning."

What does that mean? *We'll know more in the morning.*

Darcy follows the doctor down a series of corridors. He stops at a door and waits for the nurse to depart the room before motioning Darcy through. At first, Darcy fears the doctor led her to the wrong room. She hardly recognizes the man on the hospital bed. So frail. Tubes and wires cover Julian's body. A monitor beeps to the side, his vital signs streaming across the screens. It's too much for Darcy to swallow. She collapses into the bedside chair and sobs into her hands.

"I'll leave you with Mr. Haines," the doctor says on his way out the door.

Darcy's body wracks with tears. Why does tragedy follow Darcy and her family? Regrets fly through her mind. At any point, she could have refused the case and stayed in Genoa Cove with Julian, Hunter, and Jennifer. When Julian arrived in Veil Lake, she should have sent him home, ordered him to stay away from the case and chastised him for protecting her. Doing so might have caused an argument, but it would have kept Julian safe. And why didn't she stop him when he offered to guard Kashana Dorney's house?

This is her fault. All of it.

When her eyes clear, she pushes herself up and stands beside her husband. The monitors provide the only evidence he's alive. When she lays a hand on his arm, careful not to disturb the wires, his skin feels cool to the touch.

"I'm sorry I did this to us, Julian." Darcy wipes her nose on a tissue. "You're a hero. Faith Fielder got away. She's upstairs with her family, and she wants to see you when you're ready."

She cries again when the nurse touches her shoulder. Darcy didn't hear the woman come into the room.

"Let him rest," the woman says as she leads Darcy out of the room.

They all look at her as she slogs past the nurse's station. She senses their eyes until she rounds the corner. The same nurse brings her to a different waiting room, this one closer to Julian.

She sits Darcy on the couch and offers her coffee and a pastry. Unable to stomach food, Darcy refuses.

Rubbing the chill off her arms, Darcy doesn't notice herself slipping into sleep.

47

SATURDAY, JULY 5TH 5:20 A.M.

Darcy stumbles down empty hospital corridors and past vacated stations as Julian calls her from somewhere inside the building. Every turn takes her further away from his voice.

She sprints past a patient's room and freezes. A man she recognizes lies on the cot. Darcy walks back to the room and leans in the doorway, her mouth hanging open. Tyler, her late husband, opens his eyes as though emerging from a restful sleep.

"Tyler?"

"It really is you. I miss you and the kids, Darcy."

Darcy hitches and clutches her chest.

"How are Jennifer and Hunter?"

"They're well. Hunter looks more like you every day, and Jennifer—"

"She doesn't remember me, does she?"

A tear trickles down Darcy's face.

"A part of her remembers. You're her daddy. You'll always be..."

"Don't let him go," Tyler says.

"What?"

"You know who I'm talking about." Tyler makes to rise from the bed, then grabs his forehead and falls back. "Don't feel guilty. I loved you from the day we met. That will never change. All I wanted was for you and the kids to be happy, and they love him as much as you do."

"I still love you, Tyler. I miss you so much."

His eyes redden with sadness.

"Go find him. There's still time."

"I can't say goodbye to you again."

"You must. Besides, I'm always with you."

Darcy wipes her eyes. When she looks up, the room is empty.

"No, Tyler. Don't go."

Julian's voice brings her head around. Somewhere on this floor. But where?

Darcy runs past the rooms, her shoes slipping on the slick floor when she turns corners. She blasts through doors, cuts across lobbies, Julian's calls always just beyond reach. When she pushes through another set of double doors, she pulls up.

There's a pulsing, blinding light at the end of the corridor. He's somewhere near the light, calling goodbye to her and promising he'll wait until the day she joins him.

"No, Julian. It's not time yet."

Darcy hurtles toward the light. It caresses her skin with an odd electrical current.

"Where are you, Julian?"

$\sim$

THE HAND on her shoulder shakes her awake. Darcy struggles to her feet as Ketchum grabs hold of her.

"It's okay, Darcy. You were yelling in your sleep."

Darcy blinks. Gray light washes over the window, the parking lot blanketed by fog.

"Where's Julian?"

"He's in his room. You can see him after you speak with the doctor."

"No, I need to see Julian immediately."

Darcy pushes past Ketchum before he can stop her. As she hurries down the antiseptic hallway, she's carried back to her dream. The hospital appears identical, except now it bustles with activity, nurses and doctors passing each other in the corridor. She skids to a stop outside Julian's room and expects to find his eyes open. They're not. He hasn't changed position since she last saw him, the wires and tubes taking away a part of his humanity.

Darcy breaks down and cries into the crook of her arm. Ketchum sets a hand on her shoulder and leads her away.

"I know it doesn't look like it, but he's doing better," he says, an arm wrapped around Darcy as they make their way toward the stairwell. "After they released me, I snooped around and overheard the doctors talking. Julian keeps overcoming the odds. He won't let go."

He hands her a cup of coffee. This time she accepts the warm drink. Still wearing damp, mud-covered pants, she can't escape the cold rushing through her veins. After she sips from the cup, Ketchum leads her to the cafeteria where he purchases Darcy a bagel with cream cheese. The cafeteria smells like eggs and bacon, but Darcy can't stomach heavy food and can't imagine ever wanting breakfast again. Not until her world stops spinning off its axis.

At a table near the back of the cafeteria, Darcy watches people shuffle to their tables with trays of food. Some hold hope in their eyes. Others appear lost. They received bad news this morning, and their lives will never be the same. When Ketchum rubs his temple, shame washes over Darcy.

"I'm sorry for not asking. How's your head?"

Ketchum shrugs.

"The doctor says it might be a concussion, but it's minor if it is." He taps the back of his head with his knuckles. "My father always said I was hard-headed. For once, it worked in my favor."

A laugh forms in Darcy's chest, but worry weighs it down.

"What's the latest on Iglesias?"

"He's awake and barking at the nurses. Say what you will about his leadership ability last night, but he's a beast. Doctor expects him to leave later this morning." Ketchum cups a secretive palm over his mouth. "I'm sure they can't wait to push his ass out of their hospital."

Darcy chuckles for the first time in days. A pound of stress falls off her heart.

"Do you recall who hit you?"

Ketchum shakes his head.

"Could have been Oswalt or O'Grady."

"I can't believe the Doll Face Killer worked with a partner. That doesn't fit the profile."

"He didn't. As we suggested, O'Grady figured out who Oswalt was before the police had. The crazy bastard followed Oswalt around, even took pictures of the van."

"But he didn't upload the pictures to the message board forum."

"Because he worshiped the Doll Face Killer and didn't want to blow his cover. Still, he would have shared the pictures once the cat was out of the bag. He'd be an Internet hero for capturing a famous serial killer on the hunt."

Darcy takes a bite from her bagel.

"But it wasn't enough. Given time to develop, Phillip

O'Grady would have become a serial killer. He interjected himself and aided Richard Oswalt."

"He did, and from what I can gather, the Doll Face Killer didn't expect the aid and had no relationship with *FM-Kill-Her*. But together, they murdered almost every member of the siege team." Ketchum stares at the table and brushes a hand through his hair. "Dammit. I should have seen this coming."

"You couldn't have known O'Grady would—"

Darcy stops when the doctor she met last night turns inside the cafeteria, searching the tables with alarm on his face. Darcy stands. Ketchum, sitting with his back to the door, glances over his shoulder. Noticing them, the doctor motions Darcy to the door. Her stomach drops out from under her. Each step through the cafeteria makes her feel like she's still inside the woods, struggling through swamp and mud. How long has the doctor been here? Is he working the overnight shift, or did he return at the break of dawn to treat Julian? When Darcy reaches the doctor, Ketchum stands beside her, a supporting hand on her back. From the corner of her eye, she sees her former partner and friend, Eric Hensel. Hensel died trying to save Darcy and her children from the Full Moon Killer when a tornado struck the forest. The illusion wavers, and it's Agent Ketchum beside her again.

Then the doctor's face relaxes.

"Julian is awake. He wants to see you."

48

Sunlight through the open blinds forms a halo around Julian's head. Already, he looks stronger, less frail. His tired eyes hold clarity, and he can't stop smiling at the woman beside his bed. Darcy holds his hand, unwilling to let go. She wants to tell him about her dream, and strangely, Darcy wonders if Julian already knows.

"How's Faith?" Julian asks, his voice parched and little more than a whisper.

Darcy turns back to Ketchum, who watches from the doorway. She's been wondering about the girl too.

"The Fielders took their daughter home at three in the morning once the police heard her side of the story. The abduction went down as you theorized. Oswalt posed as Glen Filmore from North Chadwick and phoned Faith at the restaurant. He couldn't talk Faith into the van without the fake audio. After he recorded Zoe Fielder's voice, he rearranged the sentences and made it sound as if Zoe gave her daughter permission to ride with Filmore...or Oswalt."

"He didn't hurt Faith, did he?" Darcy asks, swallowing the lump in her throat.

"Not at first. According to Faith, Oswalt was kind to her initially. He told Faith how proud he was of her accomplishments, built up her confidence. Then he forced her to research serial killers and view photographs from murder scenes."

Julian shakes his head.

"Why would he make her do something so horrible?"

"Oswalt tasked Faith with determining why the serial killers stopped murdering people. Faith told Oswalt they never stopped on their own. The police captured the killers."

Darcy touches her mouth.

"Oswalt wanted to stop."

Ketchum nods.

"After Faith failed him, Oswalt escalated. He would have murdered Faith beside the lake had Julian not intervened and saved her."

Julian's eyes clamp shut.

"Faith saved herself," Julian says, clearing his throat. "She was the one who retrieved the knife while Oswalt berated her. I wouldn't have escaped without her aid. And she came back when Oswalt had me dead to rights AND slammed the psychopath in the head with a lamp."

Ketchum eases into the room and slides into another chair beside Julian's bed. Sitting forward with his elbows on his knees, the FBI agent holds Julian's eyes.

"What role did Phillip O'Grady play last night? Did he do this to you?"

Julian looks toward the window.

"O'Grady is the one who stabbed me. It was my fault. I had the situation under control, but I let my anger get the best of me. Had I tied Oswalt up and left him for the police instead of attempting to beat the life out of him, O'Grady wouldn't have taken me by surprise." Julian's monitor beeps faster. "He dressed himself as Oswalt's mother and hid inside her bedroom."

Darcy's heart races as she pictures the horror unfolding. The crazed eyes of Phillip O'Grady. The madman throwing himself at Julian to save the Doll Face Killer.

A male nurse holding a clipboard struts into the room with the doctor on his heels.

"Sorry, but everyone needs to leave the room," the doctor says. "Mr. Haines needs his rest."

Variegated oranges and purples color the sky over Genoa Cove. Tonight is the first night Julian finds the strength to sit beside the water. Darcy drives the Prius to the neighborhood pathway near the cove and parks in a neighbor's driveway to avoid the inevitable ticket for leaving her car close to the beach, She carries two chairs under her arms to the shore. Then she returns for Julian and connects her elbow with his. He shuffles like a man sixty years older, battling through the sand as Darcy urges him to take it slow. Beside the water, they sit with their bare feet in the tide, the salty ocean washing around the chairs. The illusion makes Darcy feel adrift at sea.

"We're two peas in a pod," she says.

"I always thought so, but it sounds like you have a new reason."

"We've both survived stab wounds from serial killers. Yes, O'Grady counts."

"And we both watch too much Netflix."

The waves cover their laughter.

"I made a full recovery, Julian. Give it time."

The water reflects the sky's endless colors as night creeps up from the eastern horizon. For a long time, they let the calming waves take their troubles away. In the gloaming, Julian speaks.

"The city is paying me for the next two weeks, but they're forcing me to take unpaid leave after that. The union fought them on it. But I don't have a leg to stand on. My injuries didn't occur in the line of duty, and the city won't pay me to recover at home."

"That's bullshit. You saved a girl's life. They should take that into account."

"Maybe if Iglesias hadn't thrown me under the bus when the city contacted him."

"I'll speak to Chief Iglesias. He needs to stick up for a fellow officer."

Julian gives a defeated shrug. The color drains from the water, switching from orange to dusky blue.

"I've been thinking," Darcy says, looking down at the sand. "The private investigation business slowed down this summer, and Hunter's tuition increased by five-thousand dollars. And Jennifer will be in college before I know it."

Julian stares at her.

"You can't take on a second job. You're stretched thin as is."

"Not a second job," Darcy says, sighing. "I know where my talent lies, and government benefits are too good to pass up."

"Please don't. You left the FBI for a reason. Why put yourself through the nightmares again?"

Darcy crosses her feet at the ankles, drops her head back, and stares into the abyss of coming night.

"Because Ketchum needs me, and we need the money."

"What about this?" Julian says, motioning around the cove. "What about your house and the life we're building? Quantico isn't within driving distance of Genoa Cove, and you can't uproot Jennifer again."

"Ketchum says I can work from home part of the week provided I'm in the office at least two days. The Behavior Analysis Unit is desperate for an experienced profiler, someone who specializes in serial murderers. They're willing to work with me and get me a cheap apartment." Darcy swallows when she sees the hurt in his eyes. "It would only be two days per week. The rest of the time I'll be home."

"What about investigations? You forget how much time you spent away from the kids during your first run with the FBI."

Darcy chews her lip. Is she doing this for their financial future, or for herself? Since Eric Hensel's death, she hasn't been able to rid her mind of his urgings. Hensel wanted Darcy to return to the FBI once she overcame her addiction demons. Though he didn't live to see it, she's been clean for over a year, no longer terrified to be alone in the dark.

A whippoorwill calls from the trees separating the neighborhood from the cove. Dusk turns a shade darker.

"We'll make it work, Julian. If the job takes up too much of my time, I'll retire and return to private investigations. This time for good."

His lips pulled tight, Julian peers over the ocean, staring at an uncertain future.

I hope you enjoyed Find Her Before Dark.

In "Don't Breathe" (Darkwater Cove 6), a series of strange and gruesome murders pull Darcy back to the FBI's Behavior

Analysis Unit. But these murders are beyond Darcy's worst nightmares. And now the killer has his eyes set on Darcy.

Read Don't Breathe today

GET A FREE BOOK!

I'm a pretty nice guy once you look past the grisly images in my head. Most of all, I love connecting with awesome readers like you.

Join my VIP Reader Group and get a FREE serial killer thriller for your Kindle.

Get My Free Book

www.danpadavona.com/thriller-readers-vip-group/

SUPPORT INDIE THRILLER AUTHORS

Did you enjoy this book? If so, please let other thriller fans know by leaving a short review. Positive reviews help spread the word about independent authors and their novels. Thank you.

ABOUT THE AUTHOR

Dan Padavona is the author of the The Darkwater Cove series, The Scarlett Bell thriller series, *Her Shallow Grave*, The Dark Vanishings series, *Camp Slasher, Quilt, Crawlspace, The Face of Midnight, Storberry, Shadow Witch*, and the horror anthology, *The Island*. He lives in upstate New York with his beautiful wife, Terri, and their children, Joe, and Julia. Dan is a meteorologist with NOAA's National Weather Service. Besides writing, he enjoys visiting amusement parks, beach vacations, Renaissance fairs, gardening, playing with the family dogs, and eating too much ice cream.

Visit Dan at: www.danpadavona.com